Hive & Heist

Book Two of the Hive Queen Saga

by Janine A. Southard

Cover by MaeIDesign and Photography
Editing by Cat Rambo
Copyediting by Rachel Lynn Solomon
Layout by Stacy Booth
ISBN: 978-1-63327-002-2

Steal back their ship's engine... or be stuck on this foreign station forever!

Keeping her tone hushed in case a local wandered too close, Rhiannon outlined her plan. "We have seven days till we take back what is ours," she said.

There was a small cheer. This, *this* was what she was made for. She could strategize; she could organize; she could direct her people along the optimal paths.

"Gavin." Her voice was sure, commanding, and he straightened to a near-military posture. "You'll have the theatre's production vehicle, so I'll need you to be the getaway driver."

He coughed. "Ah, but, the sheep?"

"You'll bring the lorry to me *after* you drop off the sheep, so be sure to pick them up early and to take Gwyn with you. She'll keep the lambs quiet."

Next. "Alan."

He acknowledged her with a mumbled *my lady*, overbright excitement turning his hazel eyes almost entirely green.

"You'll go along with Gavin and Gwyn to make sure we get all the parts. If the jet's been dismantled or damaged, determine what to take and what to leave behind. Put the jet in the truck as soon as you have it."

Trust. "Luciano." He fixed her with grave, dark eyes. She, the center of his attention. "You'll keep in touch with everyone. I trust you to be my eyes and ears."

Luciano went to his knees before her, pressing his forehead to the back of her hand. "I am honored, my lady."

Soon all four Devoted were on the floor, each bending one knee. "My lady," they said in eerie unison.

Acknowledgements

Gigantic thanks go out to my Kickstarter backers. Without you, *Hive & Heist* would be a very different book. Thank you for believing in this novel and for sharing my passion for ensemble space opera. In particular, I'd like to thank the following backers for their contributions (in alphabetical order by first name because you have to order things somehow):

Aaron Giddings	Jill Seidenstein	Rachael
Anders Monsen	Jon Foulds	Sherwood
Andreas	Lisa Bloch	Rodney D Bonner
Gustafsson	Luke Johnson	Scott & Sandra
Anon	Mark Kadas	Kurtzeborn
Avery L Heart	Melissa Louie	Steven Mentzel
Benjamin Abbott	Melissa Pagonis	Susan A Parker
Derek "Pineapple	Michael Shaw	Thomas Zilling
Steak" Swoyer	Mike Skolnik	Tiffany Lutnick
Django Wexler	Miriah	Coleman
D-Rock	Hetherington	Trevor
James Truher	Patricia D. Eddy	
Jess Downs	Philda	

I'd also like to thank my physical therapist, Terri Sullivan, PT, DPT. Not only is she wonderful (and patient) at helping me to move better, she also happily answers questions like, "So, if I have a character who got shot through the shoulder in book one, what should he be worrying about in book two?" I've done my best to take her advice, but (as with my daily exercises) all the mistakes are mine. And all the brilliant medical stuff in this book is hers.

And, of course, special thanks to Jeremy Barton, my "main investor" and spouse.

◆ Chapter One ◆

M3L-15-A

Criminals couldn't escape justice. Not with a dedicated Ranger after them.

Out on the frontier planets, any Ranger was a good Ranger, synthetic or not. People needed Star Rangers, even ones with metal arms and insectoid legs. So six years back when Melissa (original designation M3L-15-A) chose to join the outfit, she'd gravitated towards frontier assignments.

This night, she ran all systems dark, the better to keep her suspect from catching a silvery glimpse of her in the street before she made her move. The serial art thief would target a private collection on the penultimate floor of this commercial building. Melissa would stake her reputation as the best tracker in the American Star Rangers on it. All the data lined up.

In the moonless silence, she ran thermal imaging cameras up and down and around the building where she expected the thief. As soon as she found a trace of his entrance or exit, he'd be hers.

There! On the roof. The thermal image from the building was consistently blue-green, blue-green, blue-green, except for a bright-hot yellow flash. Since the roof plans didn't contain any windows or hatches in the relevant location, it could only be her thief's escape route.

The yellow spiked and writhed like a flame, like a smoke-signal to her Ranger cameras saying, "I'm here, I'm here! Collar me!"

The two unlit lamps on the sides of her head, designed by a long-forgotten engineer who thought they'd make her look more human-friendly, cocked upwards. Her aftermarket sensors chased and confirmed a signal. The criminal probably thought the roof would be stealthy, a place to hide from local law enforcement; pursuers would need to ascend through the locked building, giving away their intentions and allowing him to run off before the law reached him.

If she'd had a human mouth instead of a speaker-grille, Melissa would have grinned. As it was, she slipped her four pick-sharp legs out of their flat-bottomed sheaths. Her *shoes*, as it were. Her thief hadn't accounted for the only robotic Ranger to be chasing his tail, didn't know she had an insect's knack for climbing sheer surfaces.

She tested her limbs, bending her four knees even closer to her face. "Backwards," some disturbed citizens of the Core worlds called it. Well, she wasn't here to argue for the beauty of the engineered form or AI rights. She was here to catch a thief and a murderer.

One last flex. She leapt for the building wall, swarming skyward on four legs and four arms. Her legs speared into the mortar, giving her leverage. She didn't need all eight opposable thumbs for extra grip, so she freed two hands— four thumbs—to wield her pump-action rifle.

The weapon was a tad old-fashioned, but she was an old-fashioned kind of gal. She'd read up on her Ranger history the moment she'd found out she would be allowed to join them. She'd gotten hooked on the *old* stories, and that tendency displayed itself in her choice of weaponry.

The roof was empty when she made it to the flat top, and she tapped her right front leg spike on the cold concrete. She'd chased his criminal body across three planets and five cities, always one step behind. Now that she was a step ahead, he made her wait?

She hated criminals. She hated thieves.

Things Melissa hated, in ascending order of detestation:

- Needing to socialize with coworkers
- Paying for air on her single-user spaceship (she always ran with life support turned off because *why bother?*)
- Judgmental looks from anti-synthetic lobbyists
- Going to dinner with coworkers who expected her to eat or drink things (she wasn't built for food, but give her a can of Dallas54-brand oil any day)
- Kids who climbed on her back and asked for rides (somehow she couldn't ever say no; still, just because she had a low-slung bench structure, that didn't make her a pony)
- Murderers
- Thieves who escalated to violence (they were never any good at it, and everyone who got hurt was an unnecessary casualty in *everyone's* opinion)
- Criminals who got away

There! The thief emerged from his hole in the roof. Her cameras told her he'd dressed in deep grey, the better for staying unnoticed. He'd even wrapped his ill-gotten gains in highly durable, tencel cloth. Unfortunately for the criminal, she'd left most of her cameras on the thermal imaging setting. To her senses, he lit up like a beacon of villainy.

She stayed utterly still as he approached the edge, imagining she could feel the smugness radiating off him, seeping through her worn joints and patches. He crept closer, and *perfect!* She snatched out with her unoccupied hands, grabbing his wrist and cuffing it.

The thief thrashed and whirled in her grip, his dark evidence clattering to the roof. He kicked at her plated side (as if that would do anything to an impact rating 9 out of 10), and cursed when his steel-toed boot clanged off her skin. With her top two arms, she pumped the rifle, letting its menacing tone talk for her, but the criminal in her arms continued to squirm and twist.

Then he was still, facing her with a pistol in his hand.

She growled, an ugly and throaty sound intended to unnerve him, made all the more disturbing for the way it echoed out of her speakers. Surround sound. All he had to do was surrender, let her finish cuffing him. They both knew how this would play out. But no. He had to do things the hard way.

Well, Rangers were schooled in the hard way.

He fired his pistol into a leg joint, the easiest target for him at waist height and the one most likely to do actual damage. But that wouldn't stop her from doing her job, getting her collar. He had to hold still to fire and aim, and she didn't give him the chance at a second shot.

Predator-quick, she reared back and slammed a leg spike through his gun arm's shoulder. He screamed his surprise and pain, pinned to the rooftop.

She extracted her limb precisely, to keep from tearing anything.

The fight was over. She had no reason to cause further damage. He'd be fine with medical attention.

Using internal communications channels, she sent a pulse to the U.S. Marshals she'd seen in town. Then she rolled him over, affixing the cuff behind him to his free wrist. She holstered her unfired pump-action across her upper back and took the moaning criminal in her topmost pair of arms.

By the time she hit the ground and slipped back into her practical walking shoes, a team of Marshals had arrived. The Marshals came out in force with vans and containers and who knew what else, all illuminated by headlights.

She passed her bundle over to the lead Marshal. "He'll need some medical attention," she said, voice husky but nonthreatening, no trace of the earlier growl. "Left shoulder's punctured through and through."

She was finished here, but *You're only as good as your next collar*, her training officer had said. One down, an unknown number to go.

The lead Marshal was practically an advertisement for the uniform bomber jacket he wore. His teeth sparkled white in the electric lights, and his shoulders were as wide as her own... and probably almost as hard.

"You're all right, Ranger," he said. "Good work."

His team echoed the sentiments. "Nice job, Ranger!" and "Way to lighten our workload!"

One able-bodied beauty with her hair in a shoulder length blond braid and an air of confident camaraderie tried for more. "Come out with us for a celebratory drink after we get this scumbag squared away?"

Melissa didn't answer her. Rangers worked alone. Had done so since the 1800s. Everyone knew that. No one expected them to be social, not so long as they got the job done. And she'd gotten the job done.

She headed back to the Port Authority and her ship, the *Cold Night*, home of her hat collection, library, and memorabilia from both this life and past ones. Before she left the planet, she'd use its network to find herself another criminal to track, and then she'd take him (or her) down like the rabid blight on society he'd turned himself (or herself) into.

Behind her, she heard the Marshals punching each other in the shoulders and a lilting female voice say, "Hey, I tried."

They'd be all right. And she'd find a way to protect them all from some other crime wave so that their lives could stay well-oiled and efficient.

A multi-stage hunt through the frontier crime databases netted Melissa information about a rash of thefts and killings across a slew of planets. Each crime moved farther and farther from the American Core. The crimes weren't necessarily linked, but she synthesized her reasons and thought it was the way to bet. All the thefts had something to do with frontier living, from experimental seed plants taken from a private research lab to blank homesteading certificates acquired from a planetary bank vault.

The attendant killings seemed more incidental, but that only made Melissa mad enough to cross all her arms tight over her trunk, a mannerism echoing her favorite maintenance engineer when he worried about his college-bound daughter. *Damned thieves who didn't understand violence.* They wasted human lives the way actual murderers didn't. At least murderers had a reason, even if Melissa didn't think it was a particularly good one.

It seemed a giant coincidence for anyone to be connected to more than three of the crimes in her web, and she had three suspects connected to at least four of the seven crime scenes. By location, or family, or work, or happenstance. Of those six, three had bought passage out to John Wayne Station over the planet Kessel. So that's where she'd head.

A few keystrokes, and she jacked herself into symbiosis with her ship. She didn't need controls or readouts, not the way the ship's builders had intended. It was just a machine, and she had plenty of ways to control it with her mind alone.

She had one more piece of business to take care of before she could officially start the hunt. Before she could be sanctioned by Ranger HQ and unhindered by any of her peers. If she wanted this crime spree to be hers, she'd have to call it in. Though the *Cold Night* was already underway, she was still close enough to the Port Authority to use their networks and report in to Dispatch.

Someday, when she was too old and slow and beaten down, maybe she'd join Dispatch too. She could meld herself with the computer there and live on forever as part of the Rangers. If she lived that long. If her mind survived till her body became that decrepit.

As far as she was concerned, she'd only been *alive* for seven years, although her body was somewhere around forty. It was hard to tell exactly how old her original hardware might be, what with the filed-off serial numbers, but no one had made a PersonalRobot™ in decades.

The Dispatch computer transferred her call to her boss. He just went by Jon, no last name. His weathered face filled her visor camera with its dark, lined skin and greying hair. He wore an old-fashioned cowboy hat, Stetson, even though he was clearly indoors at the moment. He liked traditions, and she had to agree with him on all that Ranger nostalgia. She liked to nod to the old days too, sometimes with an accent module and sometimes by flashing an actual badge (carried in her vest) instead of a digital one.

The picture she sent down the packets to his comm console showed her face as it truly was: nearly spherical with a gunmetal grey eye visor, round headlamps where ears might be on a human head, and a round grille for her mouth speaker. She didn't bother to hide from him. They'd worked together for six years, and they were both *Rangers*.

She didn't actually talk, didn't bother in her spaceship's vacuum atmosphere. But she sent the waves to be transformed into words in her own voice, free of the reverberation she'd put on for the art thief.

"I want this manhunt," she said as she flashed Jon the data she'd collected on the crime spree, amping up her sometimes-drawl because she knew he liked it. She'd be more likely to get what she wanted if she kept him sweet. "I'm going out to John Wayne to look into some suspects."

Courtesies observed. She hoped no one else had already claimed the case.

The older Ranger nodded, cream-colored hat bobbing. Then it changed direction, as he shook it from side to side like a bull at the rodeo. "We can put Satryani on that. I've been meaning to talk to you about taking a vacation."

She didn't let her avatar show annoyance, no flashing visor or rotating headlamps. She did, however, up her volume, just a bit. "I don't need a vacation, sir." Discussion over. "I'm the best tracker in the department, and I'm going to track down these murderous thieves and bring them to justice."

Jon frowned, the lines around his mouth going a dark brown that clashed with his whitish lips. "You've gone six straight years with no breaks, Melissa. You're a great Ranger, but part of being a great Ranger is knowing when to take a break from Rangering."

She let space's chill leech the heat from her frustration. She knew that! Even the great Frank Hamer took breaks from being Ranger, back when they'd been Texas Rangers and not American Star Rangers. Why, he'd been out of the corps for years before he went after Bonnie and Clyde.

But she wasn't a human. She didn't need breaks. Even if she did, she'd be the one who chose when she took them.

"Trust me to take care of myself, sir. And please deed over the Ranger quarters on JWS."

He blew out a loud breath that came to her as vibrating waveforms, but it was only a few seconds before she got a notification message saying that she had custody of the quarters in question. "Take 'em down, Melissa." Jon dipped his hat's brim to her. "I know you can do it."

"Yes, sir," she said. She cut the link. Her connection was about to get too spotty for real-time conversations.

But it wasn't too spotty for looking at stored data. And if she was going to hit the station at full tilt, she needed someone to open up and rewire that Ranger apartment before she arrived at JWS.

What Melissa wanted, in descending order:

- Someone who knew how to update wiring
- Someone trustworthy
- Someone who could deal with administration issues on station so that she didn't have to
- Someone who'd be around to do more work if necessary (or fix mistakes)
- Someone with references

She grabbed the résumé listings coming out of JWS to see what was available. Lots of *just passing through* types who didn't have any proof of ability. One brilliant engineer who was much too good for her, but planned to relocate to the planet beneath the station in the next few days. A bunch of explicitly unqualified types.

And... *what's a Devoted from Dyfed doing out on the American frontier?*

Most Americans wouldn't have heard of Dyfed, she knew, except in a vague "the Welsh were the first to leave Earth" kind of way. And they certainly wouldn't know about that colonial planet's society, the best and brightest males rising to the top of the food chain only by attaching themselves to a charismatic Queen or Commander. But Melissa wasn't most Americans. She had a computer's ability to speed-process data and an upgraded memory that kept her ahead of the crowd. Plus, she could translate to and from any language she'd received a module for.

So, yes, she knew about Dyfed, as much as had ever been written and exported about it. Which meant she knew it didn't matter if the man whose résumé she'd found, a Gavin Reynolds, had official references or not. Devoted were brilliant, rigorously vetted by their home governments and universities, and the most resourceful men their planet could offer. Apparently he'd been trained as a Creative Technologist.

She messaged him, text only, saying she wanted to speak about possibly hiring him for a job. She couldn't just snatch him up, not until she knew what he was doing looking for work.

When she was only two days out from John Wayne, Melissa swerved into range of a communications array with near-instant connection to the station. Three hours available to get in a call to the unemployed Devoted.

She lucked into a connection on the first try. His face filled her screen, young and innocent, reddish blond hair falling in a mess to below his shoulders. His wide eyes and trembling smile made her yearn to soothe him. She wouldn't. She had to play the tough, would-be employer. But she saw no reason to scare him with her actual appearance, not just yet. She sent back a picture, a nondescript woman in her forties, all browns and symmetry.

"Hello?" Gavin said. His voice came out higher than expected.

Yes, he was young. She found herself leaning forward even though her avatar stayed still on the screen. No reason to treat him like a child, though. She'd get straight to the point.

"I need someone to upgrade my quarters on the station and be available for general maintenance and engineering jobs for the foreseeable future. Your documents show applicable education and proven electrical expertise across multiple planets from your travels with the Stage One company. The position includes the salary I'm sending you in another packet, as well as room and board. Any questions?" His questions would tell her more than asking outright what a Devoted was doing out here looking for work.

He heaved in a giant breath, enough that his rib cage expanded. The boy had been taught to breathe from the diaphragm, even when he was nervous as a cornered informant. "I can definitely do all that." He looked to the side, but didn't inhale again. He had enough breath. "But does that offer of room and board extend outwards? I have five, ah, dependents?"

He made the last word a question, more as though he weren't sure he should call them dependents than as if he were expanding on the previous thought.

Ah. So that's it. Room and board for an entire Hive. They'd be expensive, and six people taking up her personal space could get exhausting. Melissa didn't flip back through the other résumés. She knew what was there. But he was good, and he was responsible. And she wouldn't have to worry about him getting in trouble if he was always busy with his Hive.

Besides, maybe she could help these young people to find themselves, if she had the time, and that'd be a useful endeavor good for all civilization. She could protect them from themselves as well as from the criminals. Plus, it never hurt to have powerful allies, and any Hive connections would be powerful if she ever found herself out Dyfed way.

"Can you sign a contract now, or do you need to clear it with your Queen?" she asked. Her inner deliberations had taken a bare femto-second.

He tilted his head down and looked away from the camera, then back. "Who are you really?"

What? She widened her avatar's eyes.

"Whose skin do you wear?" he clarified. "For the flesh on those digital bones moves on the tick and not on the beat."

She knew the playwright he quoted, knew that the *beat* was the heartbeat. Her lack of practice with realistic conversational avatars had caught up to her. This Gavin Reynolds had a sharp eye for details.

Impressed, she switched from false picture to actual live feed. The image she provided came from above, looking down to show off her four arms and her four insect-style legs. She hid nothing, not her lower body's bench nor her hands with their dual opposable thumbs.

He sucked in a breath through his teeth. Would he scream? Cut the connection? But no. He grinned wide and so big for his face that his eyes had to scrunch to make space.

"That makes so much sense," he said.

Dyfed hadn't been part of the PRob marketplace, she recalled. He'd likely never seen a walking, talking robot, never internalized any opinions about them—good or bad.

"Room and board for a Hive," she agreed. Her visor turned pale blue with her pleasure. Job well done. "I'm sending you the details now."

She cut the connection before he could reply. Business concluded.

Chapter Two

Money
(That's What I Want)

"Place your bets!"

Provocatively clad men and women stalked the aisles between the gaming tables, delivering drinks and innuendo.

To blend in, and because she was thirsty, Rhiannon accepted the drinks when offered. She blushingly tried to ignore the innuendo. It was a bit more blatant than she'd been used to on Dyfed. She'd adapt quickly enough, she hoped.

There are three kinds of Queens, Rhiannon thought as she rubbed a warm red chip with the edge of her thumb. Her nail caught on the striated edge. *The precious, the self-interested, and the careful.*

Precious Queens tended to be the subjects of films. They were sweet and charismatic, but helpless. Their Devoted doted on them with a fondness that was, frankly, creepy. They were cared for, but did little caretaking of their own. Their life purpose was simply to bring their Devoted together into a cohesive whole.

Self-interested Queens were usually found at political rallies or shareholders' meetings. They had brains and talent. Sure, whatever they angled for, whatever they negotiated their way into, would benefit their Hive, but they didn't do it for their Devoted. They did it for the *fight*. They did it for the love of manipulation. If they didn't have Hives, they'd be the very shareholders they worked so hard to convince.

Careful Queens, that glorious third kind, they were what Rhiannon wished to be.

Careful Queens cared for their Devoted and created opportunities for their Hives to thrive and grow. They *earned* adoration and love, looking after their Devoted with all the talent and drive of the self-interested. In return, they were treasured. They inspired and aided their Hives to work in perfect time and harmony.

Since arriving on the American station, though, Rhiannon hadn't managed careful Queenhood. For days, she'd been locked in the medical bays, sedated. Oh, she'd brought her people to safety. To oxygen. To a foreign land.

But now they were stuck.

The docking fees, the medical bills, the *just till you get on your feet* apartment. She needed money to pull them out of the sucking pool of debt into which they'd stumbled. Not to mention money for food.

She wondered what kind of Queen the captain of *Llyr's Llambo* had been. Rhiannon's Hive had barely escaped from that crazed, Queen-less bunch with their lives. Between running from those criminals and running out of air, she hadn't been able to do anything to help the poor souls. If the older Hive were right, if some strange group were *stealing* Queens, Rhiannon wanted to be as far from her home world as possible. She was much too young and inexperienced to help other at-risk Queens, so the only thing she could do was to remove herself from the danger. She wished she knew who to tell back home.

"Place your bets!"

If she wanted to provide for her people and get even farther from Dyfed, she needed funds. Which was why she'd come to Cleopatra's Palace, the tri-level brothel and casino at the heart of John Wayne Station.

Cleopatra's Palace was comforting, and somehow cozy for all its immensity. It was warmer than the rest of the station, in heat and in lighting. *A place to part with your money and not even care.*

Not that Rhiannon planned to lose any money. She aimed to win at the gambling tables. Win her Hive's freedom from debt. Win the ability to provide treatment for Victor, medical training for Luciano, and materials for Alan.

She put two chips on green felt, waited for the cards to come out of their nine deck shoe. Today, her game was poker, Cleopatra style. All statistics and cunning. Perfect for a Perceiver-Analyst, which she still felt like underneath her Queen-Commander veneer.

Pair of fours, jack high. *Not the best hand in the universe.*

But they were two-thirds through the cards now, and these were the first fours she'd seen on the table.

She tried to think positively. *The odds are in my favor.* Every good druid knew the first step to becoming a magician: learn to bless and to be blessed.

She kept the fours, put the remaining three cards face down on the table, and increased her initial bet by two green chips. When her turn came to bet next, she'd add another two chips to the pile. But no more than that. She had to play it safe, and math could only take her so far.

She hadn't yet learned her opponents' tells. She'd thought, at one point an hour ago, that she'd discovered a consistent twitch in the man with skin the color of freshened dirt after a life-giving rain shower. He sat at the end of the table and tended to study his hand, thumb the side of his nose while looking up, and then bet a chip.

But she'd discovered this focus had nothing to do with the cards and everything to do with whether he'd spotted a particularly attractive server on the casino floor.

The dealer gave her another three cards, face down. *May the dealer's evening go as he wishes. With tips and tasks aplenty.* She tucked the new cards beside her existing pair. *Two fours and a five. Marvelous.*

Behind her, a woman cleared her throat. Rhiannon turned to see a server, her skin the color of a rum and coke. The tray bore a single drink.

"Someone here had a lemonade?" The woman's voice was husky and perky all at once. Inviting and secretive.

Rhiannon raised her hand till it hovered shakily at her jaw line, almost waving. "I had a lemonade." The drink on the tray looked nothing like any lemonade Rhiannon had ever seen. It was a near-orange color—*sepia*—in a glass full of perfectly cubed ice. Despite the ice blocks, which ought to provide many nucleation sites, the drink had no bubbles from carbonation whatsoever.

How strange these Americans are. This lemonade is nothing like the stuff at home.

The lady put the tall glass at Rhiannon's elbow, warm skin brushing against Rhiannon's in direct counterpoint to the ice-cold glass behind it. Rhiannon shivered at the sensation, and the woman's mouth curved into a gentle bow. Her tray folded out of sight and she leaned on the table, interest and enticement combined.

This close, Rhiannon could see the server wore nothing underneath her jumpsuit, made of a lightweight transparent material that bloused all over but hid nothing in its folds and shadows. Rhiannon wondered if even Gwyn could make a garment so floaty yet durable enough for working a busy room.

"Like what you see?" The woman angled her body so it was more open to Rhiannon's gaze. "You could spend those winnings on a game far more fun than poker."

She pointed at the stack of chips Rhiannon had amassed, more than she'd entered with.

Rhiannon knew she was supposed to look at the serving woman, part of the casino's other business arm, with a lascivious eye. Rhiannon knew she was intended, even encouraged, to shower the lady with amorous attention. Knew most people her age would jump at this opportunity to forge a sexual connection.

But she didn't feel the desire that films told her she ought to feel by this point. Rhiannon could appreciate the woman's interpersonal talents and astonishingly precise eyeliner, but that enjoyment came purely on an intellectual and aesthetic level.

She looked away to the ceiling, which lofted upwards, three stories high and opulent in a station otherwise crammed for space. Ivy and holly wrapped pointlessly, beautifully, around rafters.

Ivy and holly? Is it winter down on the planet? We just finished celebrating Beltane a few weeks ago back home. But any good druid knew it didn't matter what the season was at home, only what the season was where you were. *If I can't be in the land of my heart, I'll respect the land I stand on.*

Not that a space station counted as land. With heavier gravity than Dyfed and colder air, with lights that never went out and so few windows, with plants that came cut from somewhere rather than grown into place—well, it didn't feel like a planet. But maybe that was because it didn't feel like *home*.

The lady readjusted her stance, no longer attempting to seduce with a glimpse of hip and breast, shifting so her back leaned against the table at Rhiannon's side. Her new position invited friendly confidences rather than a lover's whisper. The difference was dramatic.

"I'd never want to make you uncomfortable." Her voice made Rhiannon think of high-pitched children at play as well as more adult versions of play. She was *good* at what she did. "Don't feel like you have to humor me. Really."

The dealer cleared his throat, laid his own hand palm down on surface. "Any final bets?"

Two table mates folded, the dark man with the nose-thumbing habit amongst them. He walked away, leaving no one whom she could read.

Rhiannon raised her planned two chips.

The woman at her side sighed and tapped a coral-lacquered nail against the lemonade glass, all but forgotten in the game's focus.

"My name's Cinna. Call for me if you want another drink. I promise to keep it purely professional." As if realizing *professional* could be taken a few ways when it came to practitioners of the universe's oldest profession, Cinna tapped the glass again. "Virgin lemonade. And only virgin lemonade."

She sashayed away, and Rhiannon collected her winnings from the dealer and from the other players. The chips grew her pile up to... still not enough to pay for food, medical, and docking fees. But they'd cover rent on the station-provided housing. That was something. She'd take care of her Devoted if she had to stay in here for months. At least it was warmer in the casino than on the rest of the station.

"Place your bets."

She put five chips on the line. The farther into the shoe the dealer got, the more information Rhiannon had about which cards had been played before.

"Hey now!" Shouting from two tables over caught the attention of all the players in the place, except for a very serious couple still throwing dice.

Three burly men with buzz cuts, all wearing jumpsuits in deep burgundy with creeping ivy patterns on the sleeves, surrounded a fourth man, this one in the jeans-and-tee-shirt uniform of a pioneer who planned to head down to the planet.

The incensed pioneer banged on the table.

"I demand to see the manager," he told the dealer in front of him. "These men have no right—"

His movements revealed a slight woman standing behind one of the burgundy three. Her bright red bodystocking matched her shockingly red lipstick. Dark brown hair slipped in waves over her left shoulder, baring her neck on the other side. She made a perfect picture of power mixed with vulnerability, and had a body with curves Rhiannon couldn't even hope to someday own.

One burgundy wearer asked her, "This man bothering you?"

The woman nodded. "I told him no. He forced the issue." The lady, clearly part of the casino-brothel, rubbed a palm with the opposite thumb. *Did he hold her too tight? Did she slap him?* "I want him blacklisted."

The people closest to the situation all backed away.

"Is that how it happened?" The burgundy three looked to the dealer for corroboration.

He nodded. Spooked silent.

The woman smacked the burgundy-wearer closest to her, but lightly and with the back of her hand. "Isn't my word good enough?"

The one she'd smacked ruffled her hair. *They know each other, then.* "Enough to kick him out for a week. Enough to tell him to get lost. But enough to blacklist him? We need a second witness for that."

The woman nodded, regal.

Grabbing the pioneer man's shoulders and legs, two of the burgundy three picked him up bodily. The third rifled through his pockets and drew a quick blood sample.

Then the three 'escorted' him to the entrance and, after he'd been ejected, melted away.

It only took five seconds for the murmur of *place your bets* and the clinking of chips to resume. Rhiannon picked up her cards. The next time she looked over at the table where the altercation had happened, it was full of Pai-Gow players.

Three hours later, she'd earned enough to pay Victor's extensive medical bills—though no one else's—and learned that being blacklisted from the casino-brothel also meant being unable to attend the station theatre or to borrow money from any but the most unscrupulous lenders. Plus, no romantic interest would even look at you twice.

When she asked her dealer, the charismatic brunet said, "You have to do something *really vile* to get full-on blacklisted, as opposed to just bounced out for the day or the week." The dealer leaned closer, voice turning into a gossipy whisper that didn't preclude anyone from listening in. "He must've done something extra awful if she didn't want to clarify it in public. Like overstepping some pre-agreed boundary."

They take contracts and consent seriously here. It was good to know. In the casino, at least, she could count on rule of law. Even if the law wasn't necessarily the same as Dyfed's.

The dealer shook his head as he leaned back into his place behind the table. "I wonder what he *did*."

Rhiannon laid her starting bet on the table for another round. Ten red chips this time. She'd do better now that they approached the shoe's end.

"Excuse me, ma'am." A burgundy-and-vine clad gentleman waited at her elbow. He was taller than any of the players, broader around the shoulder than any of her Devoted.

She looked away from him briefly, fingers flitting over the cards in front of her but not picking them up.

I wonder what I did.

"Can I help you?" She barely refrained from adding a *sir* on the end of the question. She had to remember that she was a Queen. Even if she'd only just passed her sixteenth year, Dyfed calendar.

He gestured to the large chip pile in front of her. "The management would like to invite you to leave."

Not until I acquire the few thousand credits left to make my bills. She twisted a lock of hair around a finger and forced herself to look the man in the eyes. *The texts say to pay attention to everyone's eye color. It makes them think you care. Makes them preen.* The bouncer's eyes were dark brown, much like everyone else's she'd seen on this station. "I'd rather not."

Behind her, the dealer asked whether she wanted any cards.

"She folds," the man in burgundy answered for her.

She flew to her feet. *How dare he make that choice for me?* Even standing, she barely reached the middle of his chest. *Though, perhaps he knows the local customs better than I.*

"I fold?" She arched a brow, trying to seem cool and collected. An adult. Queens were automatically adults on Dyfed. Sixteen-year-olds might not have the same luxury in American space.

He dipped his head, a deference she hadn't seen from the hospital staff or the accountants. "The management requests you move on, ma'am. Or else I'll be forced to throw you out for cheating."

"Cheating?"

"They've been watching you on the monitors." He drew her attention to the cameras that dotted the walls. Unobtrusive, but obvious.

She shook her head so hard that the world filled with strands of near black. "You can search me, if you like. I didn't bring extra cards or communicate with an accomplice or... how else do people cheat?" She'd been aiming for a childlike exuberance. Where dignity didn't work, perhaps cuteness would create compassion.

He didn't even smile at her innocence. "Cameraman says you've been ratcheting up your bets hard now that you're nearing the end of the shoe. Says you're counting cards."

How else does one play poker?

She said as much. "It's a game of skill and statistics."

The man nodded, apologetic frown casting wrinkles all the way to the back of his shorn jaw. "That's not how we do things here." He spread his arms as if to say *what can you do?* "Tell you what, for a first offense, we'll just exile you for a little bit and let you keep however much you walked in with."

But I earned this! She spoke slowly, too calmly. "How about you explain a different way to play poker, allow me to keep today's winnings in good faith, and I don't break your strange American rules again?" Never had she felt more like a Dyfed citizen than in the presence of people who clearly were not.

His biceps bulged under his tunic. "How long will you be on John Wayne Station, ma'am?"

"Indefinitely...?"

He nodded, not the deferential head dip she'd seen before, and gripped her elbow firmly. With that implacable, impossible hand, he pulled her towards the entrance. "If I see you again in the next month, I'll throw you out a lot less nicely than I am today."

What? She struggled against his inexorable strength, but it did no good. No one even looked up to watch. She wasn't the spectacle a true blacklisting had been. "But what did I do?"

He deposited her at the door, but then held her shoulders gently, looking down with a direct gaze to soften the words. "Look, kiddo, I get that you're not from around here, so I'm not too mad. But you cheated. And then you tried to deny and negotiate. Just read up before you come back, and everything will be fine, okay?"

There was nothing to do but nod. He was right that she needed to figure out where things had gone wrong.

Now I'm outside the casino without so much as my initial stake. She was even more broke than she'd been at the start of the venture, with no idea how to raise the money she needed. That her *Hive* needed. *They're all counting on me, and all I can do is get thrown out of casinos.* If she'd been outdoors, somewhere that only the stars and the trees could hear, she'd have screamed her frustration to the cosmos.

She breathed deeply of the hallway's just-too-cold-for-comfort air, centering herself as best she could. *Visualize the stars, then narrow down to your place in them.*

But she didn't know where the station was, what the planet below looked like. How could she ground herself in the closest earth, if vacuum and metal and uncharted space separated her from that earth? No wonder only Dyfed's craziest Hives could withstand long turns in space.

The meditation helped, even if she couldn't do all the visualizations. Slightly calmer, she cast a *thank you* thought to her patron god, Manawyddan, and another to Ceridwen that she hadn't been tossed out like the abuser before her. That she hadn't had all her money stolen, only her stake. That she hadn't died *en route* to John Wayne Station.

Good enough.

She began the long trudge from the multi-story casino-brothel towards the station-owned apartments where her Hive resided. Where they waited for her to fix their problems. Where they worried about their freedom and education and quality of life.

Her boots thudded on the off-white plastic—*that can't be strong enough to keep out the stars in case of emergency*—step after step after gravity-heavy step. Another set of thudding boots joined hers. A sidelong glance netted a splash of evergreen linen overlying a sleeve of cream and lace. *Gavin.*

"My lady," he said. Even as they walked, he played with the frayed belt holding up his billowing trousers, almost in fashion on this station. "I've solved our boarding problems."

"Oh?" For a problem-solver, he seemed twitchy. For a Devoted, he seemed willing to usurp his Queen's place as provider. "You didn't have to."

"Didn't I?" A line ran up and down his forehead, radiating tension. He hunched forward even more. "*Someone* had to. We can't stay in the station housing much longer, and no one else is finding jobs or rooms or board." He tore at his belt's dangling end. Savagely. "And what were you doing? Playing in a casino?"

She came to a stop in the hallway, making him meet her eyes. Tilted up her square chin and too-pointy nose. Talked slowly so that he'd have to pay attention, have to let her words and her seriousness sink in. Have to respect her, both her position and her anger. "I was earning money to move us out. I can take care of my Hive. If you don't think I can, maybe you shouldn't have Devoted to me."

Even as she said the words, she realized he'd never actually Devoted. It hadn't seemed like a major problem on Dyfed or on the *Ceridwen's Cauldron*. He'd acted like a Devoted: following her suggestions, working for the Hive's need, bonding with the rest. Now it struck her as a huge oversight. How could she be sure of his loyalty and constancy? What if he planned to leave them all? He had no true ties. Just a planet-formed friendship with Victor and what little bonding he'd done since.

He growled, throwing the edge of his shredded belt away from him. "And has it done any good?" Even as his voice grew louder, his posture grew smaller. Slouching. He drew closer to her, rather than shrinking away, as if burrowing into the comfort of her presence. Like a good Devoted might. "What have you won us?"

There was the crux of the problem. She *should* provide. She should save Gavin from his own good intentions and misplaced responsibility, but she couldn't. She wished he'd go away and leave her to her failure in peace. She leaned into him, as he leaned into her, until their shoulders touched: warmth and comfort through five layers of cloth.

"Absolutely nothing. I was doing well until I got kicked out."

He straightened, his mouth a flat line. "Who dared touch you? I'll go and—"

"No, no." She kept her voice low, soothing, and put a hand on his forearm. *He's so touch-starved,* she thought when he curled into the small motion. "I apparently broke some American rule. I should have researched first." She offered a small, conspiratorial smile. "I was winning till then." She patted the arm beneath hers, half expecting him to purr like a cat. "You don't have to worry. Don't have to do my job for me."

He shrugged and slouched a bit more, but turned into her body, not closed off. "It's not a big thing." He moved forward again, her hand still on his arm sliding back towards his elbow, making her scurry to keep up for the first few steps. "I got a job doing maintenance work for someone on-station who has space to put us all up."

A salary and a rent-free place to live! It was perfect. But it wasn't Gavin's place to find such a situation. Much less without telling her. "You didn't have to," she said again.

He lengthened his strides and kept talking as though she hadn't said a word. "I've already told the others, and they're packing for our move."

"Without *asking* me?" All right, maybe she hadn't managed calm and gentle. Yet. She tried again, "I'm proud of you for finding a sensible situation." That sounded much more Queen-like, even if she only barely meant it. She *was* glad he'd found a good path, assuming... "This job *is* something you want, isn't it?" By his hesitation, she could tell it wasn't. "You're not responsible for the Hive's well-being." He should know this; he wasn't from some foreign culture. "I am."

"Please," he whispered. He grabbed her closest hand in his dry one, but didn't look at her. "Please let me do this."

Regardless of her own successes and failures, regardless of the way she wanted to protect him from this choice, she had to honor that plea. Regardless of her selfish desire to be her Hive's savior. "All right. But the moment you change your mind about this position, don't you dare hesitate to cast off the chains of fiscal responsibility. That's what I'm *for*."

Gavin pushed red-blond hair behind his ear, the strands immediately falling out of place again, forward into his blue eyes. Loose and sweet and utterly unbound. Free. "We're going to be living with an American Star Ranger. Maybe you can bless her apartment. I heard an audioplay about one once."

She tuned out his recitation of the Ranger audioplay, what he remembered of it, complete with sound effects. *Bless the apartment?* She hadn't even blessed the ship she lived on. Would the gods even listen to her, useless and ineffectual as she was? Well, it was something she could offer to the Hive's newest benefactor, at least.

It was probably *all* she could offer to a Star Ranger. Whatever that was. Something in law enforcement, it sounded like.

⟋ Chapter Three ⟋

Acknowledged, Alone

Victor's Queen slammed the door to the station-assigned quarters as best she could and stalked past him. "If you're not already packed, hop to it. *Apparently*, Gavin is moving us out." She slammed the door to her and Lois's (nominally) shared room behind herself.

"Good afternoon. How're you? My shoulder's doing well, thanks," he whispered in her wake. He shrugged the aforementioned shoulder. Gavin had told him the same a few hours earlier, and he'd already packed.

It wasn't like he had much. They'd only been on the station for a week and a half, part of which he'd spent in Medical. So before they headed out to their new flat, he had plenty of time to do both his sets of physical therapy exercises—one set from Luciano, who'd patched him up as best he could and who knew the standard treatment for *miner's shoulder*; and one from the American doctors who'd knitted his shoulder back together with some crazy tech unheard of on Dyfed.

Gavin blew in, red-blond hair sticking every which way and cheeks pink with exertion. Or annoyance. "I can't believe she walked away from me!"

Victor pressed at the tender spot where he'd been mended by the Americans. *I'm not getting involved in that discussion.* Rotated the bone in the socket. No pain yet. "When I finish these exercises, you want to work on some stage combat with me?" The Americans said the activity should be fine and help build muscle. "We can find gym space today and keep going back whenever we want." Then again, Luciano said it would be too much and that Victor needed to work on not-scarring the damaged tissue.

Two doctors was really one too many.

Gavin threw himself into a plastic chair, white with swirls of dirt—well, composite strengthener, the same thing the station itself was made of, but it looked like dirt—and held his arms out like tree branches. His presence radiated outward from the tense place between his eyebrows. "I'm doing everything I can for this Hive, and augh! She's like to drive me mad."

He pulled his pad out of a pocket, flicked the screen a couple of times, and crumpled forward to stare at it.

Victor waited. Gavin would explain himself soon enough, and Victor would be there to help with whatever his Hive mate needed. Victor might have taken longer to Devote than some others, but he'd prove himself and earn his place in the Hive. Supporting Gavin was an easy place to start.

"I need an escape." Gavin flicked his pad's screen again. He flipped it to show Victor. "Maybe this is just the thing." Hands freed, he tore open a Tribute packet and bit into one viciously. He didn't offer to share.

The corners of Victor's mouth tightened. *You need an escape from the Hive? You can't leave us!*

Everyone was leaving him today. Gavin wanted to escape. Rhiannon had just returned from who-knew-where. Alan was off giving an academic lecture to the locals. Last Victor had seen Luciano, the other boy was hunched on his bed, tapping single-mindedly at a tablet.

And Lois, Victor's dearest darling Lois. He'd woken that morning with her shampoo's citrus-and-mint scent teasing his nose. Her mink-soft hair was strewn across his mouth, and her sleep-soft body curled against his side. She'd woken slowly, vulnerable, blinking sleepy eyelashes that brushed and tickled his skin.

They'd had nothing to do, no plans for the day, and he'd hoped to hold her and talk about their brave new future, but it wasn't to be. In minutes, lines appeared between her brows and she extracted herself from the comfortable bed to thud her feet against the hard floor. She was dressed and gone before he managed to ask what she wanted to do with their spare time.

Victor schooled his face into blankness and read Gavin's announcement.

Locals and visitors, old and young, ladies and gentlemen, Cleopatra's Palace is proud to announce our annual performance. This year, you will be entertained, amazed, and (dare we say it?) titillated by

The Cleopatra's Palace Brothel Revue and Odyssey Recitation

The date and time followed, and then in very small print on the left edge:

If you'd like to be involved as a member of the stage crew, please contact Cleopatra's Palace. Serious inquiries only. No compensation offered (of any kind).

Victor handed back the pad and picked up the squishy ball Luciano had made for him from lentils and an emptied pillow. He squeezed and released. Squeezed and released. "Aren't you going to be busy enough with the Ranger's quarters? I don't know if you'll have the time for this." He rotated his forearm, parallel to the floor, keeping a firm grip on the mass in his hand. "We can escape from seriousness together. You love quarterstaffs."

"I love stage combat. Because of the theatre." Gavin jabbed a finger at the pad. "This is *theatre*." He nodded firmly. "I'm going to do it." But he still toyed with the end of his belt, mangling it.

Victor raised his arms over his head, pressing up tenderly. *What about our Hive? Shouldn't we do stuff together? Are you even going to invite ME?* He tensed too much, and the squishy ball fell to the floor. "Argh!"

It looked like Luciano was right after all. Because the American doctors didn't think he'd have any problems with things like that. Then again, they hadn't gotten him into their flesh knitting machines until after Luciano had done gods knew what and they'd all passed out from hypoxia for gods knew how long.

Gavin didn't rush to help. When Victor stood from picking up his therapy prop, the other boy was on a call with a formidable woman. Her nose was long and thin, and her curled hair piled in a tower on her head. Somehow, she seemed the scariest person Victor had ever seen, even though her face was perfectly neutral. Maybe that was the scary part. No one was ever perfectly neutral.

"—my mother is Audra Reynolds, Madam—"

Victor folded into a chair, rubbing his shoulder with tentative pressure. *Gavin trading on his mother's name? I never thought we'd see the day.*

"—experience with smoke machines, of course, and livestock—"

Victor picked up the squishy ball again and started over. *The easy exercises should get me warmed back up.* He squished and released. Rotated his forearm. Started to make a circle from the shoulder.

Searing pain pushed through him like the bullet going in all over again.

A whine strangled out of his throat. Short. A nanosecond. Hardly noticeable. *Luciano told me not to push it.* It was time for Victor to find some ice. In a second. As soon as he felt less shaky and like he wanted to get out of this chair.

Gavin bounced over and hugged him. "I got it! I'm going to go interview to be the lead set and special effects designer!"

He stuffed his pad in his pocket and dashed out the door without so much as a *See you in a bit.*

Their Hive was drifting apart, and they'd only been on the station a few days. Gavin was making it worse with his *escaping* to the theatre. But what could Victor do? It wasn't like he could force togetherness. Not like Rhiannon could.

Victor sighed. Maybe set design could be fun to learn.

Already packed for whenever Gavin led the Hive to their new quarters, Victor had nothing left to do. *This official housing is so boring and sterile. I'm going out.*

He'd finished his physical therapy for the day, so now it was time to do something fun. Freeing. *Who's available? Rhiannon's mad. Gavin's out. Gwyn's ignoring us. Gods know what Luciano is doing right now.*

That left Alan, the man who'd saved them all with his mind, carried Victor's unconscious body to safety, and epitomized the kind of Devoted Victor longed to be. From the time he'd been a child reading about Hive achievements and watching his father in public (never at home), Victor knew his path: he wanted to be the super-smart man who loved his Queen and whose mind brought honor to both his Hive and his family.

Barely two months off Dyfed, and he'd already had to revamp that plan. Not just because Alan—followed by Gavin—was the super-smart Devoted with brainpower to spare. But because he'd found a new purpose. The stage combat had seemed a gentle hobby at first, something to pass the time and improve his fitness. But when he'd been able to *use* it in service, to be his Queen's physical *shield*...

Well, that had clarified things. Victor wasn't meant to be as engineering-style brainy as the rest of his Hive mates. No. He'd Devoted in a pool of his own blood, and his place was in front of his Queen. Keeping her safe from physical harm. He'd train his body in all the martial arts and make *battle strategy* the thing that made him super-smart instead.

Even so, watching Alan's successes made him pull at his shirt hem and look away. *He's probably not even going to appreciate my picking him up from this meeting.* Victor grabbed his squishy therapy ball one last time and gave it a few good squeezes. *I'm certainly strong enough for this. Physical stuff is my forte. I only have to be better than Alan at this one thing.* He tossed the ball in the air, caught it, and deposited it back on the table. He had a Hive mate to track down.

Two elevators and one overcrowded cart ride later, he'd worked his way to the inner spokes and the office block where Alan's shared calendar claimed he was giving a talk about his Alcubierre drive.

Victor slipped into the back of the room, which was full of people in uniforms and a few locals who wore floppy streamers for clothes. *These local fashions elude me. Give me a grey tunic and black trousers any day.* Unlike flamboyant Gavin, Victor only ever wore grey and black.

Behind a podium at the room's head, Alan waved his hands above his shoulders like a madman. It reminded Victor of his physical therapy exercises from the American doctors.

Alan breathed in heavily, baring a few teeth in a dismayed sneer. "No!" Alan emphasized his answer with a downward slash of his arms that made Victor's shoulder twinge. "You may *not* have the jet from my ship." The bags under Alan's eyes stood out, heavy and dark. "Not only would you need to ask Queen-Commander Ceridwen, which, gasp"—He said the word *gasp* and gestured down at himself with eyes mockingly wide—"isn't me, but it won't do you any good. It's Professor Cantor's design, from the University of Cardiff."

Victor slouched against the wall, his suddenly pounding heart thumping against the plastic at his back. *That may be the first lie I've ever heard him tell. Why would he give his Professor credit for this?* Victor schooled his features into blankness.

One chiffon-streamer-wearer raised a hand. "Mister Jones, will you be giving any private demonstrations or interviews?"

Alan's arms flew upwards again. "Manawyddan give me patience!" he cried. "This very conference is an interview. I've already demonstrated the maths." The wall behind him was, indeed, coated in messy scribbles that could have explained tensor motion. "Any of you who care about the theory can talk with me later." He stuffed his pad into the pocket at his back. "For now, I'm *busy*."

Alan stormed off the miniature stage, stomped down the aisles of murmuring Americans, and caught Victor's good elbow. Their arms locked together, and Alan pulled them out the door and down the corridor.

"Let's go," he growled. "And thanks for coming to save me."

A smile quirked at the right corner of Victor's mouth. Alan could be an unsubtle mess of frustrated emotions, but he was the Hive's mess. "Let's go get lunch." *Teambuilding has commenced!* Their arms were still linked.

Alan grumbled, "And pay for it on credit. Again." But he didn't tug Victor away from the markets, so Victor called it success. They rode an empty elevator down from the administrative-business floor.

Slouching down to his companion's height and leaning lightly on Alan's shoulder, Victor asked, "Why'd you lie about your professor being the one to make the mini jet?"

Alan shrugged, jostling Victor's lower ribs. "I may want universal recognition, but they weren't really listening to me. Better Professor Cantor get the credit than have my ideas stolen by some foreign pseudo-intellectuals." He huffed a breath upward, and his hair swayed in its wake. One displaced strand pushed into Victor's eye.

I didn't realize he was this much shorter than me. Short enough that, this close, I'm getting a good view of how messy his hair is.

They stepped off on the market level, where short-term visitors mixed with the long-term locals. The crowding press of bodies, picking up fruits at one booth or sweating to lift containers from another, should've heated the area, but some smart administrator had anticipated this and set the air temperature even colder.

"I miss our nice, warm ship," Victor said. His only warm part was his elbow, still cradled in Alan's. Determinedly, he pretended not to notice they had stayed attached to each other for so long. *Better not to get cold or lost. Or be alone in this sea of strange.*

Alan pointed with his free hand to a booth at the end of the row they were approaching. "Corn dogs?"

A man in denims, flannel, and trainers knocked hard into Alan, pushing him more strongly against Victor's side. Not even mumbling a "sorry" in passing.

"Rude," Alan whispered. He kept the new, reduced distance between them.

Victor held their joined arms tight against his side. *Solidarity*. He both loved the market's strange smells and colors, and hated its overwhelming population and presumptuous shoppers.

Case in point: a young girl, maybe eight, wearing pale purple streamers over her darker purple bodystocking jumped in front of them. The jumping moved her streamers in tangled patterns. When the Devoted pair attempted to dodge her, she jumped again. Stopping them.

Victor looked around, eyes darting almost too quickly for him to process the data, trying to find whomever she belonged to. *Ah, there.* An older woman with black hair and charred tree-bark skin wore almost the same outfit as the girl in front of them, but in blue. She watched, a fond smile on her face, and didn't interfere. *You let your kid accost strangers like this all the time?*

Alan waved his free hand like he was having a seizure. "What!" he yelled at the little girl.

Her face scrunched up, making her look like pictures of miniature dogs from Earth. It smoothed and she tried to climb Alan's closest leg. "Is it true you have a queen?"

Head tilted down further than needed to look at her, Alan scratched at the bridge of his nose and sighed. "Yes." He sounded more resigned than joyous. And that was just *wrong* for a Devoted. "I do have a Queen. I don't need a new one, no matter how cute your mam says you are."

The girl let go of Alan's leg, but didn't run away. Wasn't put off by his brusqueness. She ran in circles before them, spun to get caught up in her streamers, then spun the other way. Breathless, she came to a stop. Panting, she reattached herself to Alan's leg. Victor could smell her sickly sweet child sweat.

"Is she pretty? Do you love her? Does she live in a castle?" The girl's eyes widened. "Do *you* live in a castle?"

Alan put his free hand over his eyes and buried his head in Victor's good shoulder. "Yes. For a given definition. No. We live on a space ship." *He's really good at humoring kids. Or he hates them. One or the other.*

Victor nudged Alan, not dislodging him from his hiding place. He led his Hive mate forward, slowly, and was pleased when the girl gave ground. "And now we're going to lunch. I think your mam is looking for you." He pointed at the girl's mother, even though pointing at a person might be rude. The older woman blushed, but kept her head high.

The girl shook her head so hard that her whole torso moved with it. "Nuh-uh!"

However, she moved out of their path and let them progress, skipping along at Alan's side and asking what Rhiannon looked like and whether she was born a princess instead of a queen and about her crown and a love story about a prince "because princes mean *true love*." Victor tuned out the monologue.

But he had to watch the path ahead of them, what with Alan avoiding eye contact with anything, especially little girls. That meant that Victor saw what Alan didn't: they'd acquired a crowd, all of whom hung on Alan's sharp words about their Queen.

A man in green-slashed chiffon—the color of new shoots at the shoulders, darkening to midsummer shade grass at the ankles, gold cuffed—over a black bodystocking joined the conversation unexpectedly. *Have they no manners in this place?* Ostensibly to the little girl, the man agreed with Alan. "Hell yes, their queen is pretty. She's more than pretty. She is *hot*. I would dock my bits there."

Victor's hands clenched. *I'm just doing my therapy exercises.* He blanked his expression and watched the guy mug for the rest of the crowd. *He's not a threat.*

The man continued to school the little girl. "It's just a rank on their planet, honey. Like doctor or captain. Nothing to be intimidated by."

The little girl asked the man, "Are you a prince?"

He smirked. "I don't need to be a prince to take a woman home with me."

Alan's body went totally still at Victor's side.

The girl's mother spoke up. *Oh, so NOW she gets upset.* "Don't go ruining her dreams," she admonished the man who thought Rhiannon was just a normal woman. Someone to treat like everyone else.

And she was just a woman. But she was also a Queen, their Hive's keeper and their lives' motivation. She was the earth and the ocean and the sky, the intercessor for the gods. Rhiannon couldn't be compared to normal women, not to the women in the corridor nor even to exceptional ones like Victor's beloved Lois.

The man defended himself to the girl's mother. "Do you still tell her that Santa brings her Christmas presents?" He jabbed a finger in the woman's face. "No, no you don't."

While the crowd argued, Victor pulled Alan around them all. Towards the end of the row where they could find corn dogs they'd originally come for.

Unhappy lines spread from Alan's nose down to his flat mouth. He kept his voice down, though, when he exploded. "We can't let them think that. Get away with that. The things that man said about our Queen!" He didn't manage to find a predicate for that sentence, but he didn't need to.

Victor knew exactly how he felt. *This could be the nudge that brings us all together.* He extricated his arm from his Hive mate's and shook out his cramped hand. "They don't understand us, don't know what it means to have a Queen. The little girl had the right idea. We need to make it clear that Rhiannon is a *Queen*, and that it means more than some everyday title."

They needed to remind themselves just as much. On Dyfed, he would revel in the Devotion that almost seemed an imposition here.

Alan nodded enthusiastically. "Something obvious and immediately visible. Something that makes it clear to everyone that she's important and loved." He slouched, an odd move for Alan. "I hate to admit it, but I might want to go home."

"We bring home with us wherever we go. And we've got to bring a taste of Dyfed to the Americans." Victor sucked his lower lip. Rolled his shoulders in their sockets. *What can we do, though?*

The answer hit him. It was so obvious. Even the little American girl had wondered about it.

"We need to make Rhiannon a crown."

The scent of corn and grease and pork filled the air, weighing it down with oily heat. They'd finally reached the end of the row.

Alan cocked his head to the side. *Smelling lunch or thinking about the crown?* "We'll need to make it ourselves. I've got some gold. Inert metal for coating wires and so forth."

Victor's heart shivered in his rib cage. This was going to work.

"We can use branches from the garden to weave a crown of leaves. Our love and Devotion made manifest. A crown made from nature and science. Grown and crafted."

Victor had always intended to avoid Queens who *wanted* crowns. He'd watched his dad live a double life, torn between his all-encompassing Hive and the family he left behind for days at a time. He'd never wanted to be that kind of man. But with Lois in his Hive, and with such strangeness attacking his way of life at every turn... it suddenly made a kind of sense. His dad had been so involved with his Hive, his Queen, because it gave his life purpose and provided him with strength to face the exterior world. In contrast, the family provided him with internal acceptance and familial affection.

Besides, Rhiannon hadn't *asked* for a crown. She only had to accept it.

Chapter Four

Longing for Home

Luciano sunk down on the cot in his bare little room and hid his face in his hands. They'd moved into the Ranger's quarters, though she herself hadn't reached the station yet, and Rhiannon had promised the Hive would go to the ship to pick up some personal touches for their new home.

He wasn't sure he believed her. She'd do what she wanted in her own time, and her Devoted would simply have to wait on her whims.

Mother Mary, I'm becoming bitter as chicory. It wasn't becoming in a man not even in university. He drew himself taller and pulled out his pad to write a fresh letter home.

Dearest Mother and Aurelia,

I hope this letter finds you well. Although I can't send money from my paychecks right now, my prayers are with you. Aurelia, please know I'm doing everything in my power to make sure you can finish your education on Dyfed. You have so much potential. (I don't say that solely as your older brother, but also as a highly regarded Devoted.)

Ah, Devotion. I'm starting to think I made the wrong choice when I hitched my fortune to this Hive. The memory of the choice sits heavy on my stomach, but that's past now.

In happier news, the wounded Hive mate I told you about in my previous letter is improving. The Americans here on John Wayne Station—above the planet Kessel—have very different medicines than we do at home. They claim they've completely healed the wound in Victor's shoulder and that the man needs only to exercise the new fibers. You and I, of course, know better ever since that year with the lamed worker who lived in our house. (Mother, you are too kind to strangers with sad faces and tender eyes.) Don't worry. I have him doing all sorts of rotational and stretching ex-ercises. No one's muscles will scab and scar into uselessness when I'm the attending physician!

I'll send more letters and more money when I can. Unfortunately, there's nothing enclosed with this message today.

Baci e abbraci,
Luciano

He saved and bundled the letter into a single flash packet with the others he'd written in the past week.

Now to find out how to send these back home.

At one point, he might have believed Rhiannon would find a way. He might have believed she'd use her brilliance and tenacity to gift him with this thing he so deeply craved.

However, he'd been part of her Hive for months now and had yet to get anything he wanted. He still acted as her pilot, for instance.

Though, he had to admit that she'd finally taken lessons to relieve him. Also, she'd *finally* allowed him to do something medical when she'd assigned him Victor's wounds.

Too little, too late... and goodnight to the bucket, as far as he was concerned.

No, no. Rhiannon could still be his perfect Queen. All these troubles of the last few weeks, they could be growing pains.

Even as he thought it, it sounded like an excuse. *She's just been busy.*

He'd done his best to take some of the pressure. He'd flown the ship and tended the sick. He'd discussed mathematics with Alan and cross-linguistic singing styles with Gavin.

A quick search of the station directory showed that Rhiannon's Hive was not the only Dyfed presence. There was a junior consulate on the third level, far from the main elevators. *They don't need to know anything about us in order to send letters with the diplomatic couriers.* He firmed his jaw, trying to exhibit courage he didn't feel. If he went, he'd be walking into the lion's den, tempting the consulate employees to ask who he was and why he was so far from home.

A scratching came at his chamber door.

"Luciano?" An angel's voice, muted through the door, carried perfect vowels and the touch of a caress. "I thought we might go about the station together and find you an internship."

Too little, too late.

He opened the door and strode out, chest puffed as large as he could make it. "This place gives me milk in my knees," he told her, shaking his head in negation. *Please, God, let me go home where they know my worth and accept my desires.* "I'm heading out on my own."

She ran a hand through her hair, pulling her face into strange shapes, and stepped back to let him pass. "If you'd rather." She sounded remarkably unenthusiastic.

He gave her a flat smile, body rigid as salted cod, and went off to make an appointment with the consulate.

I'd rather not be here at all. If that comes up in conversation with whoever takes my letters, well, it's just chatter.

Chapter Five

Oath Breakers

In the heavy gravity, each step felt weighted by depression and despair. Rhiannon marched her Hive towards the last view of their home, their freedom. They stumped a circuitous path to imprisonment, stagnancy, death. This was no journey on the season wheel. It was a serpentine line with a definite end: the loss of their ship-home.

Now that her Hive had acquired *permanent housing*—as far as the station administration was concerned—and now that they'd gone eighteen waking days without paying their bills... well, the station was allowing them one last trip to grab necessities before locking the *Cauldron* down. And Rhiannon planned to take advantage of it before the Ranger arrived. It would give them a chance to be better settled in. Harder to evict.

Two months ago, Rhiannon had led her Hive off Dyfed and into a whole new world. She had led ideas to conclusions. Right now, she led her people down the docking spoke to the *Ceridwen's Cauldron*, possibly for the last time until she paid the docking fees.

Gavin started singing pieces from *Les Misérables*, which only earned him a poke in the ribs from Victor. So the baritone changed to *Fare Thee Well Northumberland*, barely an improvement. Alan tried to kick off a nationalistic round of *Hen Wlad Fy Nhadau*, but that didn't take.

After that they all trudged in silence.

Yeah, the station authorities can't banish the harp from your hand, but they can certainly encourage you to silence it for the time being.

Well, Rhiannon wouldn't have it! Her responsibility for her people meant she looked after their health and well-being—physical *and* mental. She could get them out of this fix. She just needed to come up with a money-making scheme or a way to barter favors, and the ship would be free. They could move on.

And while they had to live on John Wayne Station, they'd learn something. They'd learn skills. They'd learn American culture. Maybe they'd learn what they wanted to do with their unscheduled lives, free of adult interference.

Her boot heels thudded on the dirty-white plastic walkway.

"I think it's getting warmer," she said, encouraging a positive conversational line. They were walking away from the station, *towards* their *Cauldron*, and the docking spoke felt more and more like home with every step.

Alan hummed agreement. "They flash-heat ships on lock, for decontamination and de-icing. We're getting close."

Silence. Well, that was a short-lived discussion.

"So, Gwy-Lois." Rhiannon had so much trouble not using her best friend's nickname. They talked less these days.

Gwyn had barely spoken to her since she'd awoken. "What're you looking forward to rescuing from your quarters?"

The tall blonde's shoulders lifted and fell, ever graceful. No more answer forthcoming.

Rhiannon would have to pin her down for some bonding when they could next be alone. She had a nasty suspicion that Gwyn was still upset about Victor's getting shot on the *Llyr's Llambo*. Well, not so much that he got shot as that he bled out in her hands, more interested in cementing his Devotion than in reassuring his girlfriend. Rhiannon hoped reforging her own relationship with Gwyn could lessen that sting.

Maybe they could go shopping in the station's central market, the way they'd done at the capital's covered market back home. For years, they'd gone to sort through trinkets, piled precariously high on wobbly tables that didn't have enough surface area to display the wares. It'd be a happy, nostalgic activity. Extra benefit: window shopping didn't cost anything.

"Oh, good. We're here." Alan could not have sounded more forced. Or more relieved. He reached into Rhiannon's personal space to snatch the day pass from her hands, but she smacked the questing fingers away. This was *her* ship. *Her* responsibility. *Her* hard-won pass.

The airlock hissed open. More white plastic hallway. She counted the threads of dirt-grey swirls. *One, two, three, four.*

At *five*, the party reached the *Ceridwen's Cauldron*'s exterior door, their last taste of *home*, inhospitable and locked down as she was.

The ship's communication system wasn't on—why bother?—so she made sure all their pads were connected, so they could talk with each other as they went their separate ways. Over the past few days, they'd spent most of their time apart. Gavin working on their quarters, handing them over to Alan when he went to the theatre. Victor doing his physical therapy and walking around the station. Luciano and Gwyn doing who knew what, though not together (of course). But here, on board the *Ceridwen's Cauldron*, they belonged together. Melded.

It felt too quiet. The engines didn't thrum. The air didn't rattle. Alan's singing voice didn't fill any rooms. The internal communications channel didn't have one person asking about food preferences for dinner while someone else, unrelated, attempted to start a discussion about epic poetry.

Rhiannon's favorite epic poetry was a modern series about a space marine from a society where Hives didn't exist. Written by a Dyfed native. Now Rhiannon wondered whether the author ever went off-planet or simply had an active imagination.

Earpiece in, she debated aloud, "Should I bring sheets, or just my duvet?"

The Ranger's apartment was giant, with multiple bedrooms, each of which had a cot. A *cot*. Rhiannon would've understood no furniture at all, sure. She'd have understood a sumptuous display of wealth that crammed every corner, yes. But empty except for a barracks-worth of cots and some outdated security equipment? She didn't understand that at all. But it wasn't her place to understand their exotically American patron-hostess, only to inhabit her dirty-white plasticky walls that glowed with the bluish inset lights every few feet. Just like the rest of this familiar-yet-different station.

"Just the duvet," Gwyn suggested. "What would you tuck sheets into?" These might have been the first neutral words she'd heard directed to her from Gwyn in days.

Alan's voice sounded far away and cavernous when he broke in. "But she'll be cold." There was a snapping sound. "Why do we have nightshade?"

Gavin scoffed. "You know it's not dangerous to touch unless you're allergic."

Victor hummed a cheery tune in the background. A second voice joined in, probably Gavin's.

Gwyn teased, "Because it's a summer blooming plant, and it was nearly summer when we left? There's some hemlock too, if you want to wait till winter." Rustling, a zipper's buzz. "What are you doing in my garden?"

"Leaving it! Too dangerous for me."

"Mmm-hmm." Gwyn made the sound sarcastic. "Let me know if you have any trembling or difficulty swallowing over the next few days."

Alan made a strangled gargling noise. "I'm feeling it now."

"No you aren't," said Gwyn, laughing.

"Hey, Gavin, do you think you can get me in touch with your new *coworkers*"—by which Alan meant the brothel employees—"to soothe my frail psyche after experiencing what Lady Lois calls a harmless little *garden*?"

"Told you," Victor singsonged. Rhiannon had no idea who *that* message was for. "Yeah, Gav. How's the play going?"

Gavin was a strange one these days. He'd taken on the role of provider for the Hive—*her role*—with his job and his negotiation for their rooms. But outside of his work, he didn't spend any time with them anymore. All of it went to his new project: the revue for which he was lead set and special effects designer. He was simultaneously the most dedicated Hive member and the least available. She was glad he was happy and taking time for himself, for his interests, but she wished he'd be more involved with the rest of them.

"Would you believe they added another set? And sheep!" Gavin laughed. "How would they have survived if I hadn't shown up? This whole thing is spiraling out of control. But the show must go on."

"I can come down and help you paint sets later," Victor offered. "All of us can, right?"

Yes. Let's bring Gavin back into the fold. It should've been her idea.

Gwyn broke in. "Alan!" Her exasperated reprimand cut off Gavin's reply. "You moved my nightshade." She must have made it down to the garden.

"Sorry." His footsteps echoed in Rhiannon's speakers.

"Don't worry about it." Gwyn's patient tone soothed any irritation from the earlier stridency. "I'll tidy it up while I grab my summer projects." It might not be summer on the station, but it was certainly summer on the *Cauldron*.

Having tuned out of that conversation, Gavin replied to Victor. "Sounds good. I'll tell them to let you all in for painting—"

"What in Annwyn's bloody Otherworld!" Alan's shocked voice sent everyone into a silent moment before they all chimed in, babbling over one another and trying to figure out what and who and—

"*Quiet!*" Rhiannon yelled.

Into the calm, she spoke slowly. So, so slowly. "Alan. Please elaborate."

"They took it. It's gone." The sound of scrambling and heavy objects moving about haphazardly. "It's my baby. My ticket to fame. And it's gone." A heavy *thunk*, as though he'd collapsed onto a hard surface. "Oh gods. We're stuck here. Without our tensor jet, we're stuck here."

Rhiannon bunched her hands in her purple duvet. *Who would steal something like that? No, who COULD steal it?* No one had access to the ship. She smoothed the fabric, trying to use the repetitive motion to calm her fraying mind. *No one except the station administrators.* "Only the local authorities could have taken it without our knowing. Are you sure it's missing?"

A disbelieving cackle drilled into her ear. "Am I sure? Am I *sure*? Yes, I'm sure. My jet is gone!"

Victor's voice was tight but strong. "We've gotta make them pay." He'd been growing more martial lately.

Luciano countered shakily, "Alan could make another one?" *Turn the other cheek*, she interpreted.

But the real problem wasn't the jet. The real problem was the people who stole it. The station authorities. The ones who upheld the local laws, who should be the first to follow its dictates. If *they* stole from visiting ships, what else might they do? She couldn't trust them anymore. Couldn't trust their supposed generosity. Couldn't trust any law officers on the station. Couldn't trust anyone in power here at all.

She'd wanted to get her people off John Wayne nearly from the first. Wanted to give them the lives they'd expected when they'd signed onto her crew.

Now, though? Now she wanted them out of here as soon as possible. Far away from the lawbreakers. Oath breakers. And she wanted to keep them as comfortable as possible.

There was only one option.

"We'll just have to steal it back."

⟩⟩ Chapter Six ⟩⟩

The Local Law

Melissa stalked John Wayne's halls on booted feet. She had a courtesy visit to make before she found her quarters and met her employee.

Her safety-cushioned shoes made no sound on the grated floors, gave no warning of her approach. That didn't stop residents from pressing themselves against walls to get out of her way. It didn't stop children from reaching for her gleaming sides with grubby hands. Almost no kids had ever seen an old, obsolete robot like her, and their often equally curious parents didn't curb inquisitiveness.

I've got plenty of bumps and edges, kiddos. You could cut yourselves.

On the third level, in the central spire, she found the Sheriff's Office. Politely, she tapped the door with one of her four fists before pushing it open. The locals could be too busy for niceties, and such places were public enough.

She strode inside. The extra cameras mounted on her backbench and shoulders silently roused in their installations. Between their input and her visor's, she'd mapped the office in micro-seconds.

What Melissa noticed about the Sheriff's Office:

- Air inside more humid than outside
- One dispatch-and-receiving person at a standing desk, plastic
- Five deputies: two at desks in the front room, two further back, one getting coffee
- One Sheriff, consoling a distraught man who brandished a receipt from the station's brothel
- Mostly plastic furniture (she'd have to be careful about wearing her shoes if she came here again or she could stick a hole right through it all)
- Layout: large front room, three offices (one the sheriff's), break room, conference room, two (maybe three; she couldn't see them) holding cells, four bathrooms (including the cells')

It took much longer for the local law enforcement to notice her in turn. She didn't begrudge the time. After all, this was the sheriff's territory, not the Star Rangers'. He and his staff were busy at work, protecting the innocent. She could wait.

But not too long. She had a job as well. Her own innocents to protect.

The young man at the dispatch-and-receiving desk finished shelving something in the cubby behind him and turned to see Melissa. "Ah, hello?"

She cocked a headlamp in consideration. She'd bet they didn't see many PRobs out here. Obsolete, unfashionable, not-usually sentient. (In fact, she was the only sentient one she'd ever heard of, and she hadn't seen any of her less-endowed brethren outside a museum in decades.) Well, their sensibilities would adjust. She refused to have trouble with local law enforcement.

She flashed her badge. "Melissa, American Star Ranger. I'm here on business."

The young man relaxed and tensed at the same time. Not an uncommon reaction. No longer confused about how to treat her, his shoulders fell from his ears. But he shifted from side to side, and his heart rate rose by a quarter.

"A Star Ranger?" he breathed.

"Did I hear something about a Star Ranger?" The slam of metal on plastic. A rubber boot scraped on grating. All motion stopped: the sheriff was in the front office.

The sheriff was older, but still fit enough to scrabble with the riffraff and come out the victor, maybe one hundred years old or so. He scanned the entranceway.

When he spotted Melissa, he didn't betray any surprise or confusion. He headed straight for her. A good lawman never showed his reactions too soon. She could respect this man.

"I'll be damned," he said. "A PRob. Never thought I'd see one of you again."

Obsolete. Unfashionable. Once she wrapped up this courtesy visit, she could get on with the business of tracking her suspects.

"Melissa." She flashed him her badge. "American Star Ranger. I'm following some leads in a string of violent crimes."

"Ranger." The sheriff nodded acknowledgement, accepting her status as both a legal authority and a sentient robot without question.

That second was less common. As far as she knew, she was the only one. Given how rare PRobs were nowadays, though, there mightn't be the too-familiar contempt to strive against. Maybe she'd see more of this easy acceptance soon.

He asked, "Are we in danger?"

Melissa shook her head, side headlamps casting buttery spotlights on the room's corners. "Just tracking suspects right now, Sheriff. Nothing to worry about yet. I came by to let you know I'm on the station in the general quarters owned by the ASR. I've got cleared employees updating them now."

He leaned against the counter beside her. *Tired or casual?* "We'd better introduce you around. It's not every day John Wayne Station rates an actual Star Ranger."

The molecules vibrated with whooping hollers from the break room. Voices filtered in.

A young-sounding woman, probably average build, mid-30s. "There's a Ranger? Here?" Aspirated sip of coffee.

"Only one?" Very young man. Maybe 12-13 years old, possibly a visiting relative or intern. Disappointed.

Melissa always liked kids, especially polite ones. Something about them. When she spent time analyzing herself, reveling in her ability to like and dislike anything, she linked children to *protected*. And what was a Ranger but the ultimate protector? She knew how to end that disappointment. Raised the volume on her speaker.

"When it comes to American Star Rangers," she called, "you only need one."

The sheriff reached out and thumped her on the back, fingers catching briefly on her vest. "You're all right, Ranger."

Her insides froze at his touch, but her outsides displayed no change.

He's probably not planting anything on me.

Still, she swiveled a discreet camera to check her back. The armor plating there was thick, too thick for her to feel atmospheric disturbance. She'd learned to protect her mechanical heart and guts. An EMP or an internal connection could fry her like the victim of an old fashioned electric chair. But not a mere touch. She didn't think.

Better safe than dead.

Her camera revealed no new attachments. Good. She trusted her fellow lawmen, but she'd had bad experiences with the human race. They didn't always believe in the sanctity of their fellow sentient beings. Didn't recognize PRobs as people. Not that she'd ever met another like herself.

The sheriff was still smiling, calling to his deputies to come meet the Ranger who'd be on station. *So much for keeping a low profile. Any visitor or mole could be informing my quarry already.* Still, she shook hands with the deputies, who admired her two-thumbed grip. She told the young boy, a child saying *hi* to mom after school, about the daring exploits of 20th-century Rangers past.

Their hearts all pounded. Some left sweaty DNA on her appendages. But not from fear, no. Excitement. They'd never seen a Star Ranger, and they were ready to make the most of it.

She hoped they'd stay out of her way. She had a job to do, and no patience for interlopers. The sheriff invited her to stay, get a coffee. Said he'd make her up a desk.

What would she do with a coffee? Well, it was nice of him to offer.

"No. I have my own desk."

She pivoted on her right legs and moved out. She needed to drop her kit and meet Gavin-plus-Hive. Then she'd be ready to hunt down a suspect.

Chapter Seven

Enmeshed

Victor stumbled through the door of their new flat, exhausted. He tripped over a straw entry mat they'd brought from Dyfed, formerly of Lois's parents' house. It hadn't been there when he left. The only decoration, it looked tiny and out of place on the grey-blue synthetic carpet, dwarfed by dirty off-white walls that looked cheaply molded.

He anticipated collapsing in one of the uncomfortable metal chairs that comprised the height of luxury in their new living room. *This is the last time I let Gavin talk me into helping at the theatre.*

Well, no. That wasn't true. He needed a distraction from the *trapped!* feeling that crept in whenever he thought of their stolen tensor jet.

Besides, he'd sworn to be the first volunteer for anything that let him spend productive time with any of his Hive mates. He just needed a break from Cleopatra's Palace. *The next courtesan to proposition me will be...*

Actually, he didn't know exactly what he'd do about it. Victor shivered, but it was just the cold of the American environmental settings.

I can't wait till Alan and I finish Rhiannon's crown. Then they'll understand to go through my Queen first. Working on the crown took time, especially to soak the twiggy branches for malleability before weaving. They'd get it done soon.

Speaking of his Queen, he heard her voice, husky and calm from deeper into the flat.

"I'll take two, please." *Click-tap-whirr.* "Straight, jack high. I'll be surprised if you have better than two pair, maybe one face card."

A feminine voice replied through a background of fuzzy static. "Affirmative, young lady."

Victor followed the sounds, boot heels muffled by the industrial carpeting that Gavin laid the day before to protect wires from crossing. He went through a doorway, just wide enough for a broad-shouldered man, to reach the dinette area. It was as bleak as the entry room, with the same heathered blue carpets that didn't cushion anyone's feet and the same off-white walls that had been molded with pre-provided dirt streaks. Recirculating air hissed, scrubbed of all offensive smells yet somehow still disturbingly stale.

At the small kitchen table, his Queen faced off against an intimidatingly large metal construction. They seemed like perfect opposites at first glance: warm tones versus cool; soft hair and smooth metal; compact human and double-sized robot. Their cards stood between them with Victor's squishy therapy ball where he'd left it on the left edge.

He had never seen a metal structure quite like this one. It had a head, like a person, and a preponderance of arms, like an insect. From the way it faced off with Victor's Queen, it was more than just a sculpture or a remote-controlled automaton. Although he had yet to meet the American Space Ranger whose rooms they inhabited, he felt reasonably confident that this was it.

That this was *she*, if Gavin's description was correct.

Rhiannon and the probably-Ranger mirrored each other across the furniture with the same head tilts. Each leaned two elbows on the table, though the robot reserved two, and focused more on her cards than on her opponent.

The Ranger said, "Welcome back, Devoted Victor." Even their voices fell into the same husky register, though he knew he could tell them apart by accent alone.

The Ranger must have looked him up before arriving on the station the day before. On the one hand, he'd have preferred a formal introduction. On the other hand, the greeting's casual nature did cut down on potential first-meeting awkwardness. He appreciated her consideration. Were all self-aware robots so polite? His sample size so far consisted of one.

Rhiannon started and turned around, brunette hair falling into her eyes. She placed her cards face down on the table. "Have you been out?"

He slouched. *She has to know I wasn't here. Right? She's just trying to ask where I've been.* Queens noticed everything about their Devoted. It showed how much they cared. "I was helping rig a fog machine." He didn't mention that it kept his mind off the stolen jet and the uncertainty of its return, not in this company.

What if we're stranded here forever, with no hope of becoming anything more than set-builders in the theatre season?

Turning back to the table, Rhiannon ran a hand through her hair. Twirled an end for a moment. "I'm glad you and Gavin are relaxing."

She tossed her cards on the table. "I fold."

The Ranger robot's two upper arms crossed behind her head. "All right, then, Commander. I'm satisfied to report you've won half, and only half, these hands. These station people may not appreciate your statistical talents, but you sure as Hell weren't cheating in any sense that I can see." The Ranger's eye visor shaded into a paler blue, though the side-lamps didn't move or change, simply poised and ready. "I reckon your Hive is above board."

Lois would have loved the quaint language, and he ached to share this moment with her. He'd have to find her and tell her all about meeting the Ranger before he forgot.

Rhiannon dipped her head in gracious acceptance, but didn't meet the Ranger's eye again. "One more hand?"

Victor grabbed his squishy ball off the table as he passed them. *Does she want to be found out? Because we're certainly not planning to stay "above board" by the local authorities' definitions. Not if we're planning to steal things, even if they're our own.* He squeezed the ball as prescribed, though he hadn't noticed it doing him any good for days now. *I should talk to Luciano about that.* But Luciano wouldn't be around now, too busy out doing whatever he was doing. At the job Rhiannon got him, maybe, or just wandering the station. They hadn't seen him at the theatre, either.

Lois should be home.

He scratched on her chamber door, already envisioning her smile, just for him. Her silvery hair running through his calloused fingers. Her affection like a physical thing that could lodge in his rib cage to keep company with his heart.

The door opened.

He said, "Hello, beloved." His vision went fuzzy at the edges so only her perfect, pointy face came into sharp focus. He felt his heart rate slow and wondered that it had ever been too fast. He hadn't been stressed a moment ago, had he? Yet, here, with her, everything seemed slower, better, calmer. She was his talisman against all evil. His place of safety.

She said, "I thought you were out with Gavin?" Her voice was oddly muffled, and she sounded almost disappointed to see him. But that couldn't be right.

He slouched against her doorjamb and reached to take her hand in his own. *My arm isn't trembling yet today! Even after all that work with the fog machine.* He could feel the ridiculous grin spreading across his face, only to die a quick and painful death when Gwyn—Lois—leapt backwards before he could touch her.

Her weight shifted from foot to foot, and she tilted her head to hide behind a hair curtain. Then she shook it back, blowing at a strand before her face, moving it without her hands. Hands which he now saw wore tight gloves. "I'm working with poison." This close up, he could spy the small respirator when her mouth opened, protecting her from particles and shuttering her voice.

Deeper into the room behind her, three lengths of weed—all taller than he—lay flat under a long glass cover. The tiny white flowers looked shriveled. "Hemlock?" Direct skin contact against fresh hemlock was iffy, but if he inhaled any particles they'd take at most twenty minutes to kill him.

He could see why she wouldn't want him in the room with it, but he craved her companionship. Couldn't she put aside this unimportant plant and spend a few moments with her boyfriend?

She blushed and half-laughed, shoulders hunching up with the motion. "You're getting better at recognizing my plants." Her lips pressed together to hold back further laughter at his abysmal non-talent with vegetation, but it didn't keep the edges of her mouth from turning upward. "I started drying this before we left. In case we needed to make sedatives or herbicides." *Or religious brews,* she didn't say, which would be unlikely but still...

"Maybe we could go for a walk around the station when you finish up?" Victor backed up, increasing the distance between himself and the poisonous powder that might be in the air. Standing outside her room, he scuffed his boot's toe on the floor. "We could spend some time together. See the local sights?"

She scrunched her nose and shifted away.

"Some other time," she said. "I can't stop in the middle of this."

Right. "It wouldn't be safe," he agreed. He went back to the kitchen to wash his hands a few times.

Chapter Eight

Where We Belong

Papers and rocks (and God knew what else) crunched under Luciano's feet until he reached the small desk where the doctor's full-time assistant was doodling on a pad. The assistant looked up. "About time you got here."

Luciano's mouth pulled down at the left corner before he straightened it out into a thin line. "I don't have regular hours."

Somehow, Luciano found himself in possession of an internship with a physician fifteen decks away from the Ranger's quarters, down in a lower rent area. Rhiannon had arranged it for him, more of a volunteer clerk's position than a medical apprenticeship, but Luciano would take what he could get.

What he could get apparently included an arrogant co-worker and an atmosphere not ideal for a doctor's office.

The doctor's office smelled *moldy*.

On the second day of his volunteership, he'd asked the doctor about the mold and suggested complaining to the station's environmental people.

The doctor said, "We're on our own set of filters down here. Wouldn't want the sickness germs to float out into the common areas, eh?"

Luciano interpreted this to mean that he should complain to the doctor rather than the station, but volunteering to clean the filters did no good since the little office couldn't afford the correct kinds of cleaner nor filter replacements.

On this day, day four of working for the office, Luciano had left Rhiannon playing cards with the Space Ranger, taken the elevator fifteen floors down, and trekked inwards (past areas where people used electric carts to go long distances, then past where people walked on bare metal, then into the area where pedestrians navigated broken carts) until he reached the office. Even though it seeped into the vomit-brown papers that covered the walls in uneven strips, the office's moldy smell was a breath of fresh air after the tension and betrayal in their quarters.

Rhiannon was lying to the Ranger with her actions. Oh, they were true enough (Rhi *could* play poker), but her omission of the upcoming caper plot's existence tainted the experience.

The doctor's assistant, a 20ish man with unfortunate adult acne and no interest in healing the sick that Luciano had seen, scowled. "Well, I have things to do, so you needed to be here." He jabbed a flaking finger onto the desktop between a sticky soy sauce puddle and a haphazard computer paper pile. Clearly, these things hadn't included tidying the intake desk.

"Like what?"

"None of your business." That meant he planned to pant heavily at the brothel on his lunch break again.

Luciano's mouth turned up into a derisive smirk without his conscious permission. In the few days Luciano had been here, the assistant always made sure to take appointments for the brothel employees and to pet their hands *accidentally* when accepting their computer-generated conclusion cards. "Fine. Whatever."

The man rocketed from his chair. The force tipped a plastic cup onto the brushed metal desk. Thankfully it was empty, and nothing spilled onto any documents. "Don't *whatever* me."

Luciano's heart sped and he leaned his weight forward, ready to fight, but what was the point? The assistant didn't matter to Luciano, not really. The sex-starved man had no bearing on Luciano's life. He was like cabbage for an afternoon snack. He didn't even make a difference in whether Luciano got paid.

"Just go do your thing, okay? I can handle this."

Appeased, the assistant picked up his personal pad and twirled it with one hand, the other pointing at the medical confetti on the desk. "You still have to enter those records from yesterday. The doc's in the back room if you have any questions. So don't save them for me."

Oh dear Lord, why didn't he already do this? Sighing, Luciano slid into the still-warm plastic chair. He had a job to do, even if it was ridiculous. "The computer should really do this part." The computer made its conclusions and printed the cards out. Once the doctor signed the card-stock, sometimes after the patient left, the information required manual entry into the records system.

"Yeah, well, regulations. Gotta have a real person look at them." That may have been the longest, non-confrontational sentence the assistant had ever said to Luciano. He finished up with one more instruction, "Be sure to check the doc's schedule."

He's so transparent. "I'll ping you if any cuties from the brothel stop by."

Half out the open door to the station, left open to keep the moldy smell from getting overwhelming (and thus negating the point of having the office on its own air filters), the assistant spat back over his shoulder, "Fuck you."

Luciano smirked at the papers on the desk. "Not even if you paid me." He pulled his personal pad from a deep cargo pocket and opened up the letter he'd started the day before.

The conclusion cards sat in judgment on the metal surface, reprimanding him for not inputting their information to the system.

He didn't care. None of the patients yesterday had any lasting problems or damage.

Dearest Mother and Aurelia,

I hope this letter finds you well. Although I am still short of funds to send, my situation is improving. My Queen has procured an internship with a local medical professional, and I have learned so much in so few days.

I understand now how the American doctors on John Wayne Station treated my Hive mate, Victor, who I mentioned in my last few letters. They have such amazing technology here! They have machines which can replicate and repair flesh without scarring or alienation! Imagine if the mining company back home purchased such marvelous inventions.

My first day, a pair of men came in suffering from minor abrasions (and one broken bone), entirely their own faults for fist-fighting in a bar. The doctor ushered them into a diagnostic box, closed the door behind them, and pressed a button. The diagnostic box told us everything wrong with the two men. Then, the doctor took them to three other machines: one for cleaning and covering minor cuts, one for bone setting, and one for bone repair.

The men left in perfect form and ready to fight again later, I expect.

Supposedly, this office has comparatively little exotic equipment, which is why the doctor needed so many machines. Still, to someone who has never seen such speedy healing, this is miraculous! How wonderful that these annoying wounds are like nothing before the Americans' technology.

Other than that one exciting moment, nothing much happens in this little physician's office. A few ladies and gentlemen have come in for weekly check-ups (please don't judge me for interacting, on a medical level, with the local prostitutes), and their appointments are even more brief. They simply walk into the aforementioned diagnostic box and leave, not caring what the results say. The doctor rarely even reads the conclusion cards from these appointments, trusting the computer to flag any problems. It's all very <u>routine</u>.

Victor is improving, if you're curious, and I've met my very first PRob. Have you heard of them? The database here says they've been out of production for thirty years or so. They're giant, human-insectoid robots that—

"Help! Someone!" A grey-blond man stumbled through the door, clutching his chest and reeling woozily.

Luciano dropped the pad. It slid off piles and office supplies before clattering to its final resting place on the desktop, but Luciano didn't see where it landed.

He was already at the doorway. He gripped the new man's arms tightly and lowered him to the carpet. On his knees in the filth beside the supine body, Luc flattened his hand over the man's sternum and pumped at the man's chest harder than kneading dough.

From the back room, Luciano heard the doctor slamming drawers in her haste.

"Get him in the diagnostic chamber, now!" yelled the doctor as she entered the reception room.

We already know what's wrong with him. Luciano kept punching, eyes fixed on the man's blue-ing lips. "It's a classic heart attack." He took a deep breath and leaned down to artificially respirate for his patient.

The doctor dragged Luciano away before he could so much as pinch the man's nose. Together they manhandled the patient into the box. Panting from exertion, the doctor said, "Can't do anything till we have a conclusion card." She stabbed the diagnostic button. "C'mon, c'mon..." The machine spat out a paper, and she ordered, "Get him to the second... oh." She slumped against the wall of the viewing room. "Record time of death."

Through the window to the diagnostic room, Luciano could see the stillness of the man's chest. It wasn't too late. Hearts could be restarted at this point. "He was still breathing when he walked in!" Only minimal brain damage could have set in.

The doctor shook her head and clamped a consoling hand on Luciano's shoulder. "He'll never make it to our cardio massage machine in time."

Like Hell. Luciano rushed to the diagnostic box. He didn't need a machine to help save a life. It'd be nice, but it wasn't necessary. He tugged the man to the floor and pumped his chest again, gasped a deep breath and pushed air into the patient's non-functioning lungs. On the next pump, he told the watching doctor, "I can—"

She interrupted with a helpless little laugh. "Manual CPR, eh? How quaint."

She pulled him away from his unmoving patient again, this time to settle Luciano into a sitting position on the unkempt floor rather than to rush to one of the precious machines. "But let the equipment do its job next time, eh? It's better than we are. Maybe if we'd had a two-in-one combination diagnostic and heart massager, he'd still be alive. Maybe if you hadn't taken those few extra seconds to try and be a hero..." With one last passive-aggressive consolatory pat to his shoulder, she disappeared into the back again for God knew what reason.

Luciano raised his open hands in front of his face, studying the lines on the palms. His lifeline meant nothing if he couldn't share it with others, but how could he help the sick and the wounded? These local doctors could do miraculous things, but without their machines they could not practice medicine. Should he aspire to be like the doctor here, whose prowess seemed Godlike until she ran into a problem her machines couldn't fix?

With the machines, the less severe patients improved dramatically. Without the machine, the serious patient definitely died. Would the man have survived his cardiac arrest if the machine had been consulted earlier? Certainly, Luciano's CPR had done nothing for him.

His vision fuzzed, and sweat pooled beneath his arms. *Everything I've done is useless. I can't be a doctor here, not with my education.*

His lifelong dream of being a doctor had two parts: providing for his family and healing the sick. On this station, even if he retrained to become an American-style doctor, he could do neither. He needed to go back in time. If he didn't know anything about this strange way to practice medicine off-planet, then he could still be a doctor in the sense he'd always understood it. He could try to save each and every patient that came through his door.

Here, he was reduced to a scavenger at best, a procurer and operator of medical machines, rather than a proper physician. These miraculous devices rendered inaccessible *everything* Luciano had ever learned. His only choice was to go home. If he wanted to retain everything important to his life, he couldn't stay here, couldn't do these things.

He would be a Dyfed doctor, even if he had to leave his Hive to do it.

"The consul will see yah now," said the consulate receptionist. A blonde woman, she seemed out of place on a station where Luciano's dark skin and near-black hair blended better than his Hive mates ever could. From the twang of her words and her sleeves' floating quality, though, she was local. Luciano could smell her jasmine perfume.

Dyfed's junior consulate was warmer than the rest of the station, and its pinkish lighting cocooned Luciano in familiarity. It was so cozy and calming compared to the horrible existence outside. The walls displayed flags from all nine Dyfed cities, and pots of miniature trees dotted the corners. A single candle flickered in a lidded glass jar on the receptionist's desk.

Walking back into the only other room, Luciano saw the consul for the first time. The man was unmistakably Dyfed-bred. He wore his white druid's robe like a high Pope's most expensive crown. His round, ruddy face beamed paternal confidence and comfort, even as his office underscored a visiting penitent's unimportance by providing no chairs but the druid's own.

Luciano stood before the official, pad clenched in his grip. "My Hive is curious about sending letters home." *That sounds innocuous enough.* His clutch on the pad eased with every sensible word out of his mouth.

The man's head tilted, and he gestured to a metal bench along the wall. Luciano sat. "We don't see many Hives out here."

Luciano puffed out his chest, pretending pride and borrowing bravado. "We don't always make conventional choices. A good Queen seizes fresh opportunities, after all." *I may not be happy with Rhiannon, but that doesn't mean I'm going to tell you anything damaging.*

They danced around each other for a while, but still set a time for the Hive to put its letters into the diplomatic packet that flashed back to Dyfed every other week.

"Is there anything else I can help you with?"

Luciano bit back the chicory-flavored desires of his heart. *Can you help me defect?*

He raised open hands in front of his face, palms out as if to ward off the temptation. "No, no. That was all. Thank you."

But the consul would not be swayed. He'd seen something in Luciano's hesitation. His cheeks were tomato-red, but only in tiny spots like cherries or grapes. "You can tell me anything. It's all in confidence."

If Luciano were honest with himself, he'd admit to dropping hints. He wanted to be encouraged to share his darkest thoughts, so long as they didn't hurt those to whom he'd promised allegiance. He needed to word his complaints carefully, lest the druid jump on his unorthodox Hive. He needed help, needed to get home. He didn't need to get anyone else sent back in disgrace.

"I just… I think I was too quick to join a Hive. I mean, I love my Queen and everyone's wonderful, but I wasn't ready to leave home. Do you think…? Is there any way…?"

"There might be." The consul smoothed down his white robes of office. Red diaphanous sleeves in the local chiffon style peeked out from the shoulders. "We could call it *youthful indiscretion*. But you would be declared *high risk* and need to be reevaluated for Devotion."

I could be ruined, you mean.

He gripped the bench on which he sat, surprised to find lightweight plastic and paint beneath his touch rather than the knotted wood it resembled. *Aurelia would have a real chance, with my financial support.* "I just want my life back."

The consul nodded and pulled out a pad. "Maybe we can get your position back if we show how badly you were led astray by terrible influences. Now, tell me everything about your Hive."

Chapter Nine

The Unusual Suspects

Melissa's three potential suspects had all been required to list addresses and purpose-of-visit on their customs forms. She'd start with that.

She quietly shut the door to her room and sealed the edges with airtight foam, protocol in case of sudden air leaks. No need to wake her boarders. Employees. The other Dyfed CreaTech, Alan, had impressed her with his upgrades to the internal wiring. Perhaps he'd be available for other improvements. Like, say, tweaking her speakers.

She'd gone years since she'd trusted someone to touch her insides. Sometimes she thought it might be easier to just be a regular, unaware robot.

Sentience was a pain in the welding seams.

Well, she wouldn't ask Alan to give her the PRob version of a physical today. Not till she better knew the Hive sharing her space. They didn't have records, not in American space. But Dyfed was an isolated planet—*confederation of planets?* She didn't even know—and a Hive far from its support system could have its own difficulties. She'd learn everything about them long before she let them touch her insides. It had only been a day.

So, suspects.

Melissa's list of suspects:

- Michael Tong. A man with an address in the station's long-term residential area. The condo's other listed resident had a typically female name. Two bedrooms.

- S.L. Ynnesdale. A man with a high class condo. Owned outright, living on his own in two levels of luxury. Twelve bedrooms.

- Jessie Moore. A woman with an address in the area that bordered the local and planetbound populations. (Referred to as the sterile-and-dust district.) Studio.

She started with the man who had a resident companion. Maybe the woman would be a girlfriend. Melissa could work with that. Could ask questions that made the man look good—or bad—depending on how the lady felt about him.

The corridors ran concentric miles between her quarters, in the station core, and her suspect's in the residential far reaches. Turn after turn after turn. Recycled air circulated nonstop and blew across her vest-covered shoulders. Battery-powered carts, painted in airbrushed flames or bearing a rental company's pink logo, hummed past. She preferred to walk, to stay in charge of her own locomotion.

She passed the core shops catering to short-term residents—pioneers. Racks out front were the only advertisement. Tee-shirts and flannels and sneakers. Practical clothes for practical farmers pitting their common sense against unknown nature.

She went further out, past the *sterile-and-dust* area, named for the mixing of short-termers and locals. Finally she made it out to the long-term residents' domain. Here, people's diaphanous chiffon clothing fluttered in the fashionably increased breezes licking over her metal exoskeleton. Melissa buttoned her vest. Wouldn't do to have it gape open, betraying the extent of her weaponry to potential miscreants.

As she got closer to her destination, the air became warmer, moister. A human might not have noticed the gradual difference, but Melissa's finely calibrated senses felt the changes. Had Tong purposely picked quarters closer to the station's Amazon Belt to benefit from this effect or was it luck of the draw?

In between residential condominiums, the odd shop displayed SPECIAL IMPORT TOFUS and flyers for folk dance classes. She walked the spirals till she reached Level 6, row F, #6004. Michael Tong. She knocked on the door, and the sound rang out: metal on metal.

I should wear my gloves if I'm knocking on doors here. Her gloves were on her ship, underneath her backup memory disk collection in the mostly-unused-clothes section of the closet.

The door swung open, fast and practiced. The lady who'd pulled it open was a station resident, then, conditioned by regular oxygen-leak drills. She pulled a blue silk wrap tighter around her bone-thin shoulders, shifting aside her blunt black bob to highlight the pulsating throb at her neck.

72 beats per minute.

"Can I help you?" The woman barely got out the question before devolving into a coughing fit. She grabbed the doorframe to stay upright.

Mr. Tong's significant other?

Melissa wanted to reach out and steady her, but she couldn't be too careful with a suspect's loved one. Who knew what Mr. Tong had told this woman? Three of Melissa's hands clenched at her sides, a method she'd seen her old engineer employ when he knew he shouldn't touch something. The fourth hand produced her badge.

"Sorry to bother you, ma'am. American Star Rangers." She cocked her headlamps, trying to look as cute and harmless as a kitten. "I'd like to ask you a few questions about Michael Tong."

The woman waved her in, then shut and foam sealed the door against air leaks. But she didn't escort Melissa any further inside. They'd stay in the doorway.

Said doorway was decorated with black lacquer and mother-of-pearl panels depicting spring flowers growing on a mountain. Art in the Chinese style. Hip-high red vases obscured the bottom edge of the panel on the right. Five pairs of shoes—three high heeled, one ladies' sneakers, one men's sneakers—tumbled over each other under the left panel. All further inside than Melissa had made it so far.

The woman coughed again, leaning her back against the now-closed door. Melissa turned to face her.

And to look away from the interior. *Canny, keeping my focus off the private areas.* With no bodies in those rooms, she couldn't deduce their layout from thermals or sound.

"My boy's gone to the store for some medicine. You're welcome to stay." She coughed again. Coughed more. She leaned against the door harder. Doubled over. Cough, cough, *hack*. She sunk to the ground, blue silk sliding off her shoulders and onto the flower-patterned rug.

Ambient temperature check. Tong's mother—*supposed mother*—ran a temperature of 102. Lungs sounded watery. Breathing pattern, gasping and irregular, even when not coughing. Conclusion: Tong was taking care of a sick family member.

That didn't make him innocent. Only meant he had at least one reason to be on this station. A reason other than running from the law. Other than killing and thieving his way across six star systems.

"Do you know his whereabouts twelve days ago?" Melissa asked. Mother or girlfriend, healthy or sick, her questions remained the same.

The woman stayed on her knees, spine curving as she breathed. *In, rattle, out.* "He came home. A few days back. Before that, he had a job out in Solomon's somewhere. He came back when the doctors started giving me"—she coughed—"opiates. He's a good boy." She twisted her head so her dark brown eyes met Melissa's visor. "Takes care of his mother."

Melissa dipped her headlamps in acknowledgement. She wasn't going to get anything out of this woman. Whether Tong had an alibi or not, his mother would protect him as best she could.

He's a good boy for mama. "Thank you for your time, ma'am."

The woman raised a shaky hand as if she planned to use the doorframe to pull herself up, inch by trembling inch. Melissa *would* help, but the woman's motives still smacked too much of protection. She couldn't be sure of the lady's innocence. Of her desire to lash out at the Ranger in her entryway.

Melissa leaned over and unsealed the airtight foam. The thick metal panel swung open to reveal the very man she'd come to find.

His thick thatch of brown-black hair obscured his eyes, and he wore a planetbound pioneer's unfashionable jeans. "Ma!" He dropped to the floor beside the woman, too distraught to follow station safety protocols and seal the door. "Breathe." He rubbed circles on her still-heaving spine.

Ambient noise check. Breathing elevated, heart rate 100. Facial muscles, tightened. Conclusion: the man was concerned. This wasn't a trick. He might or might not be Melissa's quarry, but he was definitely a man who cared about his sick mother.

"Michael Tong?" Melissa had questions. The man had better have answers.

He looked up at her from his mother's side, eyes pleading. If he really was innocent, she shouldn't treat him like this. Shouldn't make him worry more.

"Tell me where you were twelve days ago," she requested, voice firm and unyielding. No judgment, no comfort. The perfect neutrality only an artificial body could manage.

"Solomon's sent me to Luxor. I was on a business trip. You can ask around. I had to leave early to come home. Ma needed me." He rubbed the woman's back again, as though making up for forgetting her while he'd spoken.

No raised heart rate. No overheating. The man was either a brilliant actor or he told the truth.

If the truth, well, Melissa couldn't help liking him. She didn't need to ask more questions right now. She'd check with Solomon's and learn whether his story was true. Till then, he could take care of his mother in peace. Otherwise he wasn't going anywhere, not if that concern was real. She could always find him again.

"Thank you for your time," she said. She picked her way over the kneeling pair on the ground, four legs clearing their hunched bodies. Once in the hallway, she turned to make a final request. "Don't leave town."

She took the elevators up three levels to a cooler and dryer section of the station. Half the people in these corridors dressed in floating chiffons like Tong's mother. The other half were more like Tong himself, preferring sturdy jeans and thick-soled sneakers.

Sterile-and-dust, where long-term residents and pioneer passers-through mingled.

Her second suspect was female and lived in a studio just off a hallway boasting late-night bars and discount alterations. Some enterprising souls had taken it upon themselves to knock out half the blue lights, and now illuminated signs flashed and glittered in this corridor, enticing anyone with money to spend. It reminded Melissa of photographs from Earth's 1960s Las Vegas.

Her suspect had moved in a week prior and was new to John Wayne Station. She'd paid four months' rent in advance, so she wasn't hurrying to get down planetside to Kessel.

Melissa picked her way down the hall, dodging sandwich boards with halogen bulbs attached to them. (Those were probably fire hazards. She'd have to check the local fire codes when she wasn't as busy with important work.) Hawkers in shop doorways called out to the throngs, but ducked back amongst their racks of clearance clothes and aisles of knickknacks as she approached. Whether to hide from the law or from the bizarre robot-that-wasn't, she didn't know. Shrieking knee-high children pelted down the throughway, circling the teaser merchandise and jumping all over each other.

#1803A. Jessie Moore. Today, she only needed to make contact and get the most cursory overview as quickly as possible. Leads sublimated in space's vacuum; no need to give them the time to gas away.

Melissa knocked on the door, striking metal on metal. The tone rang deeper and louder in this cold dryness than at Michael Tong's place, closer to the station's Amazon Belt.

She was about to knock again when a hidden speaker crackled. "Who's there?"

Melissa expected that the woman could see her just fine. She produced her badge and panned her arm slowly over the doorway, hoping the five-star pattern would catch any cameras.

"American Star Rangers, ma'am. I have some questions."

The door still didn't open. "How do I know that thing is real?"

Melissa put the badge back into her vest pocket without looking at it. "If it's real, and you won't talk to me, you could be in serious trouble." Because that was what the woman really meant. *What's the consequence of ignoring you?* Melissa's fingers stretched out, shaking imaginary dust from the joints and displaying her frustration to anyone who knew her.

No one knew her here. No one who'd grown up with experience of insentient robots expected one to pick up gestures from the people around them. Four hands, sixteen fingers, eight thumbs. *She* knew it was real. She knew *she* was real and not just a figment of someone else's coding genius.

Her emotions hid themselves from the suspect all the same.

Pause. "All right." The door's foam sealant retracted. "But I'm going to take precautions."

The precautions appeared to be armament. A distinctive *krr-chink*, and Melissa found herself torso to gun barrel with a small hand pistol. It looked old and slow, too slow to penetrate her armor plating. But she had no reason to antagonize the suspect, yet. No reason to find out whether the 9 out of 10 impact rating could hold off this woman's pistol.

Jessie stood in a staggered Isosceles stance with her left leg ahead of her right, legs slightly bent and shoulder width apart. "Step back." She leaned forward with her arms extended from her shoulders, left one bent to absorb some recoil. Perfect stance for a shooter who expected to need accuracy over quick movement.

Melissa did as she'd been bid. When she got far enough into the hallway, Jessie followed her out, door slipping shut behind her. As was her right. Melissa didn't have any papers allowing her to search the studio.

Jessie was shorter than Melissa expected. Her arms held steady at shoulder height, the gun leveled on Melissa's torso, where her middle ribs would be if she had a human skeleton. Melissa cocked a headlamp, her harmless tell for *thinking*.

If: Jessie stood on her tiptoes and slit a standing man's throat.

Then: How far would the blood spatter?

Not far enough for the pictures from the crime wave Melissa was following. At best, the woman could manage to kill a 6'5" victim in that manner. In likelihood, she'd top out at 5'8". Jessie clearly only used weapons she knew how to handle, and no professional throat-slitter wanted to stand on her toes more often than not.

Melissa said, "Can you tell me where you were two weeks ago?"

Jessie's arms didn't tremble. Her chiffon sleeves blew to the right, following the station breeze. "I didn't move to John Wayne till last week. Local law's got no need to question me about anything older than that." Her heart rate slowed. *Relief?* But she didn't lower the gun.

"Star Rangers, ma'am." Melissa tapped a hand on her vest pocket. "I'm following a multi-system trail. If you'd been a long-term local, I wouldn't need to ask."

Jessie jerked her chin upward. Acknowledgement.

"I was on my way here," she said.

Melissa knew the passenger manifests. It was *possible* that she'd been underway at that point in time. First report of her existence came from the orbital over Lash, only two days away from John Wayne at passenger liner speeds. "From where?"

"New Las Vegas." Her heart rate sped up, but only just. *Lying or emotional?* A human wouldn't have noticed the change. But Melissa kept a check on her suspects' vitals during questioning. "Got married. Lost some money. Got divorced." For the first time since the interview began, Jessie abandoned her stable stance. She turned her head to the side and spat on the floor plating. "Bastard."

That part I believe. Melissa didn't take advantage, didn't knock the gun from the woman's hands or push her out of dangerous alignment. Still… "I'd like to see that certificate." She gestured with two hands, open palmed and face up, to the studio door.

Jessie barked, not quite a laugh. "You can look it up, Ranger. You're not coming inside without a warrant."

It had been statistically unlikely, but she'd hoped. Melissa lowered her hands again and twitched her two headlamps down in defeated acknowledgement.

Humans liked it when she used her headlamps like animal ears. Something about anthropomorphizing cute, furry things. Melissa wasn't cute or furry, but she did what she could to get the information out of a suspect. "Don't leave the station," she said as she backed away.

"Get off my property," Jessie said. She pivoted to keep Melissa in her aim, following her down the hallway.

Melissa didn't try anything. She could appreciate a person's desire for safety. She'd protected herself and numerous innocents against assailants over the last six years since she'd joined the American Star Rangers.

The woman had paid a four month advance on her studio and already wore the fluttery outfits of station-only fashion. Unless she had hidden financial support, she'd declared herself *here to stay.* Between that and the height discrepancy on the crimes, Melissa downgraded her from *prime suspect* to *revisit later if necessary.*

She had one more lead to check out. Then she'd pool her data and decide what to do next.

Her first two suspects were less than ideal criminals, which left Melissa one more. With luck, Mr. S.L. Ynnesdale would be the kind of schmuck who had a million testify-happy enemies and who left incriminating evidence hanging from his coatrack. Melissa wasn't holding her breath, but, then again, she didn't need to breathe.

The station database said the man owned his condo and that it took up two levels.

What does anyone need with that much space?

Melissa took the elevator to long-term resident country, as far away from the docking rings and the visiting pioneers as an inhabitant could get. Out here, the station design emphasized peace and tranquility, but no one seemed to be around to enjoy it. Where she'd dodged carts and children on her way to see suspects one and two, here she was the only thing around to notice the grey and red painted walls, abstract shapes making a forgotten Picasso fade into the scenery.

The Picasso looked like the real thing: appropriately bumpy and lighting up her bio-toxin warnings with the cow's blood thickener in the paint.

Her four shoes swished gently on the plush carpet. Its swirling gold-on-gold pattern was unmarred by mud tracks or fallen gum wrappers. No detritus decorated the floor. The place was impeccably clean.

Her third suspect's address was only a corridor over from the elevator, trading view for convenience. It should have been the level's most bustling section, and maybe it was, but that only meant the people out on the even more private fringes were dead or vacationing in some other sector of space.

Melissa knocked on his door, metal to metal ringing overloud through the empty corridor. No one came out to investigate, not her quarry nor his neighbors. The whole level seemed deserted, silent. The people living up here didn't care to socialize.

Well, Melissa didn't socialize either, but that didn't make her incurious.

The condo wasn't a public place, and she didn't have a warrant. So she couldn't use her thermal imaging cameras to see if anyone was in, if the resident chose to ignore her.

All she could do was knock. Wait. Knock again.

She took the elevator up a floor to try the second-story entrance. This time, the ringing was quieter. Muffled. Her articulated joints crinkled a note on the door. Real paper.

She unfolded the note.

EVICTION NOTICE

Seven Day Notice to Vacate

For Failure to Pay Station Dues in the Amount of

$5,000,043,882.09

The notice was dated five months ago. If her suspect lived here once, he didn't anymore. Hadn't in a long time. Conclusion: Her quarry had given a false address.

Michael Tong and Jessie Moore hadn't been remotely suspicious. This new John Doe was. He had to be her criminal. She'd find him and she'd bring him to justice. Somehow.

Interlude 1

Meanwhile, Back on Dyfed

Olivia couldn't be sure how many days she'd languished in this prison for Queens. Trapped twelve floors beneath an old government building, paint peeling on its outer structure, she could only plot her escape. And she *would* escape. So far, she'd considered and discarded a multitude of plans which required her to be younger or stronger.

At first, she'd thought the neighboring Queen Marla might be an ally, but the woman in the next cell had succumbed to drug-induced catatonia after a few... somethings. Weeks, certainly, but she had no way to measure whether or not they'd stacked into months.

A variety of guards paced the halls, none on a discernible schedule. They made an odd assortment. Tall and short. Blond and brunette. Fat and thin. Bespectacled and overmuscled. Male and female. Either they came from a *rent a guard* service, or this strange plot had deeper and more diverse roots than anyone in the mainstream world would suspect.

But what monsters would abduct and torture Queens for mere politics? No, the guards were doubtless of the mercenary variety. This was most certainly not a sanctioned government operation.

"Your ladyship."

Speaking of guards. One woman stopped in front of Olivia's cell. She wore no specific uniform, but came armed and free. If nothing else, her full cheeks—absent of a prisoner's hunger—marked her as belonging to the party in charge.

Olivia's muscles locked. "My turn, is it?" In all the time she'd been a resident, Olivia had yet to be escorted to The Lab. At least, she assumed it was a lab.

The guard unbolted the door, and it yawned open. "Please cooperate."

"Or what?"

When the guards came for the other Queens, those ladies scrambled to the backs of their cells, setting up cot-forts, dignity forgotten. They'd all been taken out and brought back unconscious or screaming. *Will I be like that once I've experienced the nameless horrors?*

"Please cooperate." The guard's gaze focused on Olivia's tangled hair. Their eyes never met.

"Where are we going?" Olivia didn't expect the guard to answer, but she had to try. She had to know more. She was a Queen, and they owed her answers for that alone! More than that, she was a human being who deserved human dignity.

The flat voice, uninterested and uninformative, demanded her compliance. "Your ladyship."

Olivia evened her breathing and thrust her shoulders back from the hunch they'd crept into. "I have never shrunk from danger," she proclaimed as she allowed the guard escort her out. No reason to show an ounce of apprehension.

They marched down ten corridors, path twisting in patterns doubtless meant to distract and confuse. All the passageways looked alike: the same numbers of doors between junctions, the same grey-pink lighting. They halted at the one door that looked different. Above it a bright light shone green.

The guard raised her free hand, scratched, and entered without waiting for so much as a *we're ready for you now.*

A long, chest-high table dominated the room. Its white leather lit the dark space like a beacon, stained rust at the seams, or perhaps that was the high-powered sodium bulb above it. *No! Don't get distracted by details, Olivia. You have to keep yourself here if you want to find a way to escape and to free all the other unfortunates along with you.* She could contemplate the history of the lamp, first made on Earth in their year 1932, in her cell's unstimulating eternity. Later.

Again the guard said, "Your ladyship."

She gestured to the table. Olivia clambered onto it, almost relieved to rest her shaking legs. The leather's cold gave her a shivery shock. "I don't suppose you could turn up the heat?" she asked as the guard strapped her down in fraying restraints a handspan wide. The guard retreated out the door, question hanging.

"I thought not," Olivia said with a sigh to the unpopulated room.

She squinted against the spotlight. Beyond it, she made out banks of connected computers. Actual papers and pens rested atop those, no electronic pads in sight. A green board against the far wall bore mathematical and chemical symbols, all far out of her league. It all added up to one thing: *a research chamber but what kind?* Who would have the budget for such an operation? Especially without the wherewithal to run legitimate tests above ground?

A woman's voice said, "Please restrain the subject's head."

Footsteps. With her head immobile, Olivia hadn't even known another person was in the room.

Then an orderly stood at the tableside. At least, Olivia assumed he was an orderly, wearing hospital-style cottons with unfortunate stains. She wrinkled her nose in ill-timed distaste. *A messy eater.* Thankfully he didn't notice her displeasure, too busy doing his job. He held her skull steady and looped one belt over her forehead, another under her chin.

The strap on her forehead was wet and smelled of gymnasium. She said, "That top one's pinching my hair. Please rearrange it."

He should have obeyed a Queen's request like an order. Instead, the orderly ignored her. Much as Olivia had suspected he would.

Then she was alone again with nothing but the disembodied voice for company. "For the record, we will first take a baseline measurement."

The next hour was exactly like every doctor's appointment Olivia ever had, except that this one occurred whilst restrained. Brain activity, measured. Heart rate, measured. Four blood samples, drawn for analysis. *Apparently they take urine and stool samples directly from our cell toilets.* She found her mind floating, surprised by the way her body jerked in response to certain stimuli like a child's toy at Samhain.

Again, the voice. "Inject the standard inhibitor."

Olivia couldn't thrash or move away. Possibly that was for the better. A large needle descended, pushing at the space just forward of her ear where the path to the brain was clear. *They're injecting something into my brain!* She kept her muscles locked tight, to minimize the damage. Nothing could be worse than a hole in her mind.

The pain spiked, white-hot as dragon's breath.

"Next, the sedative."

The brain spear flew away into the ceiling, and the orderly reappeared to administer another shot. When this needle breached her skin, she bit back the scream building in her throat.

They'll never have the satisfaction.

"Oh, good," said the voice. The first editorializing she'd heard from it yet. "I do so hate the noisy ones."

And Olivia blacked out.

Holly watched the newest subject on the monitors, a security system ten years out of date, but still serviceable. If she'd been born on another planet, outside the Dyfed Hive system, she might have qualified for newer equipment and more skilled assistants. But she hadn't been. And she had no desire to leave now. Her people needed her expertise. She had a purpose—to free the oppressed.

To smash the Devoted glass ceiling. For herself, for her planet, for her beloved.

This new Queen was older than the rest. Perhaps that accounted for the discrepancies in her blood work. Holly could find no trace of the neuromodulators that tied together other Queens and Devoted. Not in the first sample, not in the second. *I'm sure she's the same as these other virus puppets!*

Though the possibility remained that the new Queen was too old. The drugs could have broken down so far that her Hive remained together out of habit rather than pharmacological addiction.

Holly tapped her stylus against her pad's side as though that might jar the data into the expected configuration. She'd watch a bit longer. When the sedatives wore off, the Queen would either be affected by the inhibitors blocking her from her connection to her Devoted, or else she'd be a medical mystery.

Sometimes, I love my job... if only it paid.

Until then, she'd keep attending her regular patients in her Senedd-determined position as a general practitioner. Still a doctor, but not a research-focused neuroscientist. As a child, she'd known she'd be a doctor someday, and she'd always expected to run her own lab where they got the really difficult cases. The brain cases. If only the Senedd (and the Neuroscientist Research Association whose form rejection had made her heart ache) believed a woman could have that level of analytical brain!

(Not counting the strange Perceivers who lived alien lives and were rarely seen outside their specialized libraries.)

Holly made a last note on the new Queen's chart before packing her belongings for the day. Left her tight-sleeved, lab-appropriate, coat on the back of her chair. She headed for the lifts, heart beating faster with every step closer to the exit.

With her personal pad, she made reservations at her significant other's favorite restaurant. She couldn't wait to share this exciting new development with Amanda. They were getting close! Soon, the Hive system could be broken, and they'd be able to live openly in the city. Holly would be invited to join the Neuroscience Research Association, based on her demonstrated fitness. Life wouldn't be perfect, but it would be on the way there.

Once the Hive system proved unstable, Dyfed would free itself of gender tyranny and romantic hypocrisy.

Chapter Ten

To Love Alone

Finally, Victor thought, *I get some time alone with Lois.* He laced their fingers together, tempted to swing their arms as they progressed down the hallway. Side by side, they took up just under half its width, though that might be attributable to his bony, but broad shoulders. A giant numeral 4—about the size of an adolescent child, pinned at eye-height—provided some context for location. When they approached the theatre, this sparse utilitarianism would give way to greater opulence. There, the floors were carpeted right at the theatre's entrance; here, they were bare grates, a griddle-hash of ecru foam-and-plastic.

For once, Victor's girlfriend wasn't inexplicably un-available or busy powdering a toxic plant. They'd gotten lunch at the giant market where he and Alan had gone the week before. He'd nibbled exotic concoctions from her bowl—not familiar with the soup known as pho—and she'd slapped his spoon away twice before giving up and giving in.

She wore a blousy summer-weight tunic, wrists cinched with ribbons so that it would quiver in the station breeze.

It approximated the local style as well as any Dyfed fashion might. *Maybe the body stockings most of the real locals wear have heating elements in them.* Her slender hand cooled his knobbier one. *There must not be much heat in the local fashions.*

She shuffled along at his side without complaining about the temperature. "How do you think they keep space out? There's no Kevlar on these walls."

A fact which Victor found disturbing, especially in light of how many locals kept private firearms. His ribs seized inward and he shrugged off the anxiety. Instead he said, "I helped Gavin set up a giant fog machine the other day." His hand in hers felt too warm and clammy.

She narrowed her hazel eyes, the first emotion he'd seen from her since his transgressions at lunch. "For the ladies at the brothel."

Victor's heart rate ticked up, pounding against its bone cage. *I didn't do anything wrong! It was an interesting project.* He felt a tug on his hand and realized he'd outpaced her. "You know I only want you," he said.

Door after door after door. One opened, and a pioneer family spilled out, all tight denim and laughter. Their happiness felt obscene in the angry silence.

Lois, never the confrontationist, pushed silvery strands behind her ear and changed the subject. "Where are we going?"

The very brothel where you don't want me spending time.

He yanked one-handed at his the hem of his tunic, a warm grey (solidly in the Dyfed style) that reached to the middle of his thighs. "To meet the rest of our

Hive." *That's a much better spin. We're just finding Rhiannon and Gavin and the rest.* Rhiannon claimed to have brewed a plan over the past few days. He hoped it was effective.

"So... the brothel?"

Victor constricted his fingers around hers, wanting to keep her captive in his grip. *Not the spin I was hoping for.* He tried for a little laugh. "Just the theatre side."

She strangled his fingers in return. "I'm sorry. I know you wouldn't be interested in throwing me over." She said it like a phrase she was quoting. Maybe Gavin? A smile appeared and withered in moments. "Me and Rhi are enough for you."

He didn't laugh. Though delivered like a joke, it really wasn't. Tightness in her quiet tone made that more than clear. He had thought they were past this. "I've done all this for you, cariad. We're a forever kind of love, tested in the vacuum of space and the crucible of society." He wrenched her to a stop in the corridor's shrinking heart, suddenly claustrophobic, and gripped both her chilled hands in his. "You know that, right?"

As he waited for her answer, Victor's eyes flitted all over the hall, landing too quickly on anything to process it. They passed white and blue. Cold and dark. Overbright and corners. Mesh grating. Nothing important. All meaningless details.

She hummed, neither agreement or refutation, and tugged him back into motion. While they'd stopped, a pair of locals—one a tall, brunette woman and the other a young black-haired man who barely came to Victor's armpit, both in dirt-brown bodystockings that nearly matched their warm skin tones, clearly a uniform—joined the hall, looming in front of them.

Victor was in no hurry, so he slowed their pace. *Why dodge around when we can politely stay a step behind them?* Maybe Lois just needed time to process what he'd said. *Love conquers all, right?* He bit his lip and slid her hand from his clammy one into the crook of his elbow.

She perked up, leaned forward and pushed her hair back. Held up a hand in his direction without looking at him. "Shhh."

He let her shush him, content to walk with her hand in his arm and her sweet, herbal scent in his nose. Maybe this was the kind of bonding she needed, just quiet togetherness. Though it didn't seem right that she knew so little about what he spent his time doing. And what had she been up to lately, other than preparing hemlock?

The woman in front of them moaned to her partner, "The fennel that new chef wanted just won't come out right. He says it's supposed to be white, but mine are growing up green. And all the plants in the bed with it are dying."

The man whined right back. "You think you have problems? It's like all mine are dying of high midsummer heat, but the temperature is no different than it was last week. I've got scorched leaves and everything." He groaned. "We're both going to get fired. Then what will we do?"

Lois slipped her hand from Victor's arm and hovered closer to the pair in front of them. "Excuse me."

The American pair stopped walking, and Lois barely avoided bumping into the short man. They three expanded into a half-hallway triangle, no one taking up too much of the others' space, but locked together in formation. Victor didn't have any place in their polyhedron, so he floated out behind his girlfriend, unsure what to do, slouching and cracking his knuckles. There was bare margin for him to resolutely avoid the conversation while remaining tethered to his girlfriend. *How long does this kind of thing take? She'll have to finish solving their problems soon.*

He didn't pay much attention. Lois was saying something about, "fennel takes over everything but coriander" and "mound of soil after it sprouts" and "did you get new sunlamps recently?" and "water the roots, not the leaves." She did this all the time in school, fixed everyone else's agriculture homework. Victor would never have passed fourth-form botany if she hadn't been available for questions and green-thumbing.

Then Lois was walking again, away from him, the central tower between the two Americans who needed her help with their homework/jobs.

"Ah, Lois? Where are you going?" And that didn't sound manipulative and annoyed at *all. Great interpersonal skills there, Victor. At least it's Gwyn, who understands and loves you no matter what.* Though they didn't seem to understand each other near as much these days.

Lois called over her shoulder, "I'm just going to take a look at their life sciences set-up." To her companions, though he could still hear her, "That's what you call it, right? *Life sciences?*"

Victor saw starry adoration in the local woman's eyes. The short man nodded like his head might fall off.

"We *need* someone like you. I've been so scared to ask my supervisor."

Lois laughed like bridle bells and dewy spring mornings. *When was the last time I heard that sound?* He hadn't realized how long it had been. He called after her, "You want me to come with you?"

She waved over her shoulder, not looking back. "I'll catch up to you when I'm done."

We're supposed to be meeting the others. You're supposed to want to be with me.

As the three walked around a corner, he could see Lois demonstrating some sort of mounding technique, mobile hands shaping the air into what looked like a burial cairn. He slouched and stuffed his fingers into his opposite sleeves. For warmth. He couldn't help noticing that their lives diverged further and further the longer they lived on John Wayne Station.

She'll come back to me. I mean, to the Hive. Lois just needed some time to work on her hobby. Then she'd return to the people who knew and loved her. It didn't have to mean anything.

Victor quickened his steps toward Cleopatra's Palace. The sooner he rejoined his Hive, the sooner he'd have company while he waited for Lois to be restored to his side. He didn't want to be alone anymore.

Chapter Eleven

The Plan

Rhiannon didn't see any burgundy-wearing bouncers in the brothel theatre's backstage area, but that didn't mean they weren't there. Lying in wait and ready to evict her. To record her identity and blacklist her forever. She tugged at the edges of her sleeves, pulling them down much farther than they'd ever needed to go.

In the wings, offstage right, where the dim lighting concealed most of what the maroon curtains didn't, she concentrated on breathing. *Inhale the musty anonymity.* Her Hive was here, safe. *Exhale the worrisome thoughts.* Everything would be fine. Gavin had reassured her as much.

The brothel-casino-theatre took care of its own. She could respect that. She just didn't want to get caught up in it. At least, not on the wrong side.

"Excuse me, miss?" A courtesan-actress faded out of the black curtains' full-dark and into the nearby shadows. Rhiannon couldn't make out her features, could only see that she was slightly taller, but she could hear her voice—husky and perky at once.

She knew that voice. *Manawyddan's Mousetrap! Am I discovered already?* She ducked further into the velvet maroon folds at her back and turned her head to the expensively imported wooden floor, letting her hair hide even more of her features. If she couldn't see the lady, then the lady couldn't see her. "Mm?"

The woman dragged her hand against something, making a *sssh-crack* followed by a pinprick of light that glowed yellow-hot and expanded. She held the light to her own face, cradling it as it sparked and turned into a teardrop of yellow and orange and red.

"I know, I know," the woman said. Her coral-colored nails looked nearly bloody in the fire's light. "We shouldn't light matches in artificial atmospheres."

That had to be an American prohibition. If someone from Dyfed couldn't light a candle or at least set an incense stick smoldering, all space-bound citizens would form a crashing, protesting wave. Rhiannon herself didn't spend much time on religious rites or festival celebrations, but she still expected to be *allowed* to observe them.

"I know you!" the woman exclaimed. Her mouth curved upward and open in innocent enjoyment, and Rhiannon felt her own lips echoing the gesture, throwing friendly endorphins into her system. *She probably practices that look.* "I'm Cinna. We met in the casino." The woman slithered closer, illuminating them both with the light of the still lit match.

Rhiannon's hands clenched, unpainted nails digging into the flesh of her palms. *Ceridwen protect me. Don't let her turn me in.* Not that she expected her ship-patron to answer.

Clearly comfortable with interpersonal touch, the woman brushed Rhiannon's hair back to protect it from the flame. "You don't have to worry about anyone hurting you here." She petted the hair underneath her still-extended hand. "You're helping with the play. You're one of us now. If the big guys come, I'll be the first to hide you." She giggled. "Though I doubt you'll fit behind my skirts."

She *did* wear a skirt, but it was tight. And transparent. A see-through red that looked pink where its tail fluttered in air.

She struck a pose when she noticed Rhiannon's gaze, brought the flame down to emphasize the red of her skirt, the shadows of her waist and thigh. Cocking a hip, she offered, "Well, you can try." She brought the match to her mouth, pursed her lips in a perfect O, and blew it out in a wisp of sharp, woodsy smoke. A whispered kiss brushed Rhiannon's cheek. "So be sure you keep helping us out."

Then she was gone. Like a breeze. Like a dream. Like a season.

A nervous giggle shook Rhiannon's ribs and throat, and she curled forward to keep it from echoing too far. *I thought she'd agreed to keep her sexiness far away from me.* Though that had been over a week before, and in a different place. Rhiannon's heart raced. What was the polite way to deflect someone's advances while asking them to hide your presence from the bouncers?

Rhiannon tugged her sleeves and smoothed her hair, straightening every part till she exuded sleek power like the controlled Queen she aspired to be. Well, as best she could.

It wasn't like Cinna forced anything other than innuendo on me. She's just playing.

Rhiannon took the courtesan's advice about helping out to heart. The prop table she'd snuck past earlier was a disorganized mess. Clearly someone had to organize it. And Rhiannon had a talent for organizing.

The prop table was situated in a much busier and more lit area. As people bustled past, Rhiannon stayed as hidden at its side as she'd been in the dark, camouflaged by the constant flow. She organized the props by time of use, checking against a marked-up script. She shifted pieces around. A sailor's hat for part of the *Odyssey* recitation. A pair of dance canes to be thrown to two girls doing a Broadway soft-shoe. A harness for one of the sheep.

On the approach, an actress called to a potential suitor. "Aww, sweetie! Don't run away! Come into the back with me. Free of charge."

Another woman giggled. "He's so adorable."

Rhiannon kept her eyes on the prop table, but a smile tugged at the corner of her lips. The ladies were harmless. Hadn't Cinna reassured her of their respect for consent on that first day they'd met, back in the casino?

On stage, an actress proceeded down right. "Lo! Over the waves, I... Over the waves, I... Damn it! What's next? *Line!*"

Halfheartedly, Rhiannon flipped through the worn script at her side. Another stagehand would probably beat her to it.

Someone barreled past her and nearly knocked her over, then doubled around to hover at her back. *Whatever makes you happy. Just don't jar my elbow.* The person behind her panted into her hair from a foot above, but otherwise didn't get into her space.

The woman onstage, Eleanor Peacock, called again. "Line!"

Rhiannon read out, *"Lo! Over the waves, I spy a rickety vessel. Please, suitors, let me pass to attend these poor travelers."*

The script was... overblown to say the least. Whoever had adapted the classic hadn't wanted to make the action too subtle for modern viewers. Not that the ancient playwrights had ever been particularly subtle.

The woman on stage swept her arms open, beseeching invisible suitors who apparently had chosen not to attend this rehearsal. "...let me pass to attend those poor travelers." She broke out into song.

Because of course they'd made *The Odyssey* into a musical too.

From behind Gavin whispered in her ear, "They're going to put you on book from now on, you know."

Rhiannon's hands flew up to her hair, coiling it around her fingers while she twisted her upper body to see the boy behind her. Her heart raced, pounding loudly enough to hear in the audience. "What're you doing there!"

She meant *why are you sneaking up behind me?* Gavin had been lead set designer and special effects man at the theatre for nearly two weeks, and various members of her Hive had dropped in to help out as time allowed. This was the first time they'd crossed paths outside of their quarters. She hadn't known *he* was the person hiding behind her. *Way to be observant, Rhiannon.*

He grinned at her, unashamed. "My lady." He swept into a deep bow. On straightening, he twined his arms around her waist, gluing himself to her back like flame on a wick. Louder than he should in the backstage area, he proclaimed, "You know my Devotion and attentions flow towards you and you alone."

Two brothel-casino-theatre ladies giggled at his dedication, and Rhiannon recognized one quality of titter. *So. He's not glued to me as a flame on a wick so much as a nervous soldier to his shield.*

Rhiannon patted her Devoted's hand where it rested on her waist, worming fingers beneath his linen and lace cuff. *He always makes the most interesting sartorial choices.*

"You know you can *call on me in times of trouble,*" she said, quoting the official words of a Queen's oath. She tilted her head and raised an eyebrow at the teasing ladies as if to say, *Are you certain you'd like to challenge me for him?* No menace in her posture or gesture, only confidence.

The ladies nodded to her. One shrugged. The giggler giggled again. As they turned away, both waved coquettish fingers, and Gavin pulled her even closer against his boney form.

His chin came down to dig into her shoulder. "Thank you." His oval chin speared the muscles when he talked.

She wormed her way out of his embrace. Easily done now that the danger had passed. "Who else is here today?"

"Almost everyone." He waved in the stage's direction, multiple sleeves dripping their linen and lace and wool down his arm. "Alan's doing something with the lights. Luc's helping the costume mistress sew things. We're here. And Victor's on his way with Lois to join Alan."

"Good," she said. They only had seven days until the show. Seven days until the whole station was preoccupied with the theatre. Seven days until the *best* time to steal back their Alcubierre tensor jet drive. She had a plan. What she didn't have was a Hive that stayed in place all at one time. "Have them all meet us here."

While Gavin flashed messages to the Hive, Rhiannon prepared.

"Line!" called the unfortunate actress on stage.

"O my husband, come home and cast out these interlopers," Rhiannon guided her.

Then the prop table was abuzz with teenagers from Dyfed. Not an American courtesan in sight.

Alan snapped, "Is this going to take long? I'm busy with the spots."

Luciano agreed. "Those corsets don't bone themselves."

Victor asked Alan, "What is it you need me to do?"

Gavin bent at the waist, directing all attention to Rhiannon.

Keeping her tone hushed, in case someone *did* happen to wander by, she said, "We have seven days till we take back what is ours." There was a small cheer, but she talked over it. "We need a plan if we hope to succeed."

Alan opened his mouth, probably to make a suggestion or to take over. But she didn't need him for this. *This.* This was what she was made for. She could plan; she could organize; she could direct her people along the optimal paths.

"Gavin." Her voice was sure, commanding, and he straightened to a near-military posture. "You'll have the theatre's production vehicle, so I'll need you to be the getaway driver."

He coughed. "Ah, but, the sheep?"

Without a nod to his trepidation, she continued, "You'll bring it to me *after* you drop off the sheep, so be sure to pick them up early and to take Gwyn with you. She'll keep the lambs quiet." Gwyn wasn't here, but Rhiannon had no problems committing her best friend to a course of action. The other girl had long followed Rhiannon's lead. Plus, she loved animals.

Next. "Alan." He acknowledged her with a mumbled *my lady*, overbright excitement turning his hazel eyes almost entirely green. "You'll go along with Gavin and Gwyn to make sure we get all the parts. If the jet's been dismantled or damaged, determine what to take and what to leave behind. Put the jet in the truck as soon as you have it."

Now for the most useless or the most important, depending on how things go.

"Victor." He cracked his knuckles and bounced, ready to get to action. "You're going to keep an eye on everything. Be ready with those combat skills you've been working on." He looked happy enough with this order, nodding vigorously so that his dark brown hair flopped all over the place.

And trust. "Luciano." He fixed her with grave, dark eyes. She, the center of his attention. The center of his universe. "You'll keep in touch with everyone and communicate even the smallest details of what's going on. I trust you the most to be my eyes and ears while I coordinate."

Luciano went to his knees before her, grabbing her hand and pressing his forehead to the back of it. "I am honored, my lady."

It was overkill, a gesture she'd expect more from Gavin than Luciano. But it inspired all her men. The other three followed their Hive mate to the floor, each briefly bending one knee.

"My lady." They said it in eerie unison. Never on Dyfed nor on their own ship had they treated her with such deference. Had she become a more competent Queen-Commander? What had changed?

She looked up from her waist-high Devoted and saw a white-blonde flash. "Gw—Lois!" she called in a half-whisper. Beckoning the other girl over, she explained obliquely, "We're talking about the thing that's happening with our stuff."

Gwyn didn't come closer or even look her way, however, idly running her fingers over a rack of costumes as if testing their worth. All spandex and sparkle for the Broadway revue portion. "Whatever you want is fine." She picked at a sequin. "Just let me know the schedule. I have things to do."

Like what?

Before Rhiannon could ask, a courtesan appeared near Gwyn's rack. The woman slid unselfconsciously out of her clothes and into something see through and shiny. To Gwyn, the woman gushed, "I love your musical accent! Can you teach me to talk like that?"

Four more women mobbed the rack, piggybacking on the first's requests. "And me!" "And me!" "You have such beautiful hair!"

Of course they loved Gwyn's hair. Iron-straight without effort. Near-white blonde. Shiny and supple. So unlike Rhiannon's ready-to-frizz brunette mess. No wonder they jumped on Gywn's accent instead of Rhiannon's own. In a profession like theirs, the brothel's ladies and gentlemen were practically required to prefer beauty to brains.

That wasn't fair. Gwyn had brains too. *But not the kind that got you any future you wanted,* a traitorous portion of her brain piped. Because Gwyn could never have gamed the Test, could never have got this far in the Universe, without Rhiannon's support.

When next she looked down, Rhiannon's feet were surrounded by hardwood planks. No Devoted kneeling. *How am I going to grow our Hive if we switch so quickly between excessive Devotion and nothing at all?* Gwyn hadn't even shown up till her meeting was over. The boys tended to go their own ways. Gavin was forging his own path and pulling her Hive along with him.

Hives grew, planting roots like a tree whose lively branches intertwined and stretched, all reaching towards a common sun.

So why does it feel like we're growing apart?

Chapter Twelve

Not A Telephone

Melissa needed a lead. Fast. Four days had passed since she'd visited the luxury condo with the eviction notice, and she still hadn't found her third suspect. She'd gone down-planet to Kessel, left the Hive kids in charge of her affairs on station, chasing a false trail. But that hadn't moved her investigation along, and she'd come back to JWS.

The trail was going cold.

Which meant she didn't have time for more courtesy meetings.

She'd received a message that morning from the Sheriff's Office: *All Station Law Enforcement. Mandatory Meeting. Sheriff's Office, 11 a.m.* After her visit to their establishment on the first day, she hadn't expected to see anyone from that office again. She had a job. They had a job. No reason for their paths to cross.

She'd briefly worried about her new boarders' reputations as troublemakers. Queen-Commander Rhiannon had been thrown out of the Cleopatra's Palace casino on suspicion of cheating. But after weighing the young woman's indignation and measuring it against her abilities, Melissa was reasonably sure the accusations wouldn't go any further. Certainly not far enough to cause Melissa trouble with the Sheriff.

She let herself into the reception area without preamble. No need to knock on the door this time. The place was overclocking, too many people doing too much and all bumping into each other while they did it.

She recognized thirteen human adults in the lightweight brown uniforms that the Sheriff's Office favored. Each traveled a helpless circuit between overcrowded desks and the front cubbies and back again. Four government investigators, all in navy blue, held white hats under their arms, trying to stay out of the bustle. Behind all this frenzy, three heat signatures huddled in the large conference room. She recognized one as the Sherriff. The other two, she didn't know.

The Sherriff's thermal blur abandoned his unknown compatriots. A scrape of rubber boot on grating, and he joined the mayhem. His employees made space around him.

"Ah, the Star Ranger." He reached out a wrinkled hand for her to shake.

She trusted him enough to extend a limb and squeeze both thumbs briefly around the sides of his hand, her four fingers sliding straight down his wrist and over his shirt cuff. Very few people shook her hand twice. "Sheriff."

He reached up to clap her on the shoulder, post-handshake. "Glad you're here. The galactics summoned us all. Won't tell us what they're fussing for. A Ranger can make sense of it if no one else can."

Melissa's visor turned a happy-pale blue at the compliment. "Galactics?" A deceptively casual shoulder rose and fell in response, but she'd checked his pulse during their handshake. She knew how excited he really was.

"Now you're here, you can meet them. Let's go find out, shall we?"

The deputies formed an orderly line to the conference room, followed by the four military investigators. The ambient noise dropped to nothing. Melissa had to admire the way the Sheriff controlled his people. She hadn't thought they'd been paying him any attention, hadn't known humans could hear his words or interpret his body language amidst so much stimuli. But the moment he'd decided it was time to start the meeting, his whole staff had risen like a single being.

They filed neatly into chairs. Eighteen chairs. One short, but Melissa didn't need a chair. Made of metal and springs, she could crouch to seated height for a meeting's duration.

The two men from the Office of Galactic Investigation—an overblown title for a purely American department that operated primarily from the Sol System—stood behind a dusty plastic lectern at the front of the room. They ignored the local law enforcement officers. Instead they bent together, face-to-face and shoulders nearly touching. Like two metal towers with curving tips that had yet to collapse into one another.

Like they didn't want to be overheard.

They were both male. The taller one was 6'2". Forty-five to fifty-five years old. Chin-length nut-brown hair. Brown eyes under bushy eyebrows. Athletic build.

Unexpectedly long fingers. American-standard peach-brown skin, bleached slightly grey by long-term space travel. He wore a Core worlder's suit, a style which had barely changed since the 1700s. A uniform for the formal and outdated.

His partner was 5'10". Near black hair with bleach-blonde tips, sculpted into two-and-a-half inch spikes. Fifty to sixty years old, or a hard-worked forty to forty-five. Muscular build. Blue eyes, no eye-correction halo she could see when focusing in closer. American-standard peach-brown skin, tanned to a darker shade. *Time on planet or in a tanning bed?* Like his partner, he wore a Core worlder's suit, but shifted about as though it fit badly. Or as if he wasn't usually called on to wear one.

The Sheriff ambled up to the lectern and cleared his throat.

Everyone in the seats sat straighter, eyes trained on the authority in the room. The two galactics continued to kaffeeklatch.

The Sheriff tried again. "Arr-hrrr-umph."

So loud and so close, the galactics couldn't miss him.

"Ah, yes. Thank you," the taller one said. His voice rumbled on a harmonic, subtle though he must have synthesized it in some way. The floors and walls pinged slightly with the sound.

Half the crowd's heart rates sped up. All gazes locked onto the tall man, abandoning even the respected sheriff. From her position to the side of the chairs, she could see some deputies biting their lips. Others crossed and re-crossed their legs. Melissa resolved to find that harmonic in her own vocal range—or outside of human hearing. It certainly got positive attention.

The tall man took up a position dead center behind the lectern. His partner faded into the background like an undercover cop or a discreet bodyguard. The partner crossed his arms, feet planted shoulder-width apart. *Definitely bodyguard.*

"My name is Agent Ward. I appreciate your all coming out," he said. He paused to make eye contact with each and every audience member. His affable smile dropped when he spotted Melissa, dragging his gaze up and down her metal body under its minimalist clothes, over her back bench. "Even the coffee machine."

His sly smile and dry tone invited the audience to laugh with him.

With him.

At her.

And they did. The sheriff shifted, uncomfortable perhaps, but he tittered all the same.

Well, she didn't have to let it faze her. She wasn't even on this law enforcement team. Rangers worked alone. She only needed to be polite, courteous. *Just like a reactionary galactic. This is why I prefer the outer worlds.* The Star Rangers didn't have the same ingrained traditions (or prejudices) as the Core agencies.

Joke over, Agent Ward continued. "We've picked up the trail of a serial criminal who's left bloodied bodies and open safes behind on multiple worlds." He shined a pen at the wall behind him. The light formed a map of locations and projections.

The galactics were following *her* collar. Well, she'd just have to beat them to him.

Agent Ward gestured to Melissa. Her headlamps retracted flat to the sides of her head. "We can start by having the telephone over there look up who's new on the station."

She could already tell him who was new on the station.

- Michael Tong (caring for a sick mother and too busy to steal things right now)
- Jessie Moore (too short to slit throats)
- Her missing third suspect (she wouldn't even pretend to know his name)
- Agent Ward and his partner (probably not the characters they wanted to question)
- A newborn child about to emigrate down to Kessel (it counted as an arrival)

But she was no one's to call on. No one's to order around. American Star Rangers answered to themselves. Otherwise, they couldn't be counted on to dispense justice no matter how far out on the frontier they went.

She shrugged her shoulders, drawing attention to her four-limbed torso, an inhuman trait which sometimes unsettled Core worlders. She pitched her voice lower than usual, adding in a hint of the animal growl she usually reserved for criminals she wanted to scare. "I'll let you know if I find your suspect."

Let you know that I've turned him in to the Sheriff. He might turn my collar over to you, but I'll make damn sure you know I'm the better hunter.

A deputy looked at Melissa and frowned. "Can't you help them out?" he asked, brow wrinkling.

Already a deputy assumed the galactics could call on her services. They couldn't. They could demand cooperation from a Sheriff, from the military investigators. Not from a Ranger. She followed only her own rules when protecting the innocent.

She gentled her voice for the hapless deputy, growl no longer in force. He was misinformed, but didn't deserve her ire. "No," she said. Flat. Unmodulated. Alien and alone. "I'm busy."

Because the galactics had the right idea. No matter how much it galled her. She needed to find a newcomer to the station. Not Tong or Moore or freshly arrived law enforcement. Somewhere out there, her third suspect, her *best* suspect, was waiting.

She'd track him. She'd collar him. And she'd do it alone.

Chapter Thirteen

The Socratic Method

When Victor stumbled into the kitchen around lunch-time, he found a bag of baby carrots in the refrigerator and took a handful. They hadn't been there the day before. He figured Gwyn had picked them up from her new plant-inept friends since the bag's stylized JWS station logo reflected in the cooler's white-blue light. She was so good at making friends, especially amongst people who loved plants.

He also found the Ranger seated beside the large kitchen table. Or standing. It was hard to differentiate. On the one hand, she wasn't using a chair. On the other hand, she'd folded her legs to assume a chair-like height, and her back formed a bench that looked like it could be a chair itself.

"Hello." *No harm in being polite.* "How goes your day?" He crunched a carrot, making his ears crackle from the inside. The explosive noise made him squirm with awkwardness.

Her visor flashed pale blue. *Does that mean happiness maybe? Safety?* She'd done that when she'd cleared Rhiannon of wrongdoing too, he remembered. "Thanks for asking, kiddo." She sank down further and rested her head-sphere in three hands. She looked like a despondent human being with too many arms and an unlikely skin tone.

In his mind's eye, Victor superimposed Rhiannon's form on the Ranger's, as they'd mirrored each other so well earlier. *Yes. This is the posture of someone who needs to talk about what's going wrong.*

He joined her at the table, sliding into a hard plastic seat. "You're doing some investigation, right?" For all that he'd lived in her flat for thirteen days already, they'd barely spoken. He'd only seen her the day when she'd arrived and tested Rhiannon's prowess at poker. "Not going well?" He cracked his knuckles. Hoped this wouldn't be seen as overstepping.

She lifted her head off her hands, letting the freed digits curl inward. Just curl, not tighten into a solid mass. *Two thumbs on each hand.* He watched in amazement, wondering if she could get the thumbs to touch over a fist if she made one. "There's something *not right* about the suspects I've questioned." She made a noise like blown breath through static, but he didn't feel a breeze. "Or maybe they're fine and I'm the thing that's just not right."

Oh. Yeah. She doesn't actually breathe. He pulled on his tunic's hem, adjusting the pocket weighed down by his squishy ball. "You've probably already thought of this"— *There's a strong start, Victor*—"but most people I know work out or do something physical to calm down and get their thoughts in order." He hadn't done his own exercises—physical therapy—today. *Are they even worth it?*

warred with *I don't want to lose motion* conflicted with *Luciano wants me to do small motions, but the Americans think I just need to strengthen the muscle.*

She cocked a headlamp at him like a dog cocking its ear. *She's a person. Not a dog. Don't go making that mistake.* "I've never worked out. What do you suggest?"

His hands fell slack from where they'd gripped his tunic. *Never worked out?* It made sense, he supposed. A robot had no muscles to condition. But half the point of working out wasn't the conditioning, but the adrenaline... Not that a robot would have that either.

"I've been working on stage combat with quarterstaffs," he offered.

She opened all four arms in double invitation. "Do you have two staves?"

As far as the chair would let him, he slouched away. He hadn't intended to volunteer himself as a sparring partner for the law enforcement officer who shared his temporary home. But he was alone—again—and could use some exercise. *What if I slip and mention my Hive's upcoming heist?* Maybe they'd become friends and she wouldn't *want* to arrest him. "I've only got one. Are your arms long enough to work?"

She tapped the fingers of one hand on the table. It was... odd in a robot. *It just proves she's more person than machine.*

"Ah, well, no. But these legs o' mine can double as knives."

Even the unexpectedly sociable Ranger couldn't find a reason to spend time with him. "I don't know anything about knives," he said.

She straightened her legs till she reached her standing height and offered him a hand up. "I'll teach you," she said.

The pair adjourned to a practice room within the large flat. Victor hadn't been inside before, it not being technically part of the common living spaces. Padding covered the walls, and dusty machines squatted in the back corner. He didn't recognize their type. Another instance of American physicality outstripping Dyfed's innovations.

The Ranger strode to the center of the mats and beckoned Victor closer, only to circle around him on astoundingly silent feet. He assumed she must be assessing his abilities or his lack of muscle, but she didn't move her headlamps or anything. As far as he knew, she just liked walking in circles.

"So, ah"—he rotated his shoulders, pleased at the lack of twinges—"what are those things against the walls? I mean, you obviously don't use them."

She made a non-committal noise that soaked into the padding on the walls instead of echoing back. For such a large room, sound dampened quickly. "They were here when I got here." Two of her hands hovered over his biceps. "May I?"

When she got here? Victor nodded his permission to touch. "Isn't this your place?"

"Sure," she said.

Her implacable palms came down hard on his arms, shoving him backwards. He nearly stumbled to the ground, catching a boot heel on a blue mat-edge, before he caught his balance again.

"Hey!"

"Now we know which way your body naturally moves." She stretched her top two arms behind her head, opening up her chest in a manner that looked somehow vulnerable and apologetic. Or maybe just overconfidently smug, Victor really couldn't tell. "These are Ranger quarters. Just because I don't want to use the stuff doesn't mean no one does. Don't tell me you haven't noticed the cots and the old surveillance gear. I don't use those either."

Victor hadn't noticed any surveillance gear, but he probably wouldn't have recognized it. "We sleep on the cots."

She *tsked* like a teacher he'd had for fourth-form agriculture back on Dyfed. "But you didn't *notice* them. I don't know if you're ready for this kind of weapon." But she poked at his knees until he bent them more deeply, right foot in front of the left and hip-width apart.

Is she serious? He bounced, feeling the creases in his knees and ankles, the stretch in his calves. "Because I didn't think about why you'd want cots." It was a statement, not a question.

"Because any weapon can be turned to vile purpose," she corrected.

When she circled behind him, he couldn't see her, but he certainly felt her push his spine in a forceful rush. This time, he flexed and swayed, but didn't fall. Anchored.

She continued as if giving a lecture, "Knives are great for concealed carry, but they're also the most accidentally deadly armament allowed on this station." Alongside him now, she nudged his right arm upward and laid her own beneath it till he could rest his limb on hers and achieve perfect alignment. "You're good at physical movement, and you might see one or two reasons to choose a knife, but will you see all the pros and cons? Who will keep you honest if you can't observe yourself?"

Victor bit his lip to keep from biting out something aggressive and angry like *If you can't trust me, why are you letting me live in your flat?*. He curled his left hand into his tunic hem, but didn't tug it down, arrested by the kind of observation the Ranger wasn't sure he could make:

She'd cocked a headlamp at him when asking the question.

He'd seen her do that earlier. Victor might not know everything about robot body language, if there even was such a thing, but he could recognize simple patterns. The headlamp thing made him think she was genuinely curious, that she wanted him to tell her why he was good enough, observant enough, worth imparting knowledge to. She wasn't trying to trip him up, he realized. She just had really horrible social skills.

He grinned, stretching his wide, pink mouth ever wider. "That's why you'll have to teach me," he said, like it was the most obvious answer in the world.

And so Victor's knife-wielding lessons began.

Interlude 2

Panic! At the Old Senedd

Olivia didn't know how long it had been. An hour, a day, a month? She'd awoken from her first experience in The Lab sure she didn't want to visit again.

Thank you for your cordial hospitality, but Queen Olivia Jones regretfully declines.

She sat on her cot, elbows on her knees, head bent forward so oily white tips hung in her sightline. *When I escape this prison, I'll wash my hair and have the split ends trimmed.* A shower alone sounded heavenly, trim or no. In fact, if pressed, she'd admit to a simple fondness for escape. Hygiene classed as a happy externality.

Everyone knew that a prisoner's first duty was escape, but no one discussed how one went about it. She'd lived in these depths long enough to know she could count on no one but herself. Her fellow inmates lost coherency with every feeding.

Even friendly Marla of the *Llyr's Llambo* had succumbed days—*weeks?*—ago to screaming and rocking. She now ate the brown-white mush provided by their captors with reckless abandon brought on by hunger and a lack of self-preservation, even knowing the gluey nutrients could contain drugs.

Olivia had no experience with this sort of thing. No help, no strength, no talent in picking locks. But a Queen made do with what wits and tools she had, especially an explorer Queen. Experience be damned. Whatever she would do, though, she had to do it soon. Olivia's intestines rumbled like thunder, constricted like a boa.

She ran a finger over the hard, raised scab in front of her ear where the giant needle had injected some substance into her brain. She refrained from worrying it with her nails. That only led to fruitless bleeding and rust-encrusted hands.

Need the bleeding be fruitless?

The plan burst into her brain like a rush of bloody crimson. Yes. She could certainly *bleed* as well as any other prisoner in a ramshackle research facility. And while the panicked staff searched for a doctor to deal with a mundane ailment—a potentially *very* gory ailment—she could sneak away. Perhaps they'd even help her along by transporting her to a hospital themselves.

She touched ragged fingertips against her hair, pushing through the oily mess, and scratched tentatively. Dead skin cells balled up beneath her nails. *You've done worse plucking your eyebrows, Olivia.*

She firmed her mouth and steeled herself for the pain.

Her fingers curled into wicked curves poised above her head. Her forearms' soft, white underskin filled her vision. She inhaled sharply—sweat, urine, bland gluten—and jerked her elbows down. Sharp keratin parted the skin under her white hair. Angry skin bunched up underneath her fingers, a squishy mess of heated meat.

Before she lost her nerve, she extracted her biological knives and slashed them down again, severing follicles. Again and again, she raked her nails across her scalp. Warm rivulets ran down to her mouth, tasting like undercooked hamburger patties, oversalted by a zealous chef.

Blood flowing freely, she started the next phase: she screamed. It was easy enough to do. Her heart pounded against her stomach. The taste of human meat and smell of human waste combined with her nerves. Her gorge rose in her throat. *Don't vomit. It'll get septic.*

She screamed and screamed. Every time her head moved, blood flew.

She screamed until her throat felt coated with bumps that rubbed each other on every swallow. She screamed until all that came out was raspy choking.

They didn't even notice.

Defeated, silenced, Olivia laid on her cot. Cold tears mixed with the dried blood on her cheeks as she watched the empty hallway.

"Doctor Holly!" An afternoon guard, Luke, rushed into her office. "Come quick!"

She threw on her white coat and raced after him. By direct route, only two corridors separated her office from the pens. In seconds, Luke skidded to a stop. He thrust a frenzied hand toward the figure behind the bars.

"She's bleeding all over the place!" he screeched. "From the head! And the screaming... I almost missed it in the shift change. Though, she *looks* all right aside from the blood." His own observations calmed him more than any words from her could.

The woman in the cell looked up at them, eyes red-rimmed, but didn't budge from her place on the cot. "Are you going to call for a doctor?" Even with her voice rough and cracked, she managed to sound haughty.

I hate Queens. They don't know what they do to the REST of us.

"Luckily for you, I'm a GP." Holly grabbed an emergency kit from the wall, and motioned for Luke to open the door. "Stand ready," she told him. To her new patient, she said, "Let's see what you've done to yourself, shall we?"

You can take the doctor out of the private practice, but you can't take the bedside manner out of the doctor.

The Queen flinched back, but collected herself enough to sit up straight on the cot's edge. Good. This one still had control of her faculties. This newest Queen impressed her with her poise and mystery.

How has she stayed unaffected by my inhibitors?

Holly cleaned the affected area. "Just a shallow wound," she said in her most reassuring tone, the one she used on adolescent girls with broken bones from keeping up with the adolescent boys. Smirking, she refrained from checking under the Queen's own fingernails. *Still impressed. It's a shame you're a Queen.* She patted the woman on that precious skull... and surreptitiously wiped the oil and sweat off on her coat.

"You should be more careful," Holly said. "Your head is valuable to my research."

Chapter Fourteen

Stagecraft

Rhiannon was coming to love her time at the theatre. The actors' dedication. The need for competent organization and direction. The chance to watch exceedingly good-looking people run about with frazzled nerves and even more frazzled hair.

She didn't, however, always enjoy her role in the production. Mostly she coordinated the prop table and ran book, but today she was giving an impromptu voice lesson.

She sat in a middle row on the lowest level, eye-height with the stage, wearing her sexiest tunic—a red one, shorter than fingertip length and whose scoop-neck bloused at the breasts—over black trousers tight in the hip. Just in case she felt the need to compete with the actors. An outfit her father had never seen.

Of all the actors in *The Cleopatra's Palace Brothel Revue and Odyssey Recitation*, the woman on stage had proven the most trouble. The only thing Eleanor had a talent for was waving her whip around in artful patterns. With only four days until the show, the actress still needed to be prompted with her lines. Rhiannon would be tempted to tell the director to give Ms. Peacock's understudy a chance, but the diva had refused to allow one.

And now this. The actress was blundering her way too thinly through an aria that should project frustration and a desire to be left alone by suitors who took too many liberties. Swan-necked. No operatic singer of *this* woman's caliber should worry about neck presentation. Not with so much more technique lacking.

"Stop!" Rhiannon called out, to both Eleanor and to the man on the piano. "You're singing too much at the top of your throat." *Gods, that whip can get louder than she can.*

Behind Rhiannon, Victor gave her shoulder an encouraging grip. She reached up a hand to squeeze back. No idea where her other Devoted might be at the moment.

The woman nodded, as though that were enough direction, and gestured for the pianist to begin again. Maybe it *was* enough. Her tone changed, became deeper, richer.

And gravelly. Not what they needed.

"Stop!" Rhiannon called again. She didn't mind working for the theatre 'family,' but she had her own work to do. When it came to her Hive's upcoming plan to get back their Alcubierre tensor jet, well...

She had a plan, but it hinged on figuring out where the tensor jet was. Once she knew that, she could schedule Gavin to pick it up; could prepare Gwyn to create a distraction with the sheep; could send Alan along to ensure its completeness. But if she didn't have a place to send them, what good was all that direction? What good was her plan?

What good was *she*?

Maybe Gwyn was right to ignore her authority. Authority without anything to back it up was just a pose. Powerless. Pointless.

On stage, Eleanor cocked an exasperated hip. Planted her gold-adorned fist on it, next to an impressive array of abdominal muscles. "What *now*?"

The abdominal muscles should help with the singing, not be pure ornament.

"You know how when you're about to do a sit up, you tuck your head a little bit? Pull it back into more into alignment with your thoracic spine?" Rhiannon waited for the woman's nod. "That also creates a straighter line for the vocal cords, so you can sing with more power. Try it."

Eleanor balked. "I'd have double chins! Triple!" As if that mattered in the face of music execution. "How can I build my clientele if they see me like that?"

Ah. Rhiannon had forgotten that the point wasn't the play itself. Well, some patrons might come for the entertainment, but most of the actors also hoped to increase their patronage in the other aspects of *Cleopatra's Palace*'s business. Not the casino part.

"Let's try breathing from the solar plexus instead."

For the next fifteen minutes, Rhiannon gave a breathing lesson. Didn't American children learn this at their mothers' knees? Partway through an explanation of *yes, it will cause minor bruising at first when you obsessively check the pressure with your fingers*, she heard and smelled Gavin drop into a seat behind her, probably right next to Victor.

Steam, heavily spiced with rosemary and lemon pepper, teased her nose, and she slanted a glance to check on the food in question. He had a savory chicken sandwich. She could just take it from him. But she wouldn't. *When was the last time I ate?*

Behind her, the boys whispered. So long as they kept it quiet. She had a rehearsal to run here. And where was the director, she might ask?

"Take it from the top," Rhiannon ordered the actress and the pianist. "And remember, you still need to breathe this way during the quiet parts. It's even more important in the beginning than when you crescendo at the point where the suitors each steal something from your house, okay?"

Here, at least, was a situation where Rhiannon knew what was best. And was recognized for it. The musician started again.

Gavin tapped her on the shoulder. He leaned forward so that she could smell his sweet, peppery breath. "You'll be pleased to know," he said in a triumphant whisper, "that I accidentally cased the joint where the station administrators are keeping our tensor jet engine."

Accidentally? Her heart rate picked up and pounded in her ears, drowning out the slightly improved singing that filled the front rows. *I've been hunting for almost a week, and he just stumbles across it?* She reached up to twirl a lock of hair. *Oh, look. A split end.*

Gavin pressed in closer, losing his sandwich somewhere so that he could wrap his arms around her waist at a doubtless-uncomfortable angle. "I went to check on the sheep we'll be using for the performances." Gavin spoke so quietly that Victor leaned in as well, steadying himself on the black plastic headrest instead of on his Queen's person. "But I couldn't find the right room. I started in a life sciences area that was all plants. *Oh, fair Lois, her passions do unfold on that altar of photosynthesis.*"

You couldn't get through a day without Gavin quoting *something*. After next week, would her whole Hive be like that? Constantly reciting lines from the *Odyssey* adaptation whenever it seemed appropriate to them, even if it made little sense to anyone else?

Gavin's left arm remained a bar slanting across her shoulder, but his right hand splayed in front of them as if giving a campus tour to incoming students. His sleeve— dark brown silk and only one layer—flitted in and out of her vision as it waved in the station breeze. "The umpire of that Babylonian wonder did exile me through a different door to find the sheep in question. But!" Here he grabbed her shoulders, tight and sudden. "The gardens had a number of glass walls and through one I spied our saving grace: Alan's jet!"

The woman onstage warbled in Gavin's dramatic silence, but she sounded well enough that Rhiannon felt no need to interfere. Not when weighed against finally discovering the location of their stolen property.

Still, no need to draw attention either. "Shhh," she admonished her Devoted.

He snugged his oval face into the crook of her neck— *Apology? Shame?*—before resuming his tale. "What's back there?, I asked the umpire. She chewed her gum at me for a moment, considering my sincerity, then replied *Who knows, who cares? It's some stupid administration thing from the core. Not local.* Oh, I said. *I leave those core people alone,* she told me, *they get incarceration-happy whenever someone tiptoes into their jurisdiction.*"

Gavin imitated a decent John Wayne Station accent for the parts with the woman who looked after the life sciences plants, but what she'd said interested Rhiannon more than how she'd said it.

"The locals don't get along with their core citizens?"

That would never be true on Dyfed, but that was partially because the only contact they'd had with Earthbound Wales for a hundred years had to do with seasonal festivals in those rare cases when they could be observed simultaneously on both planets. And in those rare cases when Wales had an interested Archdruid. Dyfed had grown apart from the home planet to the point of apathy, and that made sense really. You tied yourself to the land you lived on, not to a land millions of miles from home.

Gavin's arms slithered away so that he could recline in his seat and finish that delectable sandwich. He took a bite and shrugged, as much of an answer as he could give.

Onstage, the actress stopped singing mid-phrase. To the pianist, she said, "Can we start over?" but her gaze was on Rhiannon, who nodded.

Victor said, "Let's keep our eyes on the show. Did you ever find the sheep, Gav?"

As if *that* were the important thing.

"This is about our jet," she gently admonished. "Now we know for sure where it is." After all her efforts to look after her Hive and their interests, it was *Gavin* who found the tensor jet's location.

Where she'd failed to provide room and board, Gavin had procured it from his new employer. Where she'd failed to find money to get their ship out of dock, Gavin was earning it. And where she'd failed to find the Alcubierre drive, well: Gavin, again. *Augh!* Rhiannon clenched her hands and released them. He'd done everything in his power to be a good Devoted, to do his best for her Hive. Was it his fault that he exceeded his Queen in every way? She said in praise, "That was good work, Gavin."

On stage, Eleanor-as-Penelope sang her helpless anger at her suitors. They'd stolen goods from her house—*Tiresias took a ledger / that I bought dirt cheap / Aeschylus a mirror / But Terrence a SHEEP!*—and she wanted more than just her things back. She mourned, *"Oh, why has my Odysseus left me all aloo-o-one?"*

Gavin snugged down more firmly into velvet plushness. "Thanks," he mumbled into his sandwich wrapper. He licked a finger clean, pink tongue teasing the air. "But we can't let the brothel down either. We're part of the team now. And, yes, I did get all the details about our sheep." He rummaged in the seat well for some other food item, avoiding her eyes, contrariness spent.

Unlike the singer on stage, Rhiannon wasn't alone. Not entirely. She still had her Hive. But she didn't know how to get her goods back from the suitors who'd stolen them. Worse, she didn't have an Odysseus to return and save her. Rhiannon had to save herself. She had to be the Odysseus to the rest of her Hive.

She had to be Queen.

Victor bounced in his seat, setting it squeaking and sending musty dust motes up to make them all sneeze. "We're on the theatre team and our own team! Everything's going so well."

Rhiannon raised an eyebrow, thankfully while turned away from her two Devoted. *Going so well? Our transportation's been stolen. We're broke and uneducated. Our main benefactor is a member of law enforcement, while we're planning a heist.* She brought her hands up to bunch in her hair, feeling the silk of the strands, the crunch of the roots.

"You okay?" Victor whispered.

Rhiannon nodded. She needed an excuse for her dismay. Thankfully, the woman butchering the soprano piece onstage provided an easy target.

"Stop!" she called. "Let's try this again on a harmony line. The audience doesn't have to know we're not performing it as written."

Nothing in life gets performed as written.

Chapter Fifteen

The Worst Kind of Dangerous

Victor let Ranger Melissa correct his grip on the practice knife in his left hand. Her cold fingertips poked against his more malleable skin until he adjusted. He'd grown used to such touches, chilly and unforgiving on the surface, but always meant to teach, to aid, to improve. For Victor's sake rather than her own.

"Lunge and thrust," she ordered in her low voice, too reminiscent of Rhiannon's contralto to defy. "Again."

She'd said it was good for him to learn both hands (hence working the left today), but he thought this morning's sudden urge for ambidexterity had more to do with the way his right shoulder had started acting up after two hours of practice. It was getting stronger, but it wasn't perfect yet.

His heart pounded in time with his foot hitting the lunge. Sweat poured down from every pore of his body, splattering a line onto the ocean-blue floor mats. The room was metal and mat and muscle. Nothing more.

"Side swipe. Crab left."

His trainer's voice came as if from inside of himself, somewhere, hollow in his ears. He followed the order, letting it wash away doubts and worries. There was only him and his companion. This was a safe space. And when he had mastered everything she had to teach him, he'd have *earned* his place in the Hive by being the best bodyguard ever. He would be well on his way to knowing *every* martial art.

"Switch arms. Lunge. Thrust."

Her voice was attached to his nervous system, and he slid the knife hilt from his left hand to his right. Lunged with perfect form and clarity. His arm extended, flowing with the bent leg till his shoulder *wrenched*. Heat and blood and scars and *oh capricious gods, have I lamed myself with knife practice?*

Victor screamed.

"Halt."

He stopped screaming. Panted out exhaustion and pain till spit mixed with the sweat on the mats. He gasped, "Shoulder."

The ranger bobbed her spherical head. "Looks like you overworked it. Stay here while I get you some ice." She left for the kitchen.

Victor hobbled over to a padded wall—*See, Melissa? Working out is what the Rangers expect from their people. Just look at this room. My idea was far from crazy.*—and leaned his upper back against it. His head thudded quietly on the soft surface. His lower back slid down and down until he sat on the floor mats, knees pulled up almost too high for him to curve over. Just breathing.

"Here." A bag with the American Star Ranger symbol, five exploding stars joined by ley lines with the name of the corps across the top, stamped on it was thrust in his face.

Victor took the bag, frost-cold and barely malleable, in his left hand. Pressed it against the back of his opposite shoulder. *Cold!* He hissed, but kept up the pressure. Pushed into it, tentatively, more trying to make his shoulder move than to get optimal coverage. "Let's take a break?"

She huffed—well, *synthesized a huffing laugh*—and folded herself down to the floor till her back bench laid flush on it. They sat, side by side, in the oppressive quiet.

Without activity, padded rooms are kind of creepy.

Minutes passed as Victor breathed into his shoulder, contemplated his place in the Hive if he couldn't be a martial expert, and wondered when Ranger Melissa would get bored of sitting here with an invalid when she could be detecting things or orchestrating her own workouts.

She should have left me ages ago. Her mind processes information so quickly.

She said, "I got that knife you're using from a thief." She tapped fingers on the floor mats, clicking. "It was my first solo case. At first, the perp only stole things: money, art, transport. It was only a case for the Rangers because she did it on multiple worlds. Then she got jittery. Stole herself a knife and a pistol. Didn't know how to use them."

Melissa crossed her arms and tucked her head, compacting herself. More quietly, she continued, "Once the first body turned up, they didn't stop. Like her first hit was free, and now she'd gotten addicted to killing."

Melissa's headlamps flattened against her head, and Victor couldn't help reaching out to pat the nearest part of her, to be company against the memory. He leaned back against the wall to keep the ice bag in place while he gripped her foreleg.

"Thieves who go armed are the worst kind of dangerous." Her headlamps flared out. "They've got no focus for violence."

He slouched harder against the wall, shooting well-deserved pain through his exhausted shoulder.

I'm probably going to use these skills—THIS VERY KNIFE—to be the sort of person you hate.

"The *worst* kind of dangerous?" he echoed. Victor knew she would have noticed his sweating if he hadn't already been drenched from exertion. *Yet here you're teaching me, and I'm about to be a thief in six days.*

She nudged her leg against his hold in what felt like solidarity. "I'll protect you from them as best I can," she said. "Till then, you keep the knife."

Oh gods, I can't. He felt his arms trembling and was sure he'd given the game away.

"I really wore you out, huh, kid?" She sounded lighter, freer, even though he knew she'd kept her voice pitch the same. "Well, rest up. I'm giving this knife to you so you can practice, so we can do more things together. It doesn't have to be some big important symbol of duty and killing." Unsaid was *anymore*.

Victor's lungs sank down into his stomach, overfilling the space and leaving his chest cavity empty. Here was his newest friend, the robot woman teaching him to be a better Hive member, trusting him with pieces of her history, letting him polish the edges off her old rages. And him, planning to heist back their Alcubierre drive, knowing she'd never approve. His acting against authority made him a criminal. His choice to steal made him a thief. And his newfound knowledge of knife play made him everything Ranger Melissa hated.

No matter how much he liked her, appreciated her insight and attention, or bonded via activity. No matter all of that. She was going to hate him.

Stop making this all about you, Victor. She needs to let go of the knife, so help her let go.

He took his hand off her leg to press it against his shoulder. He deserved the red-hot pain where he shoved fingers too hard.

"Thanks," he said. And tried to mean it.

Chapter Sixteen

Not a Shipping Container Either

Melissa had a lead—*finally*—and she was going to follow it. Even if it took her out to a section of the station where the floors shook so hard that she had to tamp down the sensitivity of her vibration sensors. The equatorial ring.

What with the people in all manner of dress, the lightweight electric vehicles, and the sporadic farm animal on a pallet, no one noticed a robot tap-tap-tapping on the sealed doors of each storage unit she passed.

Melissa stalked the halls, building audio images of the units' contents while all around her travelers *just passing through* kept their heads bent and their shoulder bags hitched high, rubber-soled boots thudding on the plastic grating. Pioneers on their way to Kessel laughed and bounced all over the hallway with their energy, ready to start their new lives and teasing each other about sex with the livestock (this being the group with the occasional mooing or bleating companion) now that they were leaving Cleopatra's behind. Administrative staff rotating in, mail transport before and after sorting—everything went through the equatorial ring at some point.

She worked her way outward and passed into a zone so relatively unpopulated that the air's humidity dropped 62 percent from the lack of human bodies and mammalian sweat. The outer storage areas didn't get as much traffic as the ones near the elevators. Fewer people had a reason to be out there. Unless they were storing something.

She tapped the first door in this outer zone in three places. This unit belonged to a long-term resident. The clicking pingback told her it contained multiple stacks of boxes. Nothing obviously amiss.

She catalogued the number and crossed it off her list. For now.

The second door she tapped in five places. It belonged to a Kessel pioneer. Along with the expected boxes, there appeared to be a baby stroller and an illegally stored living animal. Feline, with accompanying food and waste areas.

She wasn't here to enforce station rules. Though she might report the owner if he didn't vacate the station the following day, as per his stated intentions.

Melissa's hand strayed to her lower trunk, where her knife holster used to be. She'd replaced the weapon with a second set of cuffs, so her vest still bulged in the same way. It wasn't like she *needed* the knife she'd given Victor that morning. Anyone foolish enough to get that close could be taken out by her unshod leg. She just felt odd without it. Lighter, maybe.

By tracking purchases on the station, figuring out which ones hadn't been directly traceable, she'd come up with an area where her third, best suspect might be hiding. She'd narrowed it down to the storage units on the equatorial ring.

So when she'd picked up the trail of breakfasts and magazine packets and opiate cough medicine, all scrupulously non-trackable, she'd known this was the right area. *Maybe the cough medicine has more to do with* opiates *than with criminal trespass.* But that wasn't really relevant.

Door after door. Tap, tap. Pingback, pingback.

Of rooms reportedly empty, only one had contained anything so far: an illicit stack of bricks with the density of coffee grounds. Some smuggler was doing a brisk trade. But it wasn't hurting anyone. She sent off a message reporting the miscreant to the Sheriff's Office. Then she moved on.

By the end of the hall, she hadn't found anything resembling a thief's hideout.

She doubled back to test the doors again. Sure that she'd find something. And, lo, she did. Seven doors from the curving apex of the hall, at a unit that supposedly had nothing inside. Loaned out to a *John Rodriguez* a week before. *Not a very original name.* He hadn't paid his bill to the storage company yet.

This time, she tapped harder. This time, the door pushed open. No foam seal kept it safe-tight. No lock kept out a potential intruder. *It's not breaking and entering if there's no breaking.* In the case of an innocent party, well, she'd keep anything she found a secret. Even from other law enforcement.

At first the room seemed empty. Her straight-visual cameras captured nothing out of the ordinary. Just a bare room with bare walls, waiting to be filled. But Melissa knew better. This room should be twice as deep as it appeared. She picked her way across the metal floor, careful to remain silent. A false back wall. How extraordinary.

How classic! She wished she had a six-gun and ten gallon hat to set the mood.

Thermal cameras suggested no heat signatures behind the wall. Did she trust the cameras? She'd have to. She needed to get through to the other side, to discover whether her suspect used this storage unit as his base of operations.

Sometimes you just have to take a chance.

She turned a headlamp up to full bright and dragged the beam over the structure, hunting for something different. Like a minute, darker pixilation. *There!* That was the doorway.

Once found, it was a simple matter to run a sharp appendage around its perimeter to cut the lock. Then to push it open and shut behind her. *Knife might've been handy, but nothing this damn fine body can't handle.*

The tiny room beyond had a desk with two dilapidated chairs, green upholstered cushions tufting out in places. Twelve boxes stacked in the corner, and a twenty-five pack of flat boxes-to-be. Across the desktop, a few scattered memory disks.

She picked one up. It probably didn't contain any virus that could hurt her.

Before she could find a compatible drive, she heard stomping from the outer room. Hurriedly, she placed the disk within a millimeter of where she'd found it and moved to the room's edge. She pushed the boxes and flats out from the true wall to make a few feet of extra space. Space for her to hide.

She folded her legs under her like a kneeling horse. She bent her trunk to make a flat line from head to bench-tail. Her arms, she pulled in tight across her chest. She could only hide if the entrant didn't notice his back corner had shrunk. He'd be less likely to notice that if she could keep her dimensions box sized. Box height, box width.

A man burst through the false wall, slamming its door behind him. Melissa's thermal cameras could determine that he stood hunched over something in his hand. His fingers stabbed at the air in the jerky manner of a person tapping a pad. Her supposition was vindicated when he tossed something onto the desk with a clatter. From the desk, she heard, "Garble gundingr elda?"

Damn it. Her suspect was a paranoid one, scrambling his tab connections even when all by his lonesome self in his secret hideaway.

"Don't give me that tone," her suspect said. He paced the room, lumbering gait bouncing him from wall to wall astoundingly quickly. "I need you and your partner fully invested and ready to go."

"Grrrrrinxale."

"Three days from now. During the brothel's revue," her suspect said. He paced her way.

Nonono. Turn around. You don't want to look over here.

A box in front of her hiding space shifted. He lifted out part of her cover. *Damn it again.* She could feel her shoulder sockets starting to roll and locked them in place. That was going to be Hell to unlock later.

The box's edge scraped against the one beneath it. He grunted when he lifted it.

She was grateful she didn't need to breathe. Didn't need to move. No sounds would give her away before she heard as much incriminating conversation as he was willing to make.

Not just a one-person job. That changes this whole operation.

He abandoned her vicinity and returned to the desk, bringing him back into range of her stationary thermals. With a *thunk*, he dropped the box on the desk chair and slit the opening with a knife. A knife that looked a lot like the one she'd given to Victor, not the utility kind.

"All the officials'll be holed up at that thing, leaving us free and clear to grab the gene storage. I've already scouted the room. They keep all their animal stock in one place." He rummaged in the box, grunted, and headed back Melissa's way.

Another box shifted in front of her. The one hiding her front legs. *Damn it some more.*

"Margle ishnyak vim!"

The suspect straightened up and gave the box a kick. It didn't go very far, pushed against Melissa's rigid frame, but he didn't notice. Again with lumbering alacrity, he reappeared at the desk. He slammed a flat hand against the surface. The slap bounced off walls and boxes, pinging on Melissa's metallic hide.

She didn't move.

"Don't be an idiot!" He picked up his pad and held it too close to his face. His companion would be getting a lovely view of his eyebrows. "No one's going to even think about the two of you. No, I don't care that there's a Ranger on the station. It's just a damn coffee maker."

She didn't let herself get mad. He didn't matter. Opinions of criminals didn't matter. It hadn't mattered when the galactics had called her that earlier either. That was just why she didn't work with galactics.

And when people say that you don't matter because you're just a robot, does it make it better when you say they're not human because they're just bigoted idiots? No. Let it all go, M3L. Don't let it get to you. You're in control here. They haven't even found you.

With a slam, the false door shut behind him. He was gone, and she'd missed something while she'd been calming her electronic nerves. She replayed the audio from the last few seconds.

SUSPECT: "Fine. Just be here. Two hours before the whores start their thing."

ACCOMPLICE: "Liverscramk grstle? Kivvets tomgreig gulankr."

SUSPECT: "At the store room, idiot! I don't care if they're whores, courtesans, or the President of the Russian Federation! You know what I mean!"

That solved that, then. No point in arresting the suspect right now. She'd get only him. If she waited she could get the whole ring, making the station and the sector safer for everyone. She had them now. She knew the motive, the plan, and the upcoming location of three people of interest.

She could come back here in three days. No, two days. She'd come in two days and hide again, wait for the villains to congregate. Then she'd nab them all. They could deal with the embarrassment of getting collared by a mere coffeemaker.

Hah! I'm still the best tracker the Rangers have got.

Chapter Seventeen

Queenly Accoutrements

Rhiannon sprawled over the edge of the cot in her bedroom, one leg waving in the air. Her pad was on the floor above her head, open to her mom's favorite epic poem. Sometimes, reading about fictional families pulling together in a crisis made her life seem more manageable. Other times, it reminded her that her mother was dead, her father was disinterested in the things Rhiannon cared about, and her Hive had started out as a sham. Maybe it still was a sham.

So, no, she wasn't reading the poem. Again. Her hair brushed at the tab's screen even as it dimmed to power-saving mode.

She needed to go through the plan's details one more time. *Gavin drives Gwyn with the sheep to where Victor and Alan are waiting.* Perhaps this was the fiftieth *one more time*, but preparedness never hurt anyone. *The sheep create a distraction while Alan points out all the pieces, and the boys load our jet into the getaway vehicle.*

After all, she herself had become a Queen-Commander by preparing for the Test so thoroughly. *Luciano and I have the ship ready to go as soon as the jet—and our Hive—are in place.* Without all her studying and revising, she'd have been stuck as a Perceiver, without her friends, without her cachet, without access to the world outside of numbers and graphs.

Without this crazy predicament where masterminding a heist is my best option.

A scratching came at her bedroom door, and she blanked the pad's screen. "Come in."

Victor and Alan stood in the entryway, jostling each other and the doorframe, but not coming much nearer. More nervous twitching than jockeying for position.

She rolled off the cot, which had been digging into her hipbone anyway. Perhaps it wasn't the most dignified move, but she twisted on the floor and came up straight and tall. Well, as tall as she got, anyway, being the shortest of her Hive. She wore all black—black trousers, black socks, black wraparound tunic—because she'd be back at the theatre after this short break ended. The production was in the midst of "Hell Week," and she didn't have many chances to escape that *home away from home*. Not with the performance only two days away.

Victor started forward, and the door knocked into the bag at his side when it closed behind him. "So, ah, you know we love you." He gestured to include the silent Alan, who vigorously nodded his agreement. "And we think you're a wonderful Queen..."

Oh no. Her hands clenched and she looked away from her visitors. *I'm a terrible Queen.* Not providing for their futures, nor taking control of their comfort. She forced her shoulders to relax, her fingers to lengthen back out. If only she'd been properly trained on Dyfed! She could have learned the way to be a true Queen, could have become versed in whatever mysteries were required.

"But we need..." Victor trailed off again.

Rhiannon could fill in for him: *We need more, so we're leaving you.* He was just too embarrassed, too virtuous, to say it.

When it became clear Victor wasn't going to resume, Alan took up the thread. "That is, we want to honor our commitment."

Rhiannon swayed, feeling the backs of her thighs smush into the cot's edge behind her. She tugged down on her tunic, forced her knees to lock and hold her up straight. She would face whatever news they wanted to impart with dignity, with pride. With the regal demeanor of Dyfed's Queens.

She willed her presence to fill the small room, and the boys snapped to attention. Alan elbowed Victor who stumbled forward, shuffled back, got nudged again, and said "Oh!" as if all the wisdom of the universe had dawned in front of his suddenly open and transcendent face. With a sharp *kra-thoom*, he hit his knees. Alan followed a split second after, making a more graceful—if less dramatic—descent.

This was the second time she'd had Devoted on their knees before her in a single week. Prior to taking residency on John Wayne, it had happened once for each of them: the day they Devoted. In fact, neither of this pair had Devoted on their knees in the traditional style. Victor had Devoted on his back, lifeblood flowing everywhere. Alan from his desk chair at the university.

Let no one call her Hive traditional.

Yet here they were. Two Devoted on their knees before their Queen. Freshly showered—she could smell their minty soaps. Running hot—she could feel the blushes and nerves pinking their skin. The respect, the energy, the position: traditional to the marrow.

Rhiannon was grateful for her locked knees, keeping her from making the wrong move. *What's the RIGHT move?* Twitching, moving away, moving toward them? She had no idea. She hadn't trained in traditional Queenly behaviors. She ran on textbook descriptions and the hope that she had the same power of personality as those original Queens who'd forged their own way, who'd backboned the whole system.

Victor's harsh breathing and Alan's fingers—tapping on his own thigh, as quietly as he could—kept the room from total hush. *What do they need?* She didn't dare twist her hair in thought. Couldn't bring herself to so much as twitch.

Think it through, Rhi. They came here to talk with you. They fell to their knees. In supplication, perhaps? *Gotta take the chance or we'll be stuck here all day. Ceridwen guide me because I don't know what I'm doing here.*

She extended her hands and wove them into the hair at the crowns of their Devoted heads. Her fingers didn't shake in the thick masses. Did not pet or tug. *Blessing and benediction.*

"What would you ask of me?" She hoped the words sounded formal enough.

From the bag at his side, Victor produced a golden object the size of a dinner plate, but not solid. He managed to hinge at the waist and look at the floor without dislodging her hand from his head. Arms extended, he offered it up.

She stepped back to better see the offering. A golden circlet. Either it had been exquisitely worked to mimic nature, or her Devoted had made it by braiding leafy branches together and dipping the weave into pooled metal.

She ran a freed hand through her own brunette layers, twisting the ends. *Do they want a formal Queen who wears such things? Or is this just a whim?* She reached out to touch it, but stopped short. "Is this nightshade?"

Two weeks ago, when they'd gathered their most important belongings from the *Ceridwen's Cauldron*, Alan had been inexplicably in the garden and had commented on the nightshade. *Have they been planning this for so long?* This was no whim.

The question broke their muteness.

Looking up, Victor thrust the crown towards her. "We request your Queenly guidance." The words sounded rote and practiced, as though he'd found a formal script and tried to replicate it.

Alan bowed yet lower and touched her ankle briefly. "We request your protection from the foreigners who ridicule our culture."

What have people said to him? Though the theft of their possessions was a pretty big *fuck you, Dyfed-sovereignty.*

Victor shook the crown. "We make this gift, crafted by our own hands with our own materials, to show our Devotion."

"To pledge our desires," Alan said.

Together, they finished, "To increase the nature of our relationship."

It was words, just words, but their faces were red and bright, smiles rippling their cheeks and crinkling their eyes. They panted. They flushed.

They were beautiful and entirely hers. More hers than she'd ever dreamed of their becoming.

Rhiannon had always planned to be an informal friend to her Hive, even before she'd become *Queen-Commander Ceridwen*. Back on Dyfed, she'd studied and worked and planned to make herself a Queen, but what right did a false Queen have to this type of Devotion? And yet, what right did a false Queen have to deny her Devoted the leadership they requested?

The golden circlet, the *Cauldron*'s nightshade dipped in Dyfed-imported gold from her engine room, winked in the harsh American lighting.

Wear me, it called to her. *Wear me and be validated. You are QUEEN.*

Instead of reaching for it, Rhiannon rubbed damp palms on her black-clad thighs.

An accessory didn't make her Queen. Only her behavior and her Hive's treatment of her could do that. Though Victor and Alan wished for a more traditional Queen, one who projected that she was *in charge* and *in control* and *inviolate*, they were the only two Devoted present. Where were Luciano and Gavin? Luciano who had sworn her his entire life, everything he would ever be. Didn't his opinion count? And what of Gwyn? How would her best friend take to a Rhiannon so egotistic that she set herself up as a formal Queen?

Though… Victor ought to know Gwyn's mind. And Gavin would adore the formality and the ritualistic clothing. Perhaps Luciano would find comfort in knowing his Queen planned to be better in her role, to do more.

But what if these *oughts* and *woulds* were wrong?

Victor assumed his position of ultimate supplication once again. "Please, my lady."

Nightshade and gold. Death and life. Handcrafted from space-farmed materials.

If she took it, wore it, Rhiannon made a statement about her authority over her people. Made it clear what it meant to be Queen. To her Hive and to all those who saw her on John Wayne Station.

The crown glittered at her. *You are QUEEN.*

If she didn't take it, never wore it, she rejected a gift of love from her Devoted. Rejected a request for strength and guidance from those who relied on her.

Relied on her.

Perhaps she'd been wrong earlier when she'd believed that she had to provide room and board and money to escape this foreign place. Perhaps it didn't matter that Gavin provided the physical, so long as he did it in her name.

The circlet shimmied in Victor's tiring grasp. Glinted in the light like a crown of golden stars.

Yes. They didn't need her to provide physical safety, but to be their touchstone—for culture, for togetherness. They wanted her to guide them when they were confused or faced with too many choices. Wanted her to boost them on their paths to greatness. Wanted her to be their sanctuary.

She harvested the circlet from Victor's wobbling hands, and he jerked upright as though its small weight had been keeping him stooped over. It fit her perfectly, all the sharp edges smoothed, all the dangerous berries plucked and toxic stems coated with cool metal.

"Your Queen accepts your gift and requests," she said, feeling foolish. She tugged on her sleeves, then put her hands back on their supplicant heads. "We will be as Dyfed as it's possible to be, and I shall craft our corner of safety and sanctuary in your names."

She cast about for an idea, eyes flitting from corner to corner. Something, anything, to cement this promise. *What will make this room a little corner of Dyfed culture?* Her eyes skipped over the case beneath her cot, then came back to it. *I think I have a candle.* It had been her mother's, but Mom had been a big believer in doing *anything for family*, and Hive was family. "Fill a bowl with water for me."

Alan scurried to the kitchen to get the bowl, and Rhiannon dug through her case for the candle.

"Victor," she said. "Turn out all the lights."

She led her two Devoted, the only others present in the apartment, to the common room's center and began a ritual of blessing. She pictured the station's place amongst the stars, then their ship outside of it and their apartment within it.

Never thought I'd be doing a hearth ritual. Me, an agnostic. Who knows what kind of belief the other two have?

But the point wasn't the belief in the ritual or the gods. It wasn't in how silly she felt asking Ceridwen to hear her call or Brigid to bless her hearth. It wasn't the water droplets she scattered on each corner of every room.

It was the symbolism of *this is home* and *someone did this for your house on Dyfed.* She was making this space *theirs*, one droplet of goddess-maybe-charged water at a time.

The ritual only took ten minutes, badly-done meditation included, and at the end, the three stood in a triangle and watched each other.

Victor with his desire to bring them all closer together, chestnut hair flopping in his eyes. Alan with his love of physics and Hive, apples in his cheeks puffed up so large that his nose looked comedic-huge in the small space between them. Rhiannon, feeling the mantle of love and greater responsibility settle like a veil pouring down from her new crown.

"From now on," she told them, "you will only call me *my lady* or *Queen-Commander Ceridwen* in public."

She made the demand so that they would feel *safe*, though they didn't need to know her reason.

They bowed, stilted and unsure of such actions yet. "Yes, my lady."

Her mouth quirked up on one side. Teases. "Now get out of here. I have a plan to revise." Just one more time. Before they committed grand theft tensor jet.

They left her to her own devices in the room where they'd found her. Like the rest of the American station, the Ranger's flat was too brightly lit. Too cold. Too heavy. Yet today it felt like home. Peace. Hive.

She connected her pad to the station intranet for a moment. She needed to take care of her Devoted, after all. Seeing Alan had reminded her. Other than reclaiming his work, he hadn't had many chances for career advancement lately. Unlike Victor, who had taken on their patron Ranger Melissa as a mentor.

She could find something for Alan. Maybe not here. But somewhere soon. She put a general search in place. She'd check in later to see what popped up, what she could provide for him.

She wrote a letter to her father. She'd give it to Luciano to include in the packet home when he figured out how to send his own.

Dear Father,
I'm alive and well, and my Hive is coming together. I used Mom's candle today. There's still a bit left. Thought you'd want to know.
Hope you don't miss me too much,
R.J. (Queen-Commander Ceridwen)

That done, she closed her pad and locked up the apartment. She needed to be back at the theatre. That backstage area didn't run itself. It needed a strong hand.

A Commander's hand.

Chapter Eighteen

Wherefore Devotion?

"This seat taken?"

A plate appeared in Luciano's peripheral vision, carrying bright green salad alongside something that smelled of fish and cheese and grain.

He gestured the universal *please, go ahead* and went back to his own pasta bake.

The table Luciano had picked in the main market's Eatables Square was long and communal, full of lunchers who ignored everyone else seated on either side of the espresso-colored planks. Its edges were artfully distressed to suggest that they'd just *fallen off the trees* that way even though the smallest touch revealed the wood as a plastic imposter.

This sea of strangers all looked more like him and ate more familiar foods than the members of his Hive would, but none were likely to become a friend.

He sighed into the hot steam as it pushed tomato, basil, and garlic into his nostrils. Lemon pepper wafted on the air. Victor and Alan had been pressuring him to socialize all week, more persistent than he'd have expected. Luciano made excuses at every turn. He didn't know how to act, not when he planned to leave them. They were forging closer bonds, and they shouldn't try to incorporate him in them. Whatever they were doing, be it simple teambuilding or a complicated exercise, they didn't *really* want him there.

He couldn't tell them that, of course. He needed to keep his counsel until the time came to leave.

"Okay, I know it's rude, but I have to ask," the woman with the salad said. Her breathless tone and bright smile under dark eyes—eyes the same color as Luciano's own—softened the intrusion. "No one around here wears a shirt like that, and I've got to know what it's about."

Luciano checked his bright purple tunic. *No tomato stains.* He shook his head and grinned at her. "They're all the rage on my home planet, Dyfed. There's a few of us on station right now, and we're all wearing boots, trousers tucked into said boots, and solid-color tunics like this one." Admittedly, Gavin probably wore something more flamboyant. Luciano himself usually wore tunics with a trendier cut—tighter in the shoulders—that proclaimed his allegiance to Dyfed Mining Co., but not today when he hoped to have another session with the consul.

"I heard about you guys!" She flipped her black hair out of her face and over her shoulder, then speared spinach on her fork. She sucked the emerald and dressing off the utensil and chewed. "Something about a bunch of men who're in love with the same woman or something. Can you explain it to me?"

Her hand flew to cover her mouth, burn-fast, and she rambled apologies through hidden food and flesh. "No, I shouldn't have asked. That was so insensitive. I'm so sorry. You don't have to say anything. Unless you want to."

He laughed. Then laughed harder to revel in the feeling. He hadn't truly laughed in the longest time. Briefly, not sure of the local etiquette, he patted her hand. "It's quite all right."

So he explained Devotion, his hands moving in the air as if to frame the shape of the thing. He told her about the Earth queens who had courts of their own and how they'd done amazing things to influence the world. He discussed the ethics of creating a respected class always first in line for the choicest jobs and training—based on merit, yes, but not entirely on potential. He talked about his Queen, and how she was the most understanding, most brilliant, most forward-thinking woman he'd ever met.

For a while, he forgot all the problems his Hive had brought him and remembered why he'd Devoted in the first place. He extolled the virtues of living with brilliant people who treated you like family and helped you with whatever you needed. He corrected her idea that Queen-Devoted relationships were necessarily sexual, pleased to educate an outsider on the culture he'd left behind and hoped to soon reclaim.

He didn't tell her about his plans to defect back home or about the way he'd leapt into this situation without thinking it through. *Had Rhiannon herself even thought it through?* In her defense, she had warned him about the risks before he'd impulsively Devoted to her in the street.

"I'm sorry. You probably didn't want to hear all that." He offered her a small smile.

Halfway through his treatise, the woman's sandwich had turned to crumbs. "Are you kidding? It's fascinating! I didn't realize there was such a commitment on both sides, from Queen *and* Devoted. The gossip's all about how the guys are in love with this frigid ice queen who barely cares for them. That's obviously not true."

It's not supposed to be true.

That wasn't fair. Rhiannon did care. She'd looked out for the Hive's safety, had trusted Luciano to take care of what she couldn't, and had found him the best possible work-experience learning program on this station when they'd only been here a week.

He loved Rhiannon, yes, but he wasn't like the others. He had more responsibilities than just his own future, couldn't throw away security for his mother and sister on a social experiment.

"Well," she said. "It's been interesting, but I've got to get back to work. Nice to meet you..." She trailed off as she stood to clear the detritus of her meal. "Oh my God. I didn't even ask your name!"

How nice to hear God referred to in the singular once again. He held out a hand to shake. They did that here, he was pretty sure. "Luciano."

She didn't take it, hands full with her tray. "Well, it was nice to meet you, *Luciano*." She pronounced it all wrong, with the stress on the *i* instead of the *a*, and then she was swallowed up by the crowds and the noise of people ordering lunch and knives chopping away.

He pushed his plate to the side and pulled out his pad. This was as good a place as any to spend time. He buried himself in it, trying to look as unavailable as possible. He wasn't ready for another conversation about Devotion, not when his own convictions shook so.

Dearest Mother and Aurelia, he wrote.

I wonder whether you're reading these letters all at once, spellbound by my fabulous life, or if you're parceling them out slowly to heighten the suspense.

As with my other recent missives, I apologize that I'm sending this one without gifts or financial support. However, I have good news.

Yes, your son and brother has arranged to be delivered home. I told you I was the smart one, Aurelia! You can admire all the salt in my pumpkin now.

I miss the sensibility of Dyfed, the way everyone understands my desire to Devote to the perfect Queen and doesn't question it outside of the usual *what makes a perfect Queen?* and *can't non-Devoted excel too?* that come up in philosophy classes. I miss hearing your lovely voices and providing for your comfort with my paychecks.

I've been careful not to say anything bad about my Hive, only about myself, so I might be Tested again when I return. What is another Test in the face of lifelong misplacement? For certainly, I have misplaced my way out here amongst Rhiannon's stars. I have hands made of pastry dough these days, and nothing goes right when I touch it. The exception, of course, is my upcoming return. I may return in shame, but it will be a homecoming nonetheless.

I'll see you soon, I hope, even if only in real time on my pad screen.

Baci e abbraci,

Luciano

Chapter Nineteen

Costumes In Layers

With two days till the heist, it was also two days till *The Cleopatra's Palace Brothel Revue and Odyssey Recitation*. Rhiannon often found herself backstage in the evenings. They'd had a complete tech rehearsal that day, the first one with all the spots and sounds working correctly, and now most of the cast and crew had headed home to their rooms and apartments. Some alone, some together, some with strangers.

Rhiannon, however, remained in the theatre. She wanted to reset the prop table, go over schedules, leave a note for the light person about adding another blue gel during the shipwreck scene in *The Odyssey*. She grabbed a lantern off the ledge where some less fastidious person had put it, intending to return it to its place in her prop table lineup.

But while most of the cast had gone home, she wasn't alone in the cavernous quiet.

"Psst!"

With a yelp, Rhiannon dropped the lantern. It clattered to the floor, rolling, till it came to rest with its tiny door squeaking on its hinges. She fell to her knees, black trousers muffling the thump of bone to hardwood, and gathered it up again. *Quiet quiet quiet!* This close, the lantern smelled of old smoke and melted plastic.

So far, she'd dodged four different burgundy-clad bouncers. She appreciated their sweeping the theatre for stowaways and undesirables, but she didn't have an advocate around to tell them that *she* didn't fall into the *undesirable* category.

"Psst," the voice said again, but this time in less of a hissing whisper, followed up by a chuckle. Rhiannon clutched the lantern closer, hunting for any sign of her tormentor.

I didn't hear any footsteps. Oh, and this position doesn't look suspicious.

She tried to relax her grip, to run a hand *oh so nonchalantly* through her sweat-frizzing hair. But she was stopped by the leafy bumps around her temple. *Right, my crown.* Her hand detoured to pat away dust on her black sleeve.

As though melting upward from the stage floor, Cinna appeared. She wore a faux-leather corset whose neckline—*if you could call it that*—scooped below her bared breasts and pushed them up with a thick rope trim. The corset stopped at her lower ribs, leaving her midriff bare, and a voluminous, pale blue skirt fell in lacy netting from her hips to past her ankles. A snake-shaped arm cuff hissed from its perpetually open mouth on her bicep.

The effect was jarring. Not something anyone on Dyfed would expect to see.

Possibly she's going for pseudo-Greco-Roman? To match the Odysseus theme?

Cinna's orange-glossed lips parted, revealing black painted teeth. Rhiannon could smell the oil and plastic in the colors and tried not to recoil. *Japanese theme?* "Hey, my lady," Cinna said, orange lip paint cracking a bit on the *lady*.

Oh, no no no. That's just not right.

Rhiannon returned the lantern to its wrong place on the ledge and waved her hands to ward off the misunderstanding. "You don't have to call me that." Not strong enough. "Actually, you shouldn't." Not enough information. "It denotes a certain relationship between the two of us. Just call me Rhiannon. It's fine."

She tried to run a hand through her hair. Again. But was stopped by the circlet. Again. She petted down whatever frizz might be fluffing up near the roots instead. *I bet my hair looks beautiful. Not that anyone would even notice me next to... whatever's wearing Cinna.* Her hand came away damp. *Great.*

Cinna shrugged as though to imply that names didn't matter. The gesture jiggled her assets accordingly. Rhiannon really only saw naked people on holy days, and even then only back when her mother had made her attend certain festivals. But Cinna was something special, something intentionally appealing, unlike the skyclad revelers who came to bare their flaws before the gods and the stars.

Watching Cinna was like watching Gavin's sleeves, or a sloshing tub under multicolored lights. Pretty. Mesmerizing. A little too unbound.

Rhiannon kept her eyes *up*, not wanting to send any false signals. She found Cinna entrancing, yes, but it wasn't a carnal aesthetic, and she knew someone in the brothel profession might find that confusing. If she and Cinna were going to be friends (and they had seemed to be on that path since the first day Rhiannon had rejected her advances in the casino), then there couldn't be any doubt about Rhiannon's intentions.

"I hoped you'd still be here," Cinna said. "I wanted to hear your accent again." She said *accent* the way that Rhiannon would, with the long, soft *ah* fading into more of a *gz* than a *ks*.

"Just the accent? Not my whole second language?" Rhiannon turned away to regain the lantern, smirking over her shoulder. She'd learned enough in her days at the theatre: the courtesans were *cosmopolitan*, each determined to know the most languages. As far as she could tell, the most knowledgeable one had twenty-seven under her diaphanous robes, but she'd bet none had ever heard Cymraeg.

Cinna gasped. The gasp of someone truly excited who is *not above begging*.

It made Rhiannon grin, expression hidden from her eager companion.

A loud footfall, *click*-heel to *thunk*-toe, rattled the stage, and Rhiannon dashed to deposit the lantern in its proper place. She scrambled underneath the prop table and tried to calm her racing pulse. *Breathe in, breathe out.*

A knock shivered the table's legs into her trembling hands.

Cinna appeared in her vision for the second time that night, this time at a slanted angle. The woman had bent over—*That can't be comfortable. Just look how her breasts are hanging.*—to peer at Rhiannon, half-laughing, half-mystified. "What on Earth?"

Rhiannon choked down her own hysterical laugh. Of course Cinna would vouch for her to the bouncers. "Remember when we met?" She crawled sheepishly from under the table. "I got kicked out of the casino that day. And, supposedly, from the theatre and the brothel as well. For a month." She waved a hand with two fingers sticking up. "Two weeks to go!" Tilting her head towards the counting hand, she shrugged, smile curdling.

"We can fix that! We'll make you one of us." Cinna grasped Rhiannon's hand, and pulled her into the welcoming dark. She thrust Rhiannon through a wooden door and into a harshly lit room full of musty sweat-and-floral-perfume. "But only if you do something for me." The woman disappeared behind a row of dresses.

Rhiannon bet she knew exactly what it was.

"Do you want to learn to speak in Welsh?" she asked... in Cymraeg.

A tie-dye bra flew onto Rhiannon's shoulder.

"Oit teen moy," Cinna tried. "Then what again?"

The last time Rhiannon had tried on clothes, she'd been with Gwyn who could make anything in higher quality than the mass-market items. Rhiannon's shook her head fondly in remembrance of her best friend's nose, wrinkled in disgusted dismay at the weak seams.

"Wyt t'in moyn siarad Cymraeg?" Rhiannon had never seen tie-dye worn by an adult. That didn't stop her from unwrapping her black tunic and trying on the clingy cotton bra top, blue-green starburst on one side and red-gold on

the other. No need to take off her circlet-crown. "Actually, you probably shouldn't call me Rhiannon either. Sorry." Suede trousers with fringe along the outside seams hit her in the face.

Cinna called, "That wasn't commentary!" She popped up in front of Rhiannon again, coming from behind—*How did she get back there?*—with a bright blue bandana she was folding over and over and over. "Then what should I call you?" She made another fold. *"Oyt tin moin charade?"*

Rhiannon tried to tug down her sleeves and hunch into her shoulders, but the bra top didn't have sleeves. Or shoulders, really. So her hands just fluttered uselessly about the opposite wrists. *What SHOULD friendly acquaintances call me?* She let her hands open and spread, palm up. "Queen-Commander Ceridwen, maybe." She hated the uncertainty in her voice. "It's my actual title." She gestured upwards, either to point out the crown or make the hand symbol for *crazy*. "Goes with the new hat."

Cinna didn't say anything, just began to refold the bandana. Was that a good sign? A bad one?

Rhiannon aborted an attempt to run a hand through her hair. *Fool me thrice...*

"I mean, I've never been traditional. The crown is new." She didn't have to explain herself to Cinna, but the woman was taking it so blankly that Rhiannon didn't know what else to do besides spew everything that could possibly put her mind at ease. "I suppose I should be traditional. It's what my people want. Why they gave it to me. But what do my accessories matter?"

At *that*, Cinna speared her with a withering, derisive snort. The sound went straight through to her heart. *Oh. Right. We're dressing me up so that I look like I belong and the bouncers consider me one of their own. Clothes mean something, even when they're costumes.*

Cinna replaced the bandana and grabbed a necklace instead. She slipped it over Rhiannon's head, its twig-symbol pendant lying on the collarbone. "Sounds like trying on a new role for the patrons, but you're doing it for people you genuinely love. You're lucky to have people who love you and want the best for you. Worth acting in a new way for."

She pushed Rhiannon in front of a floor length mirror that had been hidden behind Louis XIV era dresses. "Before I became a courtesan," she said, surprising Rhiannon, who hadn't heard that term outside of history texts. "I tried on a lot of different styles. And I was good at switching up. That's how I ended up in this job, where people pay me to be flexible with my identity."

She pinned extra fringe around Rhiannon's middle ribs. "Here on John Wayne, we're like a family of role-testers, all supporting each other. I borrowed this outfit from Danika, who went by Scheherazade last year when she wore it. I might get one or two of her clients out of it." She pulled the straps off Rhiannon's shoulders, scrunched her nose, and pulled them back up. "You know what I mean?"

Maybe. "You're lucky you know who you are."

Cinna rested hands on her shoulders, as if to say *You're done. Check you out.*

"No matter what you wear, you're still you." She reached out a finger to tap the golden nightshade crown at Rhiannon's temple, but pulled back at the last second. "What does this crown say about you? What does the rest of your outfit?"

Implied: *Does it matter?*

And it didn't matter, not really. Her clothes symbolized belonging at the theatre-brothel-casino. Her crown symbolized being a Queen for her Devoted Hive. Without the outfit, she was still stage manager—*and apparently Cymraeg-tutor*—without the crown, she was still Queen. But in the crown, in the bizarre getup: "It says I look damned good in fringe."

"You know it!" Cinna folded up Rhiannon's discarded clothes. "Now, say it one more time. *Oy min toy* help?"

"Wyt t'in moyn siarad Cymraeg?"

They repeated the phrase together a few times. Later, Rhiannon would have to teach the woman how to reply, but getting the sounds down would help. Then Cinna headed out, off to wherever else she needed to be or maybe to sleep. Rhiannon returned to the main stage to finish organizing her prop table, confident in her costume.

After two minutes, one of the burgundy-and-ivy men caught her eye and nodded. After five minutes, she stopped jumping when she heard footfalls. After ten minutes, she was done. *Really? That's it?* Without all the nerves, all the stopping to hide and hyperventilate, setup for the next day's rehearsal didn't take nearly as long.

She shouldered her sack of normal clothes and went so far as to wave *goodnight* to the closest bouncer when she walked out the exterior theatre doors.

...and directly into a large man. The pioneer type, recently arrived and soon to depart. Tall as Victor, but even broader than Luciano would be at that height. She was no waif, but the man dwarfed her. He used the extra height and bulk to loom, curling over her like he was hiding her from the hallway, like he wanted to make sure she knew he could envelop her twice around.

"Terribly sorry," she said. "I didn't know anyone would be standing here."

A breeze got past the wall of flesh in front of her, and her arms bumped up from the cold. She was briefly jealous of his fuzzy flannel shirt, but she'd just made this costume change. She didn't know if she was ready for a third outfit quite yet.

"Well now," he said, his voice like gravel. It gave her unpleasant flashbacks to her Hive's kidnapping by Mr. Bristow of the *Llyr's Llambo*. "You look cold, little thing. Why don't you come with me and warm up?" His tone made it clear he expected an unqualified yes.

When she hesitated, trying to craft a polite way to say *thanks but no thanks* or *I'm done for the night* or *I'm not actually a courtesan, just dressed like one* or anything at all—he reached out and

Grabbed

Her

Arm.

Her chest seized, lungs filled and emptied too rapidly. She didn't move. Didn't speak. Despite the courtesan clothes, she still wore *a Queen's crown and he had TOUCHED her.*

Bad enough when Cinna had done so, though the woman touched only under the auspices of helping out, of her job, of a friendly easy-to-break grasp. But this? This was *not acceptable*.

She gathered sour station air through her nose, forced her shoulders down and back. Breathed out over-loudly. She pulled her head back—*partway to bitchface*—to stare him straight in the eye. She didn't look away. And he didn't move, surprised perhaps by the fiery anger or confused that she neither fought nor melted into him.

Queens are too regal for any of that. Especially in the face of opposition. He was not Hive. Was not castmate. Was not anything.

Exceedingly slowly, she formed the words she needed. "Unhand me."

He smirked. "Who even says things like that? You wanna role-play with me, woman?"

Her hands twitched, but had nothing to hold onto. No. She didn't look away. She didn't change her breathing. "Unhand me at once."

"Aww, sweetheart." He let go of her arm, but only in order to wrap both of his own around her bare waist. "Don't be like that."

At least he's warm. "I'm terribly sorry, but you're wasting your time. I have no interest in going anywhere with anyone, even you." That sounded fair-minded, straightforward, non-insulting.

His arms tightened around her waist—*a reminder that he could snap me like a sapling twig?*—and he curved around her to whisper in her ear. "Dressed like that? I think you'll do whatever I want. And you'll take whatever I give you."

She tossed her head backwards and heard him curse. *I hope one of those nightshade leaves scratched your corneas.* "Let me go!" She pummeled his too strong arms with her fists. Twisted in his too tight grasp. *I'm not yours to take anywhere. I said NO!*

He didn't let her go. Instead, he picked her up. She kicked out and down, trying to smash his foot or his crotch, but it was all too far away and she'd lost any leverage she had. She screamed out her fear and frustration. He chuckled. She thrashed harder.

He said, "I know you're just playing with me. Your kind don't say *no*."

She screamed again, weaker. Harder to get air now. Rhiannon didn't know who *her kind* were supposed to be. But she'd bet *all the kinds* would say *no* to a proposition like this.

Boots clattered on the plastic floor, but she couldn't see anything through a veil of hair.

"Drop the lady."

The man holding her mostly stilled, but she could feel his hidden chuckles against her back and thighs.

"Now."

He put her down gently. Petted her bare shoulders like she was a kitten.

"We were just having some fun, gentlemen," he explained. "No problems here."

Rhiannon's rescuers were three burgundy-and-ivy-clad bouncers. The closest one was a little smaller than her attacker—*mauler?*—but held a gun in his hand. Steady.

"Ma'am?" he asked Rhiannon.

The pioneer man scoffed. "You don't need to ask *her* anything. I already told you—"

"He accosted me in the hallway," she said. Her voice steady. She picked up her dropped bag with her stage manager clothes in it. The area behind the bouncer looked so much safer, but she held her ground. He'd protect her anyway. It was his job to protect the casino-brothel-theatre employees. *But you don't really belong. You only look the part.* "I told him no. I told him to let go of me. But he picked me up and was going to take me somewhere against my will."

"Aww, come on." The man gave a hapless shrug and gestured toward her. "She's a whore. I was gonna pay. What more do you want?"

The bouncer nodded and holstered his gun.

It's your JOB TO PROTECT ME! Her breathing sped up again. Too fast. Too much. Too soon. Spots swam on the wall.

The other two bouncers came up behind the pioneer man and grasped his arms. Their spokesman told her, "You run along, ma'am. We'll take care of this scum."

To the man he said, "We're going down to the Sheriff's Office, right after I get a blood sample to blacklist you permanently." Like a tagline, he finished, "You respect the employees, and Cleopatra's Palace respects you."

The man sputtered as they led him away.

One silent bouncer looked back over his shoulder at Rhiannon, eyes narrowed. She recognized him. The man who'd tossed her out. His face cleared, like he recognized her too. *Is he going to tell them? Going to let the man go because I don't belong?* But he just nodded and winked.

The clothes, the setting, the principle of the thing.

She belonged, no matter how temporarily, within the solidarity of Cleopatra's Palace. Everyone could tell. From her clothes, from her demeanor, from her willingness to lean on the burgundy-and-ivy men who upheld the casino-brothel-theatre's peace. It was a part of who she was.

Just like she was also Queen-Commander Ceridwen of the *Ceridwen's Cauldron*. Everyone could tell. From her crown, from her regality, from her willingness to lean on her Devoted for support and to support them in return.

She was Queen.

Chapter Twenty

Also Not a Radio Player

Melissa had patience to spare. Had to have, or else she'd have gone insane by now, a computer's mind so much faster than a human's. Or so she heard.

It had been two days since she'd overheard her suspect plotting his heist. One day left until she collared the whole ring of thieves. Her surveillance records and observations were all appropriately written up, tagged, and sealed against tampering. She'd scoped out the storage facility hallway for unplotted exits. She had wire-thin ties for their wrists and ankles ready to go.

She ambled through the rings in concentric circles, swinging her arms with a jaunty practiced thirty-degree elbow bend, the way humans did when they were in a good mood. She endeavored to appear aimless. *I'm just walking the station, not trying to see if any particular room is empty so that I can break in and hide. Nope.* Around her, bustling locals enthused about the upcoming show. Anyone could watch a recording, but live entertainment commanded a premium.

She was approaching her target area, crowd thinning, when the Sheriff's Office flashed her a message.

Come in for a meeting?

If it had been a definite command, she'd have refused. But the interrogatory mark meant that the sender considered it a question. They didn't believe they had the right to demand her presence. *That* courtesy, small though it was, should be returned. She curled and flexed all four hands in the habit she'd picked up from her favorite (as far as she could remember) engineer. *Best to go now. Get it over with.*

Besides, this gave her the chance to tell the Sheriff about her upcoming collar. He'd appreciate the forewarning before she dragged three or more criminals into his cells, no doubt.

Once at the office, she dipped her headlamps to the deputy on duty at the main desk. The front room was otherwise devoid of life. Slow hour. The deputy ducked his head and gave her a tentative wave. She was already moving past him by then, though, far too fast on her four insectoid legs to wave back.

She penetrated the inner office, hunting the Sheriff. Her ambient receptors only noted four other bodies. A singing woman in one office. A shivering man in the holding cells, his heartbeat too fast. Two men in the meeting room she'd occupied days before when those horrid galactics had presumed to call on her services like she wasn't an autonomous being. Like she was a pet. Like she was a machine. *A coffee maker.*

Don't let it get to you, Ranger-girl. You're above this. You're as human as they are, and all humans need to control their anger. Still, her twenty four fingers flexed and curled a few times to uncramp her irritation.

She slowed her gait, not wanting to seem anxious. With as much Space Ranger swagger as she could pack into her springy leg joints, she sauntered into the meeting room. Her torso leaned back as if she were reclining on her own bench. A posture of self-aware power.

The Sheriff wasn't waiting. No, the two bodies belonged to Agent Ward and his crony. *Speak of the devils.* They leaned into each other like conspirators, their backs to the door. As one, they torqued their shoulders, snaking heads around to see who'd entered their domain. Had they taken over the meeting room for the duration of their stay?

Damn good thing I'm about to crack this case, then. Sheriff's gotta take back what's his.

Agent Ward gave her his smarmy, fake smile. "There she is! My favorite radio player."

Not more of this. She kept her voice a flat monotone, but tossed in his harmonic-of-charm. She could learn from everyone, even a pair of jerks like these. "I'm here to see the Sheriff."

Implied: *You two aren't worth my time.*

Agent Ward shook his head, acorn-colored hair bobbing around his chin. "No you aren't." He gave her that fake smile again, and she was sure he'd have petted her head or shoulder if she'd been any closer. "I used the Sheriff's network to call you in."

Her blue visor turned a dark navy, but she held her ground. He'd take it as weakness if she shied away or stormed out.

"You don't have the right," she said, pitching her voice lower.

"Now, now." He ambled toward her and reached out to pat her chest, right above the pocket where she kept her badge. "We need to ask you a few questions about your credentials." His partner nodded along, still silent but giving agreement and support.

Melissa wished she could sneer. She turned her visor color almost black instead, and her headlamps flattened against the sides of her head. "Your hand is right on top of it," she said. "And I'd take it mighty kind if you'd remove that hand."

He laughed, patting her again before he withdrew. Did he think she didn't mean that? No, only that he had the right to treat her like a damned pet.

When I tear his offending hand off his galactic body, will anyone care?

"Okay, baby."

Her visor flashed a furious white, and she drew her arms in and her legs up. Ready to spring, ready to rend.

He said, "We've been tracking your movements, and you have to admit that it looks suspicious. I mean, you arrived on the station just before we did, and we're pursuing a dangerous criminal." He sat on a desk, casually, as if inviting her to be informal with him. "Care to share your reasons?"

So it's just a hazing then. Her arms relaxed back out to her sides, though her knees stayed up high and ready. She brought her voice up high, made it younger, innocent, as if to say *even a child can understand my reasons*. "Well, I was following this dangerous criminal, see?" She brought her voice back down again, into the low, animalistic range she liked to use on suspects caught in the act. "So I'll thank you to stay out of my way." Sadly, her new tone didn't make him draw back in fear, didn't ratchet his blood to pound against his veins.

She turned, presenting her metal-plated back to the two galactics. They might have called her in, they might have treated her like an inhuman thing, but they couldn't make her stay. She had control of herself, had the power invested in her by the Ranger Corps. "This meeting is over. Don't call me again."

The Sheriff can find out about my collar tomorrow, when it happens. Let it surprise these two jokers when he gives them the whole criminal ring. They'll have to acknowledge me then.

Agent Ward's voice followed her out into the hall, harmonic and musical and something he didn't deserve. "Are you sure you aren't under some hackery virus? You're vulnerable, you know. This doesn't have to be your fault."

She didn't deign to respond. If he wanted to assign blame for a crime wave or believed that she couldn't tell whether she was under the influence… well, she didn't like it. All she could do was keep living. Keep working.

Melissa didn't answer to these galactic annoyances, and it wasn't her job to set them straight. She'd wasted enough time here.

She needed to get into position in that room so she could pounce upon the criminals all unawares. She'd make her arrests and send her collars to prison. Then Agent Ward would realize he'd been wrong about her.

Interlude 3

Queening It Old School

Olivia had devised a new plan during the endless opportunities for meditation her captivity provided. Her prison mates' wailings might pound the halls frequently and at volume, but they faded into the background after a while.

It's true. Humans can get used to anything.

She'd been sent to the lab twice more, where she recognized the disembodied voice as also belonging to her doctor during that first escape attempt. Twice more they'd injected her with some unknown drug, once in her veins and another time in her skull. Her vision had gone fuzzy after the latter, and she'd been as shiny and mellow as any dopamine addict. Those effects wore off after three sleeps, whereupon she'd hatched her newest scheme for freedom.

Here comes my unwitting accomplice now.

He was a male guard, broad as he was tall. Thankfully, the plan didn't hinge on her overpowering him with her aging body.

"Pardon me, young man," she called when he had half a hall yet before her cell.

Most guards avoided stopping to chat. They preferred to pretend the prisoners could neither speak nor understand them. However this particular guard had recently shown off pictures of a new niece to a coworker. A family man, then, with a love of children.

She thought his name was Luke, but she wasn't sure. She decided not to call him anything. Getting it wrong would be worse than acting the doddering old woman.

"I know you're busy with your work, but if you have a moment to spare for a sentimental old woman..." She hunched over as though her spine could barely hold her head's weight. The contortion made her spine twinge. "I just missed my great-granddaughter's birthday." She injected a tremor into her voice. Between that and the stooping, her abdominal muscles were getting a workout. "Could you get her a message from Nana Olivia? Just to let her know I love her and didn't forget?"

The guard changed course to angle for her cell. *Hooked!*

"What's your great-granddaughter's name?"

If naught else, she'd made herself human in this man's eyes, no longer an animal in a cage. "Victoria." She'd never had children, never had the chance. Many Queens found themselves in the same position, part of the role they played for society. *Your namesake is a long-dead Earth Queen, my dear, fictional child. She'll be an appropriate model for you.* "She's only seven." The lies kept coming. "I've never missed her birthday. She'll be so disappointed."

He leaned on the wall next to her cell. So close, but forever separate. He wanted to care about her family, about her pretend progeny.

Now to reel him in.

"I can imagine her tears. Nana Olivia doesn't love me anymore." She sniffed, simulating the hypothetical girl's sorrow. "No child should ever feel unloved."

The guard shook his head in agreement. "Of course not. I have kids too, and a new niece."

She suppressed a smile. "Do you?" All innocence.

"What would you like me to tell her?"

For verisimilitude: "Are you sure? Won't you be in trouble with your bosses?" These hired guards could easily find similar jobs elsewhere.

He shrugged. "We're all volunteers anyway." He pulled out his pad. "So, what shall I say?"

Volunteers! Her stomach muscles shook harder with the effort of holding her position. She coughed and went to her knees on the floor. *Much easier to maintain. Makes me look more pathetic and harmless. Just a harmless old granny.* She refused to feel shame for her physical weakness. *Let's see you look this good when you're pushing two hundred.*

"Tell her that Nana Olivia remembered her birthday, and is so sad she missed the party. She has important places to be, but she loves little Victoria." *Didn't I name her Victoria?* "Nothing will keep me from giving her a giant hug and a big present when I see her again."

The guard took down the message faithfully, not reacting at all to the see her again part. "I'll make sure she gets it," he said. Then he left.

It took her till the count of four hundred before she gave up on standing and crawled to her cot, hope radiating in her brittle bones for the first time since her head wound plot had failed.

Holly heard scratching at her office door. *Are we ready for the next specimen so soon?* She checked the instruments and removed the needles from the autoclave by hand. By hand! She didn't mind the outdated technology, though, not when it all worked. She was perfectly capable of picking up a needle and placing it in its holster.

Set-up complete, she retreated to a dark shadow and flipped the switch that would unlock her room. Green light flicked on above the door outside. Her dearest Amanda's favorite color.

Luke barreled in, mouth wide with panting pleasure. Lank hair curled under his ears. "You won't believe it! The oldest Queen just tried to get me to send a message for her. It sounded innocuous enough, but you know how these things get."

A few guards called the Queens *things*, their attempt to get distance from the work they did here.

The practice gave Holly a vicious pleasure that she tried to tamp down.

Queens were people too, underneath all the conditioning and unfair advantages heaped upon them. The virus puppets deserved her pity, not her contempt. Their free will had been stolen by the neuromodulators, all unknowing, when they performed the official Devotion ceremonies.

"How long has she been a resident now?" Holly asked herself more than Luke, looking up the Queen's chart on her workplace pad. "Not quite four weeks, hmm."

Holly might expect a play for freedom from a wily Queen, but not one who'd been separated for weeks from her Devoted. Even if the inhibitor injections hadn't had any effects, loneliness should have set in. "Have one of the others prep her for a surprise session tomorrow morning. Let her think she got away with it for now, but I want a spinal fluid sample."

This old Queen didn't exhibit *any* of the expected behaviors. Didn't have any of the recently developed peptides nor even abnormally sized ion channels near the relevant axons. True, Holly had wondered whether the woman's neuromodulators had simply broken down over time, leaving her Hive to live on time-forged bonds. *That* would show up in the cerebro-spinal fluids.

Then again, in the best case, the old Queen came by her Devotions honestly. Holly knew that in the very early days, before the viruses and the sanctioned neuro-slavery and the enforced exclusionary caste system, only choice and compatibility created a Hive.

Holly hated to stand in the way of choice. If this Queen had freely chosen her position, Holly would halt the tests and let the old dame live in a more unmolested captivity, without further pain. The tests wouldn't mean anything to her research anyway, in that case.

Not if the woman's brain had no neuromodulators for Holly's research to counteract.

Chapter Twenty-One

The Show MUST Go On

Rhiannon never imagined she'd be stage manager for a Broadway-and-classical mishmash. Held for an SRO crowd. In a giant theatre outside Welsh space. Produced by a brothel.

Perhaps if she'd ended up with artsy Devoted, she might have one day expected to be a stage manager. Since Hives only worked at the top .01 percent of society, her hypothetical performances might have played for standing room only crowds.

But to leave home so completely. To act as a Hive within a larger Hive, Ceridwen's within Cleopatra's. *That* had been... if not *unthinkable*, then at least *unthought*.

Tonight, her demesne teemed with bare limbs and superstitious prayers for good luck. Actors covered up the acrid sweat in their costumes with layers of perfumes, scented oils, and citrus spritzers. Shoes *clop*ped and bare feet *klomb*ed on the real wood planks backstage, taking their owners from one curtain to the next.

Someone called out, "I can't find my lantern."

A flurry of voices volleyed back, teasing: "You should've slept with it."

Harried: "It's probably with my flower barrette."

Sensible: "Have you asked the Queen?"

The residents of Cleopatra's took great delight in referring to their stage manager as *the Queen*. It had started after Rhiannon's run-in with Cinna. She wasn't sure if it was because she wore a crown or for the fun of claiming to know a Queen in a country that didn't have them. Surely not for the respect due to her title?

Whatever the reason, when they said it Rhiannon's joints unlocked and her eyelids perked. These masters of role-play, at the top of the local pecking order, *these* called her *Queen*.

And she definitely knew the missing lantern's location. She plucked it by the wire-strap from its appointed place on her prop table and beckoned the hapless actor over to demonstrate. She received blushes and overwrought thanks. *Ah, actors on opening night.*

Not that she'd experienced the phenomenon before, but Gavin told tales. Tales of his mother, tales of his life before Dyfed, tales of the world beyond their old atmospheric borders. She sent the actor off to touch up his makeup.

In this brief downtime, her pad flashed on her hip. Message incoming from Luciano, who'd remained behind in their rooms. The Ranger's rooms, really. Technically. Mostly. He'd be coordinating from there, keeping all the Hive up to date on the plan, till he was ready to join them at the ship.

Tonight was more than opening night for the play. This was the night Rhiannon's Hive took back what was theirs.

Just heard from G&G. Been told to turn back without sheep?

Gavin's and Gwyn's part was to pick up the sheep for the play, then detour to grab the stolen Alcubierre drive in their unimpeachable transport lorry. But why would Gavin be told to scrap the sheep?

"Gather round, everyone!" The madam's voice rang into every hidden place backstage. She probably didn't even need mechanical assistance. The woman had incredible strength and power. Of voice, of personality, of character.

Rhiannon couldn't escape the madam's tentacles, captive in the mistress's territory.

She messaged back: *Going to find out what's going on. Tell Gavin to wait in place for more information.*

She found Cinna in the actors' huddled circle, decked out for her first number as an old-fashioned showgirl. The short skirt and four inch heels displayed impeccably smooth legs to their best advantage.

Rhiannon whispered in her friend's rum-and-coke-colored ear, "What's going on?"

Cinna grabbed her hand and held it tight. She was warm, even in the chilled pre-show environment. "Eleanor Peacock, the diva playing Penelope, is sick. Pneumonia. Without her, and with fear of contagion if we call her in, we're going to have to cancel the performance." Her fingers squeezed Rhiannon's.

With the performance cancelled, there would be no chance for the heist. The getaway vehicle would have no place. The locals would be too alert. Her people would be stuck on this station with their dishonorable leaders and truncated career paths.

Of course, the one actress to get sick is the one who doesn't have an understudy. Too worried about upstagers and appropriations.

No! I have to find a way.

If they needed a Penelope, Rhiannon would give them a Penelope. Rhiannon raised the hand not attached to Cinna and spoke loudly, clearly, betraying none of the tremors her friend must feel. "I'll play Eleanor's part. I've been coaching her through the music."

Empty space formed around her, giving the madam a clear view to evaluate her fitness.

Rhiannon offered a crooked smile. *"The show must go on."*

That cinched it. The director leaned over to whisper into the madam's ear, possibly letting the formidable woman know that Rhiannon had been stage manager and line runner and general know-everything for the production this last week.

The venerable lady tipped her head, assessing Rhiannon's body and demeanor.

Rhiannon refused to straighten or slouch before the survey. A worthy actress would be calm. A worthy Queen could handle anything another alpha female wanted to deal out.

Inside, though, her stomach expanded to scrunch up her lungs and eat her body with acid. *Ceridwen guide me! What have I done?* Even as Rhiannon projected cool competence, sweat sprouted beneath her arms. She'd never acted on a stage before, and she had no idea how Penelope's part went other than the words and the music. She hadn't memorized the blocking or the emotions.

The madam repeated in her powerful, strident voice, "The show must go on."

The actors scurried about, rushing to and fro to continue their preparations.

Cinna tugged the hand joining her to Rhiannon. "I'll help you get dressed."

"I think you enjoy this activity too much."

The woman shrugged her sparkling shoulders.

Twisting the ends of her hair around her fingers, Rhiannon sent Cinna on ahead. "I'll catch up to you in Eleanor's dressing room. I need to finish up here." She strode back toward the prop table and fussed with Penelope's suitor-repelling whip until her friend was out of sight.

Then Rhiannon sent Luciano her final message for the night.

Play was cancelled. It's not anymore. Sheep and plan still on. But I'm now an actor. Will be out of contact for the performance's duration. You're on your own. I know you'll be great and take care of everything.

We're Hive. We look out for each other.

Chapter Twenty-Two

The Usual Suspects

For twenty hours now, Melissa had crouched behind the boxes in the bad guys' storage room. She hadn't needed to make excuses for her absence. Her tenants had all been at a rehearsal for tonight's show when she'd left. She'd have to order flowers for them once she finished up here.

Scritch-scratch.

The storage room had acquired a few rats since last she'd hidden in it. *Ugh.* That contraband feline a few cells down would have come in handy. Her thermal sensors tracked hot little bodies across box flaps and underneath the single desk in the room. She counted six. One in the far corner, one a mere foot from her bench-tail, and four underneath the desk.

That was a lot of rats underneath the desk, but her thermal cameras showed nothing else there. She slipped a forelimb from its safety shoe and tapped the floor. The station's metal understructure vibrated a few microns, and she adjusted her auditory and visual range to pick up the motion.

She tapped again, harder this time, and kept her senses trained on the floor under the desk. It didn't move nearly as much as it should. Something was holding it down, something heavier than four telltale rats.

Things to be thankful to the rats for:
- Amusement (counting and watching them)
- Excuse to call in backup ("I needed an exterminator. They could've nibbled through the wires.")
- Bringing the desk to her attention

She *could* check it out and come right back to her hiding spot. It would only take a few moments.

Anything to break up this monotony. What was she thinking earlier about having patience to spare?

She slid the forelimb back into its shoe and slunk across the unlit space till she'd gotten behind the desk. And came face to headlamp with a dead body.

Her visor's muted blue glow was more than enough illumination. She knew this man-boy: the reception worker from the Sheriff's Office. Blood clumped his brown hair, and more ruddy brown flaked off his nose. He'd been shoved into the cramped space before rigor mortis had set in, but now his fingers were claws.

His lower shoulder was missing a chunk of flesh.

A rat scrambled up his neck to the top of his head. It met her blue visor with its beady eyes before gnawing at a blood-cake.

A warning of danger to come? She brushed it off the kid's body, sending it scurrying. She'd be sure to check with the exterminators later, get these rats killed or moved down-planet. She didn't believe in portents. Ranger luck made itself from perseverance and talent.

She heard a *thunk* from the outside room and feet tramping through the dummy storage area.

Muffled by the false door, a woman's voice said, "What kinda genes we stealing?"

A man laughed. "Don't matter, chiquita. They're expensive."

Gruff leader suspect said, "Shut up, the pair of you. We have work to do tonight. You either trust me or you don't."

Two voices chorused, "We trust you."

Melissa didn't have time to regain her hiding space. Well, she'd have to hope that all her collars-to-be were in attendance. She patted the poor kid's head again. *I'll get them for you, for justice, for everyone.*

Her body felt springy with potential energy. This must be what Victor meant when he spoke about humanity's physicality.

The door to the false room opened. Melissa sprang forward on her four legs, jumping farther and quicker than any organic could manage. She synthesized a hoarse, animal yell and landed in a crouch in front of them.

The woman— *Jessie Moore!*—scrambled back into the main room, trying to escape. The two men were struck dumb, shocked and scatter-witted. It took bare seconds to send them to the ground. Two arms secured one's wrists with her waiting ties. Two other arms secured the second's ankles.

She couldn't let Jessie get away. Luckily, her quarry hadn't yet escaped into the station at large. Jessie had stopped in the storage room's entryway, using the communications system.

Isn't this the whole gang? If it wasn't, the remaining perp should show up soon. So long as Melissa stopped her from sounding a warning.

Melissa grabbed the woman by the arms and dragged her back into the office. Her visor turned paler blue with suppressed laughter. Tonight's collar was going well. Except that Melissa, Space Ranger Extraordinaire, was out of restraining ties.

Jessie went limp, docile. Unfortunately for the criminal, this move provided no problem for Melissa's strength.

A rummage through the desk drawers revealed police-issue restraints, the new, snazzy kind. *I wonder how they got these. A trophy, perhaps?* She took her time getting Jessie trussed up. Then she sat the other two in more comfortable positions and looked over her captives.

Melissa's three collared criminals:

- Jessie Moore (already questioned and considered likely innocent by virtue of being too short to slit the previous victims' throats)

- Michael Tong (already questioned and considered likely innocent by virtue of being on station in order to care for his sick mother rather than in order to rob it)

- Agent Ward's partner (exonerated in her head for being with law enforcement; she'd never heard him speak, but apparently he was the gruff voiced and lumbering leader)

Her arms came tighter across her body. *Clearly, I was wrong about Moore and Tong.* She curled all her fingers inward—eight thumbs on the outsides—then uncurled them. Again.

Right then. Time to get this lot down to the Sherriff's Office and lock them up. After that, she could call headquarters, report the job well done, and analyze where she'd gone wrong with Moore and Tong.

"On your feet," she ordered her prisoners.

They lumbered up, leaning against each other for support when their bound hands made it hard to keep balance. She reached out to help Ward's partner, but snatched her hand back computation-quick. Criminals didn't deserve help.

She put the would-help arm on her hip, knowing it looked cocky. *Let it.*

They shuffled across the room to the outer door, ankles hobbled and each linked to the next at the waist. She opened the door remotely and had them precede her through it.

This area of the station was empty tonight. Even more quiet than usual, thanks to the revue at Cleopatra's Palace. The Sherriff was attending, as were her lodgers. As was probably everyone other than the criminals and the workaholics.

She felt the ground shake before she heard boots stampeding her way.

What now? Who could be here? She slid in front of her prisoners, determined to protect them from any angry rioters who'd already heard of their exploits. They were going to jail, not to vigilante justice.

A squad of five in riot armor pounded around the corner and stopped in front of Melissa and her collars. Led by Agent Ward himself.

Her visor turned a frustrated dark blue.

Ready to take the credit for himself. "Agent Ward." She nodded at him tightly. Did it really matter whether she got the credit or the annoying galactic agent did? Not really. She could let him take it.

He ignored her. To his partner, hobbled at the end of her prisoner line, he said, "Well done, Agent Rodriguez. I see you've captured it red handed."

The riot teams' weapons all came up, as if that was a signal, and trained on her torso, her headlamps, her articulated joints.

Her shoulder sockets rolled, but she kept her arms steady, not letting them make tense pinwheels. No alarm-ringing or attention-gathering.

This isn't the time to panic.

She recognized one of the riot team, the woman with the teenage son who played intern at the Sherriff's Office.

"I captured this ring of violent thieves." She tried to inflect her voice with humor and jerked a thumb at the train behind her. "Shouldn't you be pointing those at them?"

Agent Ward came up beside her and grabbed the thumb she'd pointed with, but she twisted it out of his grasp.

"Keep your hands off me," she hissed, adding static to the sound.

He spread his hands before him. Placating her. Beseeching the riot audience. "No need to get violent." He reused her word, applied it to the wrong party in the situation.

Five riot guns re-aimed themselves, as though they needed it.

Agent Ward's mouth slid open in a plastic approximation of a smile. "Come along quietly."

He held out the ties to her, and she numbly let him put her wrists into them. First one, then another. *Why are they letting him do this?* Then the third, the fourth.

"Good girl."

He patted her bound hands and motioned to his posse. They formed up around her and pushed her down the hallway, not content to let her move under her own power. Her visor flashed alarmed white before she got it under control.

They'll realize he's wrong. They'll see the problem. They don't want to arrest a Star Ranger. This is a misunderstanding.

She didn't believe herself.

Chapter Twenty-Three

Nothing We Can't Handle Together

Victor's portion of the plan was easy. His job was to watch Alan grab the Alcubierre jet, then help load it into the getaway vehicle.

Gavin said their jet was being held in the life sciences area. The place should be empty, what with everyone at the play. Alan would sneak in to grab the necessary parts. Victor would be on hand as spare muscle and lookout.

Just in case the room *wasn't* empty, Gavin and Gwyn were underway with the confusion-causing sheep.

Yes, his part of the plan sounded easy, but there'd already been one unexpected complication tonight, and now Rhiannon was unavailable. Onstage. *What if we need her brilliance again later?* Victor's fingers tightened and loosened around the knife hilt in his pocket as if it were his squishy therapy ball.

I hope I don't need to use my lessons.

Rhiannon had proven right about one thing: nearly all the station's residents were attending the play. The spacious corridors were so empty that Victor could spread his arms and not touch anything on either side.

Well, not entirely empty.

"I think this is your department," Alan said and gestured toward the man standing in front of the life sciences area's main door, right beside the green leaf logo.

Of course there was a security guy. Of course. That was the way this Hive's luck seemed headed tonight.

Victor's hand slipped on the hilt. *I know that guy!* He wiped his palms on his slacks, tugged his tunic's hem. No need to start with violence.

"Well, well," Victor raised his voice, trying to add an intimidating note as they approached. Their boot heels *thunked* ominously on the naked floor mesh. "Didn't think we'd see you again."

The man tilted his head, black hair tipping down to touch his shoulder as he contemplated them. His mouth formed a square of revelation; the over-the-top recognition on his face would have been comical if Victor had wanted anything from him other than his absence. "Oh! The guys with the Queen."

Alan's mobile face flattened to *utterly unamused*. His already-too-wide nose flared as he inhaled. "This is the man who wanted to insult Queen-Commander Ceridwen?"

Victor tugged viciously on his tunic's hem. *I hope he's just playing along and not planning to eviscerate this man with the knife from my pocket.*

He pasted on a smile. "We really appreciated your views on Queens in society. How it was *just a title like doctor or hairstylist.*" He quoted the man's previous words as best he could. Let his smile open to reveal unfriendly teeth meant to rend and tear. "We'd never have realized we needed to make her position clearer without your help."

The man shifted closer to the wall, head obscuring the green leaf decal that marked the area. He looked up and down the hall for someone else to chat with. But the place was deserted. "Made it clearer?"

Alan leaned in, broader-shouldered than Victor and using that heaviness to look more dangerous, more capable of snapping someone apart if he just moved too hard. "Oh, yes. We gave her a crown."

"A crown?" the man squeaked.

"Careful." Victor crowded up on the man's left side, not quite touching. "You don't want to make him mad with all this parroting." He flicked his fingers at Alan who leaned closer accordingly, breathing mint tea-scent in their faces.

Perhaps mint isn't intimidating enough?

The unfortunate man stumbled back into Victor's chest anyway. "I, ah, didn't realize that, umm, Queens were really *Queens*. I mean, you have so many."

Alan breathed a round, baritone growl.

Victor whispered in the man's ear, "Maybe you should get out of his sight. Just till he calms down."

That was all it took. He departed, leaving Victor and Alan alone in the corridor. Unopposed, they strode in.

Again the place was empty. But that was probably normal for evenings anyway. They tiptoed, just in case, on squeaky smooth floors (no carpets or mesh grating for the organic matter factory!) with no seams for dirt or seeds to fall into.

Calves aching, they twisted between rows of saplings. They slipped in fallen mud around overflowing pots and displays of seedlings. They wrinkled their noses at the slight decomposition from the Plants 4 Sale. Behind all this, they reached a door labeled *Life Sciences Employees Only*.

Locked.

Alan compressed his lips, rolling them inward till the surrounding skin touched. Then he shrugged, scratched an eyebrow, and pulled something from his bag. "Good thing you brought me. Looks like I'll have to pick a few locks tonight, not just identify our property."

Victor leaned against the Clearance Sale display next to the door and let Alan get to work. He only had to watch for strangers and be prepared to help out with whatever Alan needed. Alan was the expert.

Life Sciences Employees Only.

He wondered if Gwyn had been invited back there to help those hapless locals with their summertime-and-fennel problems.

"Hah!" Alan's cheeks scrunched with pleasure. Or maybe it was the evening shadows. "Got it already."

Like the public spaces, no one seemed to be in residence. Unlike the room they'd just left, though, this place was brightly lit. Sunlamps floated over plant beds, some on tables and others springing tall from the floor. The ceiling lights, provided for human visitors, kept the place washed with overbright near-blue.

Alan suggested, "Do you think the lights're automatic when the door opens?"

That'd be better luck than I should count on. Victor gripped his hidden knife hilt. "Walk softly." They kept low, ducking to stay behind the cover of tall greenery growing towards the top deck.

At the end of the row, just as Victor was about to suggest walking the walls instead—even if they were less secure—Alan pointed to a window, floor-to-ceiling.

"In there!" he whispered, jabbing until Victor acknowledged the motion. Past that window, everything was man-made white, juxtaposed against the organic brown and green throughout the rest of the section.

Acknowledging they'd discovered their Alcubierre jet also meant noting the scientists working on it.

"Someone didn't go to the performance."

Three someones, in fact. They wore tight bodystockings with no overlayer of floaty chiffon for the breezes. Practical. Good for working on fiddly electronics in a clean room.

No one was supposed to be here. This was the easy part. Get in, get the drive, get out. All unseen.

Victor fingered his knife hilt.

"Hey." A deep whisper preceded a rush of warmth against Victor's back.

Trapped!

"Why are we crouching all sneaky-like?" *Crouching all sneaky-like* had the ring of a practiced phrase, for all that it tripped off the tongue.

Gavin.

Victor turned in his crouch to see the amazingly clean fuzz of a very white sheep. Gavin and Gwyn stood behind it, taller than the plants. "Get down!" he hissed.

They obeyed.

Well, it looked like Victor was in control now. That was what Rhiannon had sent him for. No big setback. He was staring at the planned backup contingency. Gwyn would loose the sheep, and everyone would stampede out or at least be distracted enough for Alan to get the Alcubierre jet.

He jerked a thumb toward the window-walled room. "Looks like you're up, Lois."

She shook her head, like this was all some childish fancy that she'd grown out of. But she dutifully circled the sheep.

Easy as before, Alan opened the door. The white balls of four-footed fluff flung themselves inward as planned.

Unlike they'd hoped, there was no screaming. No scientists threw their hands about in dismay. In bare seconds, the laughing locals hustled the sheep right back out.

"Wonder what they were doing in here?" one asked.

Another answered, "Bet it was one of Wrigley's pranks. You know how he gets."

The third said, "Nice of him. Since we're stuck here."

The first replied, "Stuck, my ass. You volunteered for this gig."

They laughed some more.

Victor's eyes narrowed. *This isn't going according to plan.*

He surveyed his troops. Alan, mouth all the way open with top teeth visible, hands around his head in frustrated surrender. Four sheep. Gavin, head tilted down to look up through his lashes at the laughing, oblivious scientists. Gwyn, dearest to his heart. She huffed, shifted her weight from foot to foot, hunched. Victor had seen that frustrated look often on his beloved, and wished he could steal it away now, make her life perfect again.

Gods, am I doomed to failure?

Nothing could make anyone's life perfect. Not if they were stuck on this station, amongst incomprehensible barbarians, with no prospects. His Hive—*his Queen*—was counting on him to get this right, and now the backup plan had been shattered.

Do we just go back to Ranger Melissa's apartment and wallow in defeated misery until she captures her criminal and kicks us out?

Gwyn pushed a hank of hair behind her ear. "I brought something with me. But it'll only be useful if they've got aggressive air filters."

Like the perfect straight man, as though they'd planned it, Gavin asked, "What if they don't have aggressive air filters?"

Gwyn's eyes went huge. "Then everyone in that room dies. Followed by everyone who breathes the recycled air."

Victor tugged at the hem of his tunic, feeling the knife in his pocket bounce against his hipbone. *Death is part of the cycle of life.* True, but he didn't want to cause it. *Us or them.* He cracked his knuckles.

"All right," he said. "Do whatever you have to do."

She dashed out of the room with a *just a moment* and returned with two respirators and a bag in her gloved hand.

"Hemlock," she explained to their trio of confused looks.

Alan backed away. Victor wished he could too, but, "What do you need?"

Handing a respirator to Gavin, Gwyn explained her plan. "We'll put hemlock powder into the air system leading to that room. Assuming the station's air filters notice our addition, the scientists'll be evacuated. Then we can go in, wearing the respirators and ponchos."

Assuming the station's air filters notice.

It was a big assumption. *I hope I'm doing the right thing.* Victor toyed with the knife in his pocket: a simple device, not necessarily lethal. Great for cutting ropes and harvesting plants.

"Let's get to it." He backed away, following Alan towards the dirt and the seedlings. She didn't need him for this, and he'd rather not get caught by friendly poisons.

Gavin and Lois did *something* with a vent on the outside of the room. Then the foursome waited. One pair in respirators and plastic tents. The other against the muddy trenchers. The scientists inside didn't say anything, making checks and taking notes.

Sweat dripped down Victor's neck as though he'd been working out with Ranger Melissa, but he hadn't moved in a long time. Uncounted time. It cooled in the station's unnecessarily chilly—to the Dyfed-raised—air, and he shivered.

The plants next to him were lemon balm, easy to tell by their citrine, minty scent. *I could pick some to make a nice, calming tea.* A tea that would kill him if it accidentally included some hemlock powder.

Alan made a noise, color high in his cheeks as he pointed at some horrible slight to his baby, but Victor shushed him.

In the room, a scientist coughed.

Gwyn said, "It's been long enough."

If the filtration system doesn't notice soon, we'll have to alert the station. Victor's bad decisions had turned his Hive into murderers. They'd be lucky if the Sherriff and their own roommate didn't execute them on the spot.

Chapter Twenty-Four

A Prisoner's First Duty

The parade ended with Melissa in a jail cell, listening to Agent Ward tell the Sherriff that she was a criminal, a non-person who had been programmed to dupe them all.

She could've told them otherwise (them being the Sherriff and the swarming deputies who squashed so tightly against each other outside the cell that none could effectively subdue her should she manage to get free), but if they already believed Agent Ward's lies, then they'd necessarily conclude her protests were part of that false programming.

She compacted herself into a long rectangular lump, legs folded beneath her on the floor.

Once upon a time, she *had* been an unwitting dupe in illegal activities. But not since she'd gained sentience. She would never. She *could* never. Never again.

Agent Ward was saying, "I've got my partner scrapping her ship right now. We don't want her escaping to call for help."

I've got no one to call, moron. She tilted her headlamps away from their position. *American Star Rangers don't work in teams.*

The Sherriff asked, "Do we have to do this now?" His heart rate elevated, but she didn't dare believe that fellow-feeling for *her* caused it. "I wanted to get to the revue."

Agent Ward sighed a musical sigh.

Is he even a real galactic agent?

"Of course, Sherriff." He managed to pack disdain into the conciliatory phrase. "We can discuss the dispensing of justice after the entertainments."

The Sherriff huffed his thanks and waved his people out of the cramped corridor. The deputies' cheers—*for justice or for the brothel*—were a muted wash, a dull sound eaten by each other's bodies. They jostled together, feet accidentally stamping on ankles and aerosol rifles kicking into ribs.

Why'd any of them bring aerosols to deal with me? It wasn't like Melissa could ingest sedatives through nose, mouth, or membrane.

The office cleared out. Agent Ward was last to leave, tossing a piece of stale bread into her cell on his way out.

Oh, ha ha. Bread for the prisoner, bread for the toaster.

She could really learn to dislike Agent Ward.

She waited a few moments, long enough that anyone who'd come back for an item—forgotten jacket, pad, lip stain—would decide to go on without it. Then she did a check:

- Thermal sensors: All same temperature. Variation right next to vents. A bit warmer next to the coffee machine.

- Auditory feedback: All walls and furniture stationary. No movement between one ping and the next.
- Visual: Well, she didn't see anybody.

She knew her duty. *The first duty of any prisoner is to escape.* She had to get out of here, make her arrests, and try not to end up as scrap metal.

She shook off a safety-shoe and used the razor-sharp tip to cut through the wall beside her prison bars. Slick and smooth, it pushed through with next to no resistance. These cells weren't meant to hold a knife wielder. Anyone could short the locks.

Her cell door clicked, and her visor lightened to triumphant pale blue. *Not even a shock through my armor plating.*

She wrapped her four hands around the bars and pulled the door open.

Escaping was easy. The hard part would be getting the criminals back under her control... and making her way to headquarters in a ship they were already taking apart.

Chapter Twenty-Five

Knife Lessons Helped After All

As Victor watched from behind the glass, helpless, the scientist most affected by the hemlock coughed again. Gasped too hard. The man was dying.

Time to turn ourselves in. He reached for his pad to figure out how to do such a thing, and the alarms finally—*finally*—rang out. They blared, tones up and down the scale. So loud that they created static feedback in his ears.

Thank the gods.

A computerized voice counted down, "Vacuum seal in fifteen seconds. Fourteen. Thirteen."

The three scientists shoved anything they were holding onto available counters and raced to the opposite wall. They went through a door into another window-walled space—much smaller—where water poured in before air blew through and got sucked out. Again, water poured and pelted. Air sucked and blew. A decontamination chamber-cum-airlock.

The cougher gasped again, but his color looked improved.

Maybe he won't die from hemlock inhalation. Victor gripped his knife hilt like a talisman. Against death. Against his own thoughts and intentions.

The computer's countdown finished. "One. Vacuum engaged."

"We've got to get to medical," a scientist said, voice muted by the glass. The other two nodded fervent agreement, and all three hastened out into the station.

"On the bright side," said Victor, mouth tilting up, "the room is empty *and* no one died."

On the negative side, a backlit sign above the door warned, *Vacuum environment. Keep second door closed.* Lois had brought respirators, yes, but not spacesuits.

Maybe they keep suits around for this exact reason?

Victor backtracked out to the public area, not worried about running into anyone this time. He searched every wall for a hidden panel, a locker room. A sign that pointed to a locker room.

But heading for the public spaces hadn't been a good idea after all. Silhouetted in the doorway to the main hall was a large shape. A familiar blob with four arms, legs that bent upwards at insectoid angles, a sphere perched atop it with lights attached to the sides.

Victor reached into his pocket for the knife's comforting weight, but couldn't bring himself touch it. *The law has come for us.* Melissa had undoubtedly been alerted by the alarms and come looking for the perpetrators. She cocked a headlamp, turned it on so they could both see clearly.

'*Thieves who go armed are the worst kind of dangerous,*' she'd said during one lesson. And what was hemlock but an armament? What was he but a common thief?

"Victor? What are you doing here?"

He pulled on his tunic's hem. *She doesn't know yet.* "It's a long story." *Please lose interest and go away.*

Her visor flashed white, a reaction he'd never seen before. "I'm in something of a hurry myself. Got the local pitchfork brigade all aflutter." She shrugged her four shoulders in a move that would've been *what can you do?* on someone else.

Victor had no idea what she meant. Sometimes her alien allusions made her as impenetrable as crazy quotemaster Gavin.

Gavin, who was once again snugged all along Victor's back and using his interpretive powers for good. "You have a mob after you?"

Her knees rose up, pulling her spine down towards the ground. She looked like a cat readying herself to pounce, but on what?

"I did. Including the rest of the law enforcers on this station. They captured me once. Now it's my turn to capture them." Her visor was dark blue.

Victor's eyes swiveled into the dark corners, followed bright dots when they raced past Melissa's headlamp again, tracked a sheep that ran past her and out into the hall.

The sheep's appearance made up his mind.

All my plans have failed. What is one more failure? He had to take a chance. They'd formed a bond in the past week. She had to know that he was more trustworthy than people who would hunt them both. The enemy of my enemy, and all that.

"Well, if you have the time to take a break..." He crossed closer to her and pulled on one of her arms. "Then you should help us."

She let him drag her inside. "What're you up to in here?" Her suspicion speared him more strongly than her spiked feet ever could. She'd never treated him as anything less than a valued comrade. All right, perhaps as a child, but no one mistrusted children with important things like honor and honesty.

"The same people who want to kill you have also stolen something from us."

He gestured to make sure she saw four-sixths of their Hive in the room. "We had a plan to get it back." He paused, grinned. *This will either cement her involvement or get us thrown in an American prison.* "I know how much you hate thieves."

Alan came closer and jabbed Victor in the ribs. He whispered, as though the Ranger couldn't hear him when he did it, "What are you thinking? She's going to arrest us."

Her twenty-four fingers formed claws in the air, like a shapeshifting Archdruid on a holy day.

Aggression or acquiescence? For us or for the mob on her tail? He knew she hated thieves, and he'd spun it as best he could, but the truth was that he was as much a thief—as far as she knew—as the people who'd taken the Alcubierre drive in the first place.

His fingers tightened on the knife in his pocket, his talisman throughout the night. With his intentions in the open, he found it comforting again. A gift from an old friend. Though she might not approve, he was content within himself. *This might be my only chance to return it, if she doesn't have faith in me.* He pulled it out and flipped it, metal blade winking underneath the light from her headlamp. Solemn, deliberate, he offered her the knife.

"Keep it, kid," she said, voice husky and low, visor turning the pleased pale blue he'd seen when he got something right during their lessons. "What've these loons taken from you? Let's make it quick, eh?"

And then Alan was dragging Ranger Melissa back toward the glass-walled room, pointing out to her the pieces he needed. The things they'd arrived on the station carrying. With a vacuum-proof accomplice in the mix, the room was simple to breach. Gwyn assured them it had been sterilized and that Melissa didn't carry any poisonous trace.

They loaded up Gavin's transport with the recovered sheep and Alcubierre drive.

"Where you headed?" Melissa asked.

Gavin threw open the driver's door and leapt in. "We're going to the theatre. Come with us if you want to perform."

Multi-layered laughter bubbled from her speakers. "Thank you kindly. I hear this play's the thing."

Victor wished he could tell his Queen about their success. Both in getting the jet and in cementing an alliance with the American Star Ranger. But she was on stage still.

Actually, he ought to let Luciano know that this part of the plan had worked out. That way they could start falling back to the ship. Someone had to tell Rhiannon at some point. She couldn't stay on stage forever, especially not if they planned to use their newly reacquired jet to get as far from this duplicitous place as possible.

Chapter Twenty-Six

In the Mouth of the Wolf

Luciano should have stayed in the Ranger's quarters. When restlessness took him over, however, he'd dashed to the junior consulate for his late-night repudiation.

It hadn't done him any good to arrive early. Relegated to the waiting room, he had to stand. They kept no chairs for visitors, and the cramped space couldn't have accommodated them anyway. The receptionist, the same local woman as before, had the only desk, and she didn't seem interested in offering up her seat so that she could stand awkwardly on the dragon-patterned area rug instead.

The receptionist said, "The consul will be with you momentarily." She kept her gaze on the barely illuminated surface before her, and Luciano couldn't make out what she was doing.

Victor flashed a message to Luciano's pad. *Objective acquired. On our way. See you at the ship!*

Luciano replied, *Good work.*

Like his Hive mates, he'd packed his bags and knew his escape route. Unlike the others, though, he didn't intend to rush for the *Ceridwen's Cauldron* as soon as he could.

They didn't need him to pilot anymore, and they had Lois for medical issues. He'd discharged his duties and done his bit for the reacquisition of the group's property. The Alcubierre jet would take his former Hive to whichever crazy alien place they chose next.

Now was the perfect time to leave them.

It shouldn't be possible, leaving a Queen, not based on the reading he'd done and the movies he'd seen. God as his witness, Luciano didn't want to desert her either. He remembered the warmth her respect kindled in his belly. His chest tightened when he thought of Rhiannon's sparkling intelligence. He'd miss Victor's teasing about his love of tomatoes and the way Alan stood up for him when that happened.

No matter how much he loved his Queen and his Hive, though, he couldn't escape the truth: they were no good for him.

Traveling with the *Ceridwen's Cauldron* prevented him from caring for his mother and sister financially. Running from Dyfed meant he'd forfeited his education and his chance to do more for society. He wished he could turn back time and warn the younger, more naïve Luciano that Devotion didn't conquer all.

As it was, he'd found a solution that let him rewind his scholastic career. He could seek his salvation in the junior consulate and in re-Testing.

"Ah, Luciano!"

The consul always seemed surprised that he had a guest, but this was clearly affectation. Luciano not only had an appointment to defect *tonight*, but there was no other door through which he could have arrived.

"Come in, come in." No alternate paths opened onto the consul's office. It was just a dim tight box adjoining the main room.

He probably built the dividing wall himself. I bet it's a fire hazard.

Luciano took up his place on the bench. "Where do I go from here, exactly? I can't live in your office until the next diplomatic ship comes in, can I?"

"You know I can only promise you so much, young man." The consul shook his head, bell-pepper red firing his cheeks. "Why don't you take that bug out of your ear, and we can discuss any questions you have about this contract?"

Luciano reached for the pad the consul held, purportedly whatever he needed to agree to and sign in order to become a free agent once again, but he didn't do anything about his availability to his Hive. They weren't free *quite* yet. He needed to keep his earpiece in, in case they required him for *one last thing*. He had a duty, borne of his own oaths. He hadn't broken those vows yet.

"You know that I love them all. I just need something else in my life."

"Of course, of course." The consul's red sleeves flapped under his knee-length white vest, like a bleeding dove. "There's nothing in there for you to worry about." The man gestured expectantly to the pad, as if Luciano should take his word and sign the document unread.

Right, then.

Luciano perched on a hip to tuck his legs underneath him. *I've got some reading to do.* He needed to make sure nothing in the document could hurt him or his family.

All the while, he kept one ear open to the Hive's communications channel.

Good luck, old Hive of mine. In the mouth of the wolf! Perhaps you'll send a little luck my way?

Chapter Twenty-Seven

Opening Night

She'd never been the betting kind, but Melissa had been lucky so far in life. Finding sentience. Getting away from the drug dealers who'd used her as a mule. Making a place for herself with the Star Rangers. Being recognized as the best tracker in the Corps.

Was she lucky enough to get to the perpetrators, convince the Sherriff he'd been had, and bring the guilty to justice tonight?

Only one way to find out. She had a duty, a calling to protect the innocent from those who would prey upon them. To take the worst out of society and lock them away.

Melissa jumped from the moving truck as it passed the theatre's main doors. The kids—*her* kids—would continue to the service entrance with their sheep. She, on the other hand, was going straight in. Her collars were in that audience, and she wasn't going to give them a chance to get the drop on her again. She'd face them head on, tie them up, and transport them back to Jon at Ranger HQ. Personally.

Her shoes swished on sumptuous red carpet in the empty lobby, sound echoing off the high ceilings and gold trim.

A bouncer, doubling as an usher for the night, blocked the doors. She flashed him her Ranger star, and he slunk back into the potted plants, hands in front of him.

Not aggressor. Not prey. Not worth her time.

Large double doors *thunked* open, a more dramatic entrance than many on the stage itself. Directly ahead and down, she saw Commander Ceridwen in a skimpy bralette-and-diaphanous-slip combination with a whip coiled at her hip, singing an incredulous lament about her suitors' stealing all her belongings while her husband was away, presumed lost at sea.

The Commander's eyes met Melissa's visor briefly before her hand slapped the thick whip handle. She slashed the thick leather at the stage boards, and the sonic boom reclaimed the audience's attention. The Commander swirled her prop in a full loop over her head, then cracked a half-wave at her suitors, driving them back with almost-erotic cries.

Melissa appreciated the attempt to distract her prisoners-to-be.

She synched up with all the unprotected cameras in the giant room. Her thermal and visual sensors swiveled. Data streamed in from her own cameras as well as the borrowed ones.

She *hunted*.

She sifted through the pictures at impossible speeds. Her processors heated with the effort to check each and every row, to inspect each and every face, in a theatre with five balcony tiers and a seating capacity over 8,000.

Ping. She found her mark in fifteen long seconds.

"Agents" Ward and Rodriguez—*Maybe those outra-geously common aliases should have been a clue, but you can't blame a man for having the same name as a full percent of the population*—sat with the Sherriff in the second balcony's front row.

Moore and Tong weren't in attendance. They couldn't possibly still be pulling off their theft while their compatriots kept the law from getting worried.

Could they?

She crouched, backlit by the lobby's bright yellow. Her four insectoid knees lifted high to gather potential energy. On stage, Rhiannon crescendoed, lifting her torso in open supplication.

The lights cut out.

The audience applauded the scene's ending.

Melissa leapt.

She'd measured it perfectly. Air breezed past her as she flew upwards, handcuffs already in her top hands. Low hanging spotlights winked by. One turned on, and the next scene started with the shadow of a flying robot.

She rebounded off a support beam and stood before her marks. Cuffs sliced through the distance and immobilized the villains.

"Mister Ward, Mister Rodriguez. By the power vested in me by the American government as a member of the American Star Rangers, you are under arrest for thievery, murder, and conspiracy."

The actors below had yet to move. They sprawled all over one another in some strange tableau, waiting for the cue to start the action. One grasping for another's ankle.

The hobbled one reaching for a pad. Another threatening to tip water over them all. The lights glowed dimly.

The whole theatre sat in hushed quiet. The actors unmoving. The criminals unmoving. The audience breathless with anticipation. The Sherriff staring in wide-eyed horror.

A loud inhalation from the stage.

Agent Ward screamed. "It's escaped!" he cried. A spotlight flashed on their position and blinded Melissa's cameras, so that she had to make do with thermal only. "It's here! I need backup!"

Is he really going to stick with this antisynthetic story? No one could possibly take it seriously. Especially not from criminals. But the Sherriff was calling for backup, and half the audience was stampeding toward the doors. The other half was pulling weapons from hidden pockets and holsters.

The air vibrated with confusion and energy. Any of those knives, guns, tasers could go from *ready* to *lethal* in a moment. Turning a peaceful night at the theatre into a free-for-all brawl of bloody proportions.

Melissa made a *throat-clearing* noise, projected it to reach all the seats.

"No need for all this worry, folks." She slid a hand inside her vest and came out with her badge. It winked in the spotlight. "I'm an American Star Ranger, and I'm bringing this violent criminal to justice. He won't bother you anymore. Please put away your weapons and take your seats. Enjoy the show."

Indeed, the Commander was back on stage. Melissa wasn't sure whether the Commander had been scripted into the next scene or not, but she *definitely* had Melissa's best interests in mind. A spotlight trained on the actress who called out for her love, shading her eyes with a hand, the better to search high and low. When she "found" Odysseus, she jumped up to wrap herself around him like a koala, but the dumbstruck actor didn't bother to catch her.

When the Commander rebounded off the man's oiled abs, she improvised a mournful monologue about how her beloved had come home and yet things were not like they once were; he didn't appear to even love her anymore. She pushed her body against him, grinding, but the actor only absently caught at her hips. Comically frustrated, the Commander drew her whip again and corralled him in with her other suitors declaring, "Penelope has to take responsibility for her own life."

Several theatre-goers laughed, a nervous titter, and sank back down, content to follow the actors' lead.

They'd been reassured. If Commander Ceridwen—alias Rhiannon—was analogous to the theatre. The theatre was analogous to the brothel. And the brothel was always in the know about what was dangerous and what wasn't. They'd capitalize on the danger, yes, but never in a way that hurt the clients... or the locals.

Riot averted.

Her visor went sky blue in relief.

Then it all went to Hell again.

Free of his cuffs, "Agent" Ward pointed his own sidearm at her.

The Sherriff tried to calm them. "I don't rightly know what's going on here. But I reckon we can sort it all out in my office."

Rodriguez stumbled into him, cutting off the voice of reason. "Sorry," he mumbled.

Melissa reined Rodriguez in, and he immediately starfished. His massive bulk took up all the space in front of her. She couldn't restrain his partner without maiming him, and she wasn't in the business of permanently injuring a man in custody. Behind her human handcuff, Ward aimed his weapon at them both.

Whatever he hit, he wouldn't do much damage to her with that peashooter. But it'd rip a chunk out of his partner and maybe ricochet into another theatre patron. She had to stop him. He couldn't be allowed to hurt more innocents.

She slipped off a shoe, baring the pointy tip of her right leg. She feinted forward and thrust, her limb flashing in the light. Bright red blood spattered onto her leg, onto Rodriguez and the Sherriff, onto the velvet seats around them

Ward stumbled back, clutching his arm to his side. "It's out of control!"

The audience stampeded again, Rhiannon unable to hold their attention anymore. The Sherriff pulled his own sidearm, though he had to know it wouldn't so much as scratch her.

"I'm afraid I'll have to take you in," he told Melissa. "For your own safety and, it looks like, riot prevention."

She shook her head. "This man was resisting arrest."

The Sherriff nodded as if in agreement. But even as he did so, he'd lifted his own ties from his pockets. "I'll still need you to turn yourself in."

Because that worked so well the last time.

She didn't have the time or the faith in him to subject herself to incarceration again. "I can't let you do that, Sherriff." She tossed Rodriguez into a seat, out of her way and largely uninjured. "I'm going to have to arrest you all for now."

Ward cried, "It's going to arrest all of us. It can't be working right. You have to help us kill it!"

A man two rows down doubled back from where he'd been attempting to exit. "It's talking crazy!" He raised his arms to Heaven. "You gonna arrest me, metal man?"

I am no man.

But perhaps this was not the time for discussions of gender and sex in AIs.

"No," she said on a growl. "So get out of here before I change my mind."

He scuttled away to join the exodus from the second balcony, whispering with the other evacuees. They looked over their shoulders and pointed at Melissa, the Sherriff, and the two posing galactics.

The Sherriff slipped the buckle on his holster, but didn't pull the gun yet. They could still salvage this together. "What's it going to take to have you go back with me under your own power?"

That she'd be willing to do. As equals. As law enforcers. He'd understand the situation in no time. She'd only have to bring up her evidence logs and call in to HQ. She gestured him towards the door. "Let's go then. All of us together."

But the door was blocked by the man from earlier, accompanied by deputies and armed theatre goers. "It's gonna arrest us all, guys!" he shouted.

There were a lot of them. Too many, even for a Ranger. And who knew what they'd brought with them?

The mob rushed forward.

"Look at that blood!"

"Did it kill a galactic agent?"

"It needs to be disassembled!"

"Memory wiped!"

"Slagged!"

"Baaa!"

A runaway sheep had wandered on stage, no longer caged wherever Gavin had delivered it. The fluffy livestock gamboled into the first row of seats.

Perfect. Melissa crouched and leapt.

Her leap coincided with shouts and bangs and the whizzing vibration of a bullet that passed too close. She landed in a cluttered walkway that was coated in lost jackets and sticky wine. She stumbled, thanks to her unshod leg, but caught herself and disappeared from her pursuers' view, slung downward to hide her bulk underneath the warm animal. With a small electric shock, she got the sheep moving toward the exit.

No pioneer would attack a healthy sheep, even if they believed she was under it.

Running away now only means you'll still be alive to arrest the instigators later.

She didn't believe that anymore. Not in this situation.

The whole thing had gotten out of hand.

Chapter Twenty-Eight

In This Together

Victor loitered in the hallway outside the theatre, one hand on the knife in his pocket. *Should I take it out and do some exercises?* That'd be good for his shoulder, maybe— *how much therapy is too much physical exertion?*—but would also probably make him look like a crazy, violent man who ought to be stopped.

And he didn't want to be noticed.

The rest of the theatre-tethered Hive had piled into Gavin's transport. They'd all be back at the ship by now, where Alan would be breaking it out of its station-enforced bondage.

Rhiannon would have been plucked from the stage. Luciano would have preceded them all to the *Cauldron*. It was clear where everyone belonged. Yet here stood Victor in the cold, blue halls of John Wayne Station. With no escape vehicle.

In a race to the finish, who will be the last Devoted on board? Will it be Victor, more physically adept but waiting for some unknown happenstance to start the race? Or will it be Luciano, whose location no one knows? The amusing announcer voice in his head did little to quell nerves jangled by an underlying truth. He *should* have left by now.

Whether he slouched against a wall outside the theatre or whether he hustled to the *Ceridwen's Cauldron*, Ranger Melissa's plans would move forward. She didn't need him to wait around to make sure she'd gotten her criminals safely in handcuffs.

And yet, she'd paused in her pursuit in order to help him.

That means something, doesn't it? His tunic hem twisted between slippery fingers. *She listened to me.* Would she have listened to one of the others? He wanted to believe she wouldn't have arrested any of them, that she'd have been reasonable about their desires and goals. But he knew better than most what difference a personal connection could make.

Rhiannon wouldn't have formed this makeshift Hive for anyone but Gwyn. Gwyn wouldn't have asked her to for anyone but family.

Perhaps Melissa felt the same way about him?

The doors across the hall burst open. They clattered and shook where they bounced off the walls behind, left open and unsealed in haste. *Ker-lack* went sheep hooves. *Grrmmrraal* went the dull roar of angry theatre patrons.

A sheep preceded all the other noise makers. It ran into the hall, blue eyes gleaming wildly and pale white coat glistening in oiled whorls. Nudge-slamming into Victor's leg, it threw him back and bleated. *Ba-hea!* It ran down the corridor to the right.

It left behind a compact metal sculpture, dropped like a biological function from its stomach. An absurd Odysseus.

The sculpture expanded like a sponge in water. Like a crab extending all its limbs.

A crab that Victor recognized.

"Ranger! What're you doing here?" Nearly exactly what she'd said to him in the life sciences area a moment, a lifetime, earlier.

"Too many." She shoved at his back to get him moving. "Time to go. You don't want them to find you here."

He pelted, one foot in front of the other. He was already on the wrong side of the law on this station and didn't need to give them more reason to notice his less-than-law-abiding ways.

"Have to get to my ship," he called back.

She chased behind him, his protector. *Makes sense that she's in the business of looking out for people.* "We're mosey-ing the right way for the docking ring," she said. She didn't sound at all out of breath, her voice pitched perfectly for him to hear her.

Oh, of course. Robot. Why would she be panting?

She volunteered, "I'll get you to the *Ceridwen's Cauldron* before I scramble for the *Cold Night*."

She'd be leaving in a rush, alone, pursued by angry locals, and without anything to show for it. Didn't seem right. Not when she'd helped him to pull off his nearly-doomed heist, with his Hive waiting for him and his Queen looking out for all his best interests. Victor pumped his left arm through the air, trying for proper running form, while his right fumbled for his pad. He flashed a *Talk* request.

"Luciano!" He tasted salt-sweet sweat each time he opened his mouth, the desperate tang tainting his breaths.

He didn't look at the screen, didn't care what his Hive mate was doing.

"What?" Luciano's already high pitched voice took on an annoyed, even higher tenor. "I'm busy right now."

The air warmed, either from exertion or from proximity to the docking ring. "And I'm running for my life."

The metallic *kray-thick* of Melissa's shoes hitting the floor behind him. The doorway on his right, decorated with ribbons for someone's birthday. The screams of *dismantle it!* and *short it out!* and *we can use electricity!*

Luciano sighed heavily with all the weight of the world.

Yeah, me too.

"Where are you?"

He couldn't make out the numbers of the doors and corridors they passed. Everything went too quickly. His eyes chased light ghosts and colors when they ought to be picking out landmarks.

"I'm with the Ranger. You can find her on a station map maybe?" He gasped for air. "Or look for the giant lump of people moving too fast. Tell Rhi."

"Can you be more specific?"

His leg muscles burned and his chest felt cold on the inside, every breath too hot. "No."

"I'll see what I can do." Luciano sighed again, a deep noise running counterpoint to Victor's own high pitched intakes.

Of course he would. That's what Hive was for. And Victor had earned his place. Rhiannon would care for him, for all her Hive, no matter what.

"Don't let them catch you," Luciano suggested.

Thanks for the insight.

⟍ Interlude 4 ⟋

Emergency Evacuation

The downside of working on a secret project for a grassroots political campaign, Holly supposed, was that you could do brilliant work, but it would only see the light of day *after* the revolution.

Once she had finished up with another subject, sent another virus-puppet Queen out of the testing chamber, she returned to her cozy office. If she could publish her current paper in progress in any industry journal, she'd surely be famous.

She tossed her coat over her chair's back—the one with the broken lumbar adjuster, still worth half her regular salary on the second-hand market—and noticed a message alert's flashing light on her work console. She ignored it while she finished filling out the data on her non-networked charts.

Stage Two almost complete. We can definitely break a Queen's hold on her minions in the short-term.

That done, she sat at the desk and hit *play* on the message.

Her boss' face filled the screen. The woman, Ffion Kendrick, had first involved Holly with the project. She was also a minister in the Department of Health and Well-Being. "Evacuate to the backup site," Ffion ordered. "You know where the evac ships are. Five subjects per ship, just in case we lose some." Short and to the point, as usual.

"Our contact in the Department of Civic Protection has reported a warrant filed for a police raid on the facility," the message continued. "Bring whatever equipment you can; what I could get you for the backup site is more than thirty years behind. Someone wanted to scrap it when they closed New Aberystwyth Urgent Care, but I got it rerouted. Don't call me back. Just go. Now."

Holly opened another pad, this one connected to the old speaker systems in the rundown building. "Attention all personnel. Attention all personnel. Prep subjects for evacuation. This is not a drill."

She'd always wanted to say something so ridiculously officious, but never at the expense of her own research labs.

Craaacsh. Shrrk. Ouhhng.

She opened her office door onto organized chaos. Orderlies in worn cotton rushed carts down the corridors, not always avoiding collisions. Guards gripped whatever peacemaking equipment they held more tightly, banging into doors and walls with their tense inability to course-correct.

She needed to find boxes for all the information in her office. It, at least, was necessary at the new facility. The shortest path to the supply room took her past the cells.

There were two types of Queens now. The crazed ones heard her announcement, a goddess's voice, and tore at their hair or pounded on the doors. The dopey ones didn't even notice the change, still staring off into nothingness.

Then there was the outlier. Olivia. The oldest Queen stood tall and regal at her cell door. Her clear eyes tracked Holly's progress down the corridor. Shoulders back, grey-white hair curling beneath her ears, she looked like a woman fully in charge of her faculties. She looked like she'd expected this evacuation notice.

She must have got a message out after all!

In which case, Holly's identity—everyone's identities—were forfeit to the oppressors. The authorities knew who she was. *Manawyddan's Mousetrap*, she's good. Holly shook her head and couldn't help the rueful smile that quirked her lips.

Holly passed the Queen, whose eyes followed her in silent judgment.

On the return trip, a box from the supply room under each arm, she studied her downfall again. They sized each other up from their opposing sides of the cell door.

One, haughty and calm. The other, worried and cornered. Which was which, *that* was open for interpretation.

The hallway bustled with workers escaping and evacuating. Luke bumped into her, stumbled but didn't stop. Three cells already stood empty in this row.

I don't need her physiologically, and she's proven herself troublesome.

No one would notice if Olivia didn't get packed up with the rest. The older woman was useless as a test subject, worse than useless as a mole, and not even the kind of Queen that Holly needed to fight against. She'd come by her position through pure personality and intelligence.

Much as Holly resented Dyfed's desire for more Queens Queens Queens, she couldn't fault someone who'd come into the crown on merit.

So long as Holly got recognized for her merit as well.

Readjusting her load, she opened the door with her personal code and grabbed the woman by a twig-thin tricep. She didn't explain, and the Queen didn't resist. It made sense. Anywhere had to be better than a cell, and the worst that could happen was evacuation. The best that could happen was anything else. Barring death, of course. But Holly had yet to kill a test subject and all the virus puppets knew as much.

Boxes under one arm, Olivia on the other, Holly marched them to an observation booth and set it to *Occupied*.

"I'm freeing you," she said, putting the best spin on it. From a cubby in the wall, she extracted the omnipresent medkit and pulled out a dose of the usual sedative-plus-inhibitors. Inhibitors had proven pointless on this test subject. "This sedative will last only a few hours, long enough for the evacuation to complete. You, however, will be dressed in my lab coat." She stripped off her coat and passed it over. Quick on the uptake, the former test subject donned it. "No one will stop to look at you."

"Why?"

Holly looked away from the clear eyes, focused on the needle. It was long and thin, delicate for all that it carried the power to heal or to destroy.

"Remember that I helped you." It wasn't quite an answer, but it wasn't nothing.

The Queen rolled up her fraying sleeve. "I will," she said solemnly.

"My keycard is in the left pocket." Holly depressed the plunger, sending liquid sleep into deceptively blue veins.

A minute later, Holly stepped into halls just as chaotic as moments before.

Craaacsh. Shrrk. Ouhhng.

Her actions didn't affect the evacuation, but perhaps they'd change her life's course, stave off potential incarceration. She looked back at the observation booth. The door light still shone red. No one would enter.

Once more in her own office, she piled papers and books, pads and knee-high cases. She started with the most important data. Then the oldest. As she worked, she used her personal pad to flash Amanda.

"Cariad!" her lover crowed. "You never call at this time of day. What fortune is this?"

Holly took a break from stacking to see her beloved's face. The lines around Amanda's eyes crinkled with thrilled joy, and her cheeks balled up with pleasure.

I don't get home enough, working two jobs. It'll get better. I promise. Amanda's greying hair curled with sweat. "You taking another set of tourists out today?"

Amanda's nose crinkled. *Adorable.*

"We just got back from the caves. It was only a day hike."

"I've got bad news." Holly moved away from her pad to continue packing. Her lover would have to make do with a view of the ceiling. Holly could imagine the pout. "I've been tapped to set up a new lab in a safer location. And I might have been identified as an activist."

Amanda gasped.

Maybe that wasn't the best way to break that particular news. "I'm sure the lawyers will have it sorted out by the time I've got the new lab running. That will only be a week or two." Ah, the beauty of being a well-funded and well-connected revolutionary. "Do you want to come? In two weeks, we can discuss how long we want to stay."

"Of course you should stay with the new lab!" Amanda's laugh filled the office, even from the reedy speakers. "I'd never ask you to leave your work. It's too important. But I need to finish up here. I'll join you when I can."

Holly returned to her pad to look on that beloved face once more before she had to abandon it for the evac site. Amanda blew a kiss at the screen. Holly returned it.

Chapter Twenty-Nine

Rage's Range

Sparks rained down, flashing hot white. Melissa attempted to shield Victor from the fiery danger with her only-slightly-less-vulnerable body. Her cameras detected new pits in her armor plating, but Melissa didn't feel a thing. No functions impaired. Armor still at full functionality.

Luciano had somehow opened a communication line between Melissa's internal channel and Commander Ceridwen, no longer on the theatre's stage but *en route* to her getaway ship. Rather than subject the Commander to frantic ducking and scampering, Melissa modulated her speech and face into perfect calm, backlit by a Casablanca sunset.

The Commander's voice vibrated along her circuits, full of portent and power. "I can help you. I want to help you, and my Hive agrees unanimously." She took a long, noisy breath.

Hurry up with your idea. Melissa's spiked leg sunk hard into the station, making her lurch to the ground. The mob behind her clamored and clattered, ever closer and ever louder. She tugged free of the white plastic floor easily enough, but they'd lost precious moments. Victor doubled back to help her up and got winged by a thrown shoe for his trouble.

The voice she used for Queen-Commander Ceridwen was collected. The face showed none of her desperation. "Oh?"

The Commander twisted her hair like a nervous perp being questioned about something she'd definitely done. "It's drastic, though, and you don't seem like you need drastic, no matter what Vic said..." She trailed off, waiting for Melissa to confirm or deny. A good interrogation tactic. Leading.

Melissa flashed an external picture of her actual location. The mob behind them. Victor sweaty and panicked beside her. Her missing shoe on a nicked leg.

Dryly, she offered, "Drastic is welcome about now."

"Then Devote to me." The Commander didn't pause, didn't twist her hair. She stood straight and strong. Defiant and commanding. Then she broke her confident posture. "You know, if you want to."

There was the crux. *Did* she want to?

No, no, a thousand times no. A Devoted followed her Hive. A Devoted was a citizen of Dyfed. A Devoted could never be an *American* Star Ranger. A Devoted could never go off on her own in a ship without air or power. A Devoted could never go off on *her* anything. Devoted were exclusively male, a category into which Melissa did not, alas for this circumstance, qualify.

It didn't matter that this Hive traveled with another female. Gwyn traveled with the other teens, yes, but she wasn't a Devoted.

But neither did Melissa want to be memory wiped or sold for parts, and that was her only other option right now. Given a choice between death and making a whole new life... well, she had to choose life. A new life, with people she trusted and who had never given much thought to her synthetic status. She could figure out how to be Devoted, how to be male, how to be something other than a Star Ranger later. She'd have the time. If the Commander got her out of this.

She'd read the words before. "I pledge you my Devotion," she said both internally and out loud. The latter for Victor's benefit. "My life and my hands are yours for a year and a day. May we choose never to part."

The Commander's eyes flicked away from the screen, and she ran a hand through her hair. "Ah, there's precedent for this. I'm sorry. You didn't know. You don't have to." Her hands twisted to convolute the words, to obscure the blame.

Beside Melissa, Victor gasped out, "Foreign expatriates can only Devote completely." He didn't look at her to say it, too busy concentrating on the ground. One foot in front of the other.

The mob was still gaining. Melissa's leg stuck again, spike driving through the off-white plastic-and-composite swirl and shearing a cable. She was embedded damn deep this time. If she had time to figure it out, she'd readjust her center of balance. But if she had time to figure it out, she wouldn't be running.

Again, Victor turned around to help extricate her from the floor.

In Melissa's head, the Commander leaned forward, fingertips turning white where they clenched her communications device.

"It's up to you," she said.

Melissa stopped the servos pulling on her stuck leg. "I don't know the words," she said. To the Commander. To Victor.

Victor fought with the grating that trapped Melissa's limb. Determined to do his best for her.

That's what Devotion looks like. That's how Dyfed's propaganda says a Hive should behave. All for one.

He said, "My sword and my service."

Over the comms, the Commander smiled. "It starts with 'My sword and my service.'"

And one for all. They weren't going to let her fail on some technicality. She told the Commander, "Victor is talking me through it."

Speaking of legality... "Is this binding if it's not in person?"

The Commander tugged her sleeves down, adjusting the bunched cloth on limbs looser than they'd been a moment ago. "It's been done in extreme situations. We'll just have to do it again in front of the entire Hive when we're reunited." She shrugged. "I think it'll work. Let Victor be your witness."

Melissa tapped Victor's shoulder where he knelt beside her stuck foot. It wasn't coming out for a while. She could tell. "You're my witness and my guide." This was more important anyway. "My sword and my service."

Victor nodded, overeager, brown hair flopping into his eyes. "My body and my blood. My agency and my anima."

Out loud, Melissa repeated the words. "My body and my blood. My agency and my anima."

"These all belong to you, so I swear."

No going back. She was going to miss being an American Star Ranger. "These all belong to you."

Her Hive mate-to-be watched her with steady eyes. She'd never seen him so still, yet his smile was wide, giddy. His heart rate even higher than while they'd been running.

A strange family that will accept a synthetic so easily.

"So I swear."

On screen, the Commander reached out a futile hand as if hoping to touch her. Of course, they couldn't. The attempted physical connection had a sense of ritual.

The mob clattered ever closer to Victor and Melissa's stationary position. A Velcro-heavy shoe winged through the air and rebounded off Melissa's armor plating.

"I accept your sword and service. Your body and blood are mine to direct. Your agency and anima are my agency and anima, now and forever more. Call on me in times of trouble, as I will call on you, but always you will be my first defense." The Commander let her hand drop.

This is my new life. My Commander. My Queen.

The Commander tilted her head and raised her eyebrows, sardonic. "Though you're falling behind on that score. Only just Devoted and already you need my defense."

Melissa had heard such one-up-man-ship from companionable Rangers before, always equally lighthearted. A sign of brotherhood and bonding. "Nope. I'm one up. Ask the others how they—we—got our tensor jet back."

The mob was louder now. Minutiae rained down on Melissa's back, protecting Victor at her feet, as angry residents emptied their pockets.

Melissa's circuits buzzed with energy. She'd never chosen something so life-changing before. Soaring off into the unknown with a group of kids she barely knew. Giving herself new citizenship. Giving herself a new goal. Giving herself a new identity.

Giving *HIMSELF* a new identity. He'd never given much thought to being female, simply always had been. Hadn't *chosen* so much as known. But it was a rule of Devotion: Queens were females; Devoted were males. Melissa had been lucky for this emergency Devotion to have a sexless body, if not an ungendered mind.

He could try it. See how it went. His Commander already had a woman in her Hive, so if the change was too onerous, no one should complain too much about a switch back.

But for this moment, for right now where they balanced on a precarious legal precedent... for right now, Melissa could be masculine.

The posse was almost on them.

"My lady," he said, having heard the others address her as such, "whatever you're planning to do, you might want to pick up the pace." Was it okay to be so informal? To give near-orders to one's Queen? Melissa would have to find out.

"Can you put me through to the station?"

Melissa piped her channel through to the loudspeakers with a loud crackle.

"John Wayne Station, I demand you release my Devoted at once."

The posse halted its forward movement, members searching the corridor for the source of the voice. They jumped and crouched. Looked right, left, diagonally.

A fashionably dressed man pushed his way to the fore. His face was round and red, glistening with effort. His diaphanous sleeves bore a gold dragon, the Dyfed-Welsh crest, underneath a hip-length white vest that expanded into a fluttering robe. He wagged a finger at the Sherriff and Agent Ward, heading the mob. But he didn't speak. He was too busy heaving in breaths.

Luciano came up behind the man and supported his elbow to help him straighten. To look authoritative. The Devoted's nearly-black brows were furrowed as though he might cry. But his heartbeat was steady and his mouth was a flat, unemotional line.

"That's my Queen's voice," he whispered in the authority figure's ears. Melissa heard him, having attuned his sensors to everything about his new Hive mate.

The red-faced man nodded, sniffed in through flaring nostrils, and stepped away from the support. "If the lady claims these two as her own, then you must let them go."

The posse roared, though the individual members only whispered amongst themselves.

The man continued, "You must let them go or declare war on the sovereign system of Dyfed."

Agent Ward growled. He waved a hand as if to shove aside these consequences. Of the mob, of the Sherriff, he exhorted, "The machine gives you pretty lies! It knows what you want to hear. Who is this disembodied voice?"

The posse bristled. It shifted and leaned forward, ready to ram and stampede once again. Ready to run over Luciano and the ambassador and Victor in order to get to its synthetic scapegoat.

Where is my justice?

But the Commander heard this rhetorical question. Was listening. Could respond.

"I am Rhiannon Jones. I am Queen-Commander Ceridwen of the *Ceridwen's Cauldron*." The young woman's voice filled the corridor like a blanket of gas. It touched every bared skin cell and sought every hidden crack between atmosphere and space. "I am revered and reverer."

Her voice wrapped around Melissa's scarred, metal skin and slipped through his mouth-speaker. For the first time, Melissa understood the expression *I felt warm inside*. He'd never felt heat or cold as such. Only noted the effects on circuits or bodywork.

But now. Now his circuitry felt a curious coziness. Not dangerous like an electrical fire about to start. Nor like overheating on a sunny planet. But an expansive warmth that meant his joints would move faster. Lubricant slid on bearings to spread that warmth throughout his body.

Revered and reverer.

The molecules beside him vibrated as Victor nodded his head along with his Queen. Their Queen. Melissa was included. Included in a group for the second time ever. A group which had not even commented on his synthetic aspect.

Rhiannon concluded, "I protect those who Devote their lives to me. I call on the stars to witness."

Chapter Thirty

I Am Queen

The stars heard her call.

She'd made Gavin redirect the lorry, and now she spilled out of it and onto the white, plastic ground. Such a flimsy barrier between her and nature's vacuum. Unnatural. Gavin and Gwyn fanned out behind her. An entourage from Cleopatra's Palace drove somewhere in their wake.

The posse's ringleader sputtered the beginning of a question, but couldn't find the words he needed. His sounds caught and died in his throat.

Good. He knew the power of her voice. The power of her existence.

The Sherriff, heretofore polite when she'd contacted him about her ship day passes, refuted her *I am*. "Now see here, young lady—"

A gasp cut him off. It came from a red-faced man in white druid's robes. The druid stood at Luciano's side at the front of the pack.

How have we been found out so soon by Dyfed? Will the station send us into custody?

But the druid didn't send his scandalized stare in her direction, didn't demand her surrender to his guardianship. No, he waved his hands at the Sherriff, face aghast. The universal panic that meant *HALT!*

"You can't speak to a Queen like that," he hissed. He bowed to Rhiannon. "Your ladyship."

Ah, a diplomat. He hadn't heard of her specifically, only knew what her status implied.

She could have traded it for a status the station residents would understand. Cleopatra's madam had offered Rhiannon a place, based on her performance and quick thinking. But Rhiannon had declined, even if it would have given her power right now. She had too many responsibilities to take permanent employment on John Wayne Station.

Oh! The druid's benefit came clear. *A diplomat!* Well-schooled in the niceties of social interaction. Better schooled than she when it came to the etiquette of Queens.

She bestowed a regal nod of her circleted head.

"You hold my Hive member hostage," she accused the gathering. "You will release the one known as M3L-15-A to me and allow us safe passage."

The druid bowed to her again. "Of course they will, your ladyship."

The leader of the wolfpack, a man about Gwyn's height with chestnut hair and angry eyebrows broke in. "Of course they will *not*. Sherriff, back me up on this. If nothing else, they've got bills to pay for the docking and the medical. Didn't that one"—he pointed at Victor—"arrive with a bullet wound patched up in *your* hospital?"

The Sherriff clucked his tongue. "I'm afraid I can't hold 'em if the consul says I can't. I'm the local law and this is too far out of my jurisdiction." He narrowed his eyes at the instigator. "Though it should be well within yours."

The man with the eyebrows nodded. "Well, then. I commandeer your weapons and your people. Destroy that robot and all its accomplices!"

No one moved to harm them. But no one moved to detain Agent Ward either.

Rhiannon was paralyzed, reluctant to break the precarious tableau lest she cut herself on the shards.

I've allowed myself to be caught in the mousetrap.

The Sherriff clucked again. "Now, that's just not the way this is going to go," he said.

I am no ordinary mouse.

She knew that Alan had remained with the *Ceridwen's Cauldron* while the rest of her Hive stood in this corridor with only the druid as their champion. She knew that he commanded its power. He had all the access they needed to their escape vessel and the knowledge to make it so.

Bolstered by such knowledge, she challenged her would-be executioner. "You'll find it easier to let us go than to make us angry."

"Wait!" Gwyn pushed forward, edging in front of Rhiannon and Gavin, into the détente's center. She stood taller than the Sherriff, yet also smaller, her tremulous voice betraying her nerves. "I'll pay the docking fees and medical bills. Then there's no argument at all with the station."

Rhiannon looked away from her *not a staring contest* with the law enforcement. *What?* "That's not..." There was no good way to end that sentence. She settled for a bewildered, "How?"

Gwyn turned her back on the slavering wolf pack. On the Sherriff. On Victor and Luciano and the druid and her new Hive mate. Reached out, beseeching, to Rhiannon and Rhiannon only. Dropped it. She shifted her weight from foot to foot, looked to Rhiannon's booted toes and then back up to her knees. Scrunched her nose. "I've been offered a job here in the life sciences division. And citizenship," she confessed. She stood straighter, tilting her head back so near-white hair fell smoothly to her waist. When her smile started, it was like a half-laugh. "I'm going to take it."

Gavin came closer, papering himself against Rhiannon's shoulders. *People don't leave Hives.* Warm and muscular, his presence anchored her in the moment.

Gwyn shrugged, as though abandoning her Hive—her beloved, her *best friend*—meant nothing. "The position comes with a sign-on bonus. What else am I going to do with that? This whole job is like a dream."

Rhiannon shook her head, feeling the crown move with the force. "You don't have to do this."

"I want to, though."

Rhiannon could tell it was the truth. Gwyn's stance was so open. She stood tall, not slouching or trying to make herself look smaller.

"We can still force our way out."

"I love the plants and the animals, and they need me here. They need expertise that's almost common back home."

Victor made a wounded noise, intruding on the two-person world they'd briefly built. Despite the pain in the sound, his face was blank, the opposite of the bouncy teambuilding enthusiasm he'd exuded since getting shot. He whined, high and reedy. "I'll miss you."

He didn't try to hug his girlfriend. Didn't move at all.

Gwyn shook her silky blonde tresses. They glinted warmly in the otherwise-harsh American light. "You haven't missed me for a while now," she told him. "When was the last time we even talked? You'll be all right. I know it."

Victor's mouth gaped open on another high-pitched sound. Rhiannon's newest Devoted nudged him in the ribs, and his lips closed into a thin, flat line that tried to betray nothing.

Gwyn stepped closer to Rhiannon and opened her arms for a hug, and Rhiannon flew into it.

"I want this." The soft voice choked off into sniffles.

We'll never see each other again.

Rhiannon had to honor her wishes. Much as she wanted to keep her Hive together, wanted to keep Gwyn by her side for all of her life and beyond, she also had to look out for her best friend's interests. Rhiannon had always championed the other girl's cause—even at such a fundamental level as giving her the Welsh nickname which, yes, she'd recently shunned, but which had also given her cachet with teachers and strangers back home.

"Remember when we were nine, and we became best friends on the day you stood up for me?" Rhiannon pulled away to look into her red-rimmed hazel eyes.

Underneath Gwyn's pinkening nose, the girl smiled. "Something like that."

Now's not the time for the old argument about exactly what happened that day.

Rhiannon pulled the newly made American into a hug. "Don't forget to stand up for you too. I love you, Gwyn."

Squeezing back, Gwyn didn't even complain about the nickname. Rhiannon had known she wouldn't. In this moment, they were the little girls they'd always been with each other.

"I love you too." Gwyn sniffed and straightened again. Eyes running, but cheeks apple-ing. "Take care of my garden."

"A-hem!" The wolf pack leader would not be ignored. "This robot is an enemy of the state and will be dealt with accordingly."

A Cleopatra's Palace lorry arrived and deposited the madam into the fray. "Perhaps, perhaps not." The venerable woman emerged from behind Rhiannon to stand by the Sherriff, looking down her aristocratic nose at the unhappy Agent as though he were a child. As though he were beneath her station. Which, in fact, anyone who wanted companionship or credit in this sector *was*. "Cleopatra's Palace is satisfied with the arrangement. The Sherriff has already backed away. That only leaves the station administrators. As they are not present and not involved, I declare this matter settled."

Like a Hive, Cleopatra's Palace looks out for its own.

Rhiannon may have been the Queen of a Hive within a Hive, but that exterior shell still granted protection from destructive elements.

The Sherriff crossed his arms, the very picture of power. "Agent Ward, these good people have a mountain of political backing, and it seems they're planning to pay all their monies owed. I reckon we should let this go."

The man choked on air again. It was very satisfying.

Rhiannon loaded her people into Gavin's transport—technically, the brothel-casino-theatre's, but they didn't seem inclined to contest her appropriation—including her new Devoted.

Not including her dearest heart.

She waved to Gwyn, who waved back to the departing Hive, ignoring the milling crowd behind her. Alan would have the ship ready to go, and they'd all get out of here. Away from these people with their strange customs and stranger beliefs about what makes a possession free for anyone to take, take, take.

Don't let them take too much from you, Gwyn. This escape has taken more than enough already.

⟫ Interlude 5 ⟫

Today Is Another Day

Olivia woke with a crick in her neck and a pounding in her chest.

The room was dark, so dark. Cautious, she felt for the door and cracked it open. Empty hallways, floors littered with the evacuation's detritus—an abandoned cart, a broken coffee mug, *a single shoe?*—testified the researcher had told the truth. Olivia had been sedated… and left behind.

Using the keycard in the left pocket, also as promised, she took herself upwards twelve floors until she reached ground level. For the first time in unknown days, she felt sunlight on her face. She closed her eyes against the brightness and offered her thanks to every single god who might listen to the prayers of an old, nearly broken woman.

But not fully broken. She didn't know why the lab doctor had let her go, but she had to make the most of it. She'd escaped, but the other Queens needed her help. Wherever they'd been taken, the tortures would no doubt continue.

"Excuse me." She found a minor functionary when she stumbled into the building's courtyard. "I need to borrow your pad."

The nameless, faceless, otherwise-useless person handed it over. Briefly, Olivia wondered what she looked like. Dirty, hungry, desperate, wearing a lab coat with no lab in sight. Then the moment was over, and she went about her business.

She flashed her Devoted a message. *Am healthy. Meet me at Senedd, second floor.*

If she wanted to free the remaining Queens, she needed to find them.

If she wanted to find them, she needed aid from someone in government or law enforcement.

If she wanted to include government or law enforcement, she needed someone she could trust. Considering that she'd been abducted by a government agent and held in an outdated, but still official, government facility, she knew lower levels of power were involved. Corrupted.

If there was one good thing, though, about being an *aging* Queen, it was years of building relationships with some *now* very important people.

She returned the pad and headed to the Senedd building, where she skipped the impressive groves and vines and stonework that made its public face. Instead, she took the back stairs to the second floor. That's where everything got *done*. The people here had the clout to make things happen and the need-to-know to find out what *ought* to happen.

With her name and contacts, it didn't take long to work her way into the Permanent Cabinet Secretary's chambers.

"I'm terribly sorry, your ladyship." The assistant bowed obsequiously low, which Olivia found comforting after weeks of having her status ignored. "But the Cabinet Secretary is out of the office."

"What about Effie? That is, where can I find Ffion Kendrick, the Permanent Undersecretary for the Department of Health and Well-Being, then?" Olivia would've preferred to go straight to the apex of her personal-contact food chain, but if Effie were out, then she'd call on another friend. Old friends in power were *old friends in power,* no matter which power they had. "Just point me at her office, if you would."

"I'm terribly sorry, your ladyship." The receptionist bowed again. *How many bows must you make? I'd prefer acquiescence to apology.* "All of the functional department heads are on their goodwill tour of Wales-on-Earth."

Is it time for that already?

The goodwill tours always made for interesting feature stories on the news. Everyone danced in groves, talked to some Earth-based druids, and exchanged gifts.

"Didn't they just do that a few years ago?"

"Yes, your ladyship." Another bow. *Good grief.* "The ministers all went three years ago. This year, it's the administrators' turn. It's been scheduled for the last six months."

Olivia nodded her thanks and walked back into the sunlight in a daze. Her Devoted rushed to her side, kept waiting by gatekeepers—*I should have thought of that*—and more anxious than ever to touch her skin and see her well.

She couldn't trust anyone she didn't know. Well, they'd only be gone for two months. Until then, she'd have to start with finding the perpetrators.

A good Queen never retires.

Chapter Thirty-One

Yesterday and Today

Melissa's old ship, the *Cold Night*, wasn't hers—his—anymore. The station authorities had impounded it as evidence.

His new ship would have to make up for the loss of everything he'd known. Of all his chosen belongings.

He reached into his vest and pulled out his badge. *American Star Ranger*, it proclaimed in an arc across the top. Five shining starbursts joined together with embossed lines to form a stylized star.

He traced a raised line with a thumb.

Other than his Ranger badge and two sidearms, he only kept one other possession on his person at all times. A copy of all his personal memory chips. He'd miss his collections of weapons and hats, his library and his mementos of past collars, his reports to HQ and their replies.

But he only needed himself. Only wanted his memory chips with their record of how he'd become a *person* time after time.

No, that couldn't be true anymore. He didn't only need himself and his chips. No. He needed himself, his chips, his

Queen-Commander, and his Hive's support. That's what Hives were for, wasn't it?

I should read up on the Dyfed-native literature about Hives and Devoted. They supported each other, and were supported in turn. *If I'm going to be Devoted, I've got to know what it means. I won't let them down.* Not after all they'd done to save him.

He'd been allowed to pick his own room in the residential corridor. Not been assigned. Not been told he didn't need space because he was just a robot. Simply been allowed to choose from the unoccupied rooms. There were plenty.

At the moment, he didn't have much in his rectangular box-home. They'd let him appropriate furniture from Gwyn's old room, so now he had a dresser and a desk.

Gwyn had taken the bed with her, but Melissa didn't much need one.

The door vibrated with scratching from the outside, and he whirled to face it, pistol in his lower left hand. Badge clutched to his torso with the top right.

"Hey, Melissa," Victor called through the metal obstruction. "We're meeting up for dinner. You want to walk together? I'll show you where it is."

Melissa had already memorized the ship map and knew exactly where the mess hall should be, assuming they ate dinner in the mess hall. But Victor's offer wasn't about directions. It was about forging relationships. Melissa had never gone for dinner or drinks with his fellow Rangers, had always brushed off the overtures from local law enforcements. Had held himself apart.

Until now.

He holstered the gun and secured the strap. He'd have to call in to Jon at HQ, let them know he was leaving the service for a while. It had been done before. Back when they'd been *Texas* Rangers. Back in the early, pre-space days. Rangers dropped in and out of service like heart rates sliding up and down.

With one last caress along the raised lines between the stars, he put his badge into a desk drawer. The Rangers had given him a home and a purpose, had trusted him to be an effective lawman. But his loyalty was now to his Queen. His Hive.

He slid his door open and walked from the unlit room into the bright blue-toned hall. "Thanks for playing tour guide."

His own voice shocked him. It was lower, deeper than he'd ever synthesized for his own words. He'd taken it down a few octaves and modulated its rise and fall to be less variable than usual. A man's voice.

He growled as though clearing his throat, adjusting the static and the waveforms till there was no static at all, till he'd equalized the tone. He was going to be the smoothest sounding man on the ship. Here, it didn't matter that he was unnatural. None of the Hive had ever so much as flinched from him. They wouldn't recoil from a sound too perfect, too sweet. "Let's take that tour, eh?"

Victor slouched and shoved hands into his pockets, left corner of his mouth upturned. "So, what do you eat? I'm pretty sure we've got lamb tonight, thank goodness. But our taste of home won't be the same as yours. Lleu preserve me from the things Luciano thinks are normal."

In the bright lights running in strips overhead, Melissa had no trouble seeing his eyes roll.

Steeling himself for confusion and judgment, he wrapped all four limbs around his chest. His visor blinked a brief white before he settled it back to blue. "I don't eat."

Victor laughed. Head thrown back to expose vulnerable tendons. Heartbeat steady. Stomach muscles shaking with the reality of it.

Melissa mirrored his openness. His top arms went behind his head, opening his chest up. Open and smug at once.

Not too strange and ugly then. His visor turned paler blue with suppressed laughter and lightness of being.

"You'll keep our food bills low," Victor said. "But you still have to come to dinner. It's mandatory."

Dinner as the essential circle, Melissa had heard someone describe it once. Perhaps he should have had drinks with former coworkers. Would he have been as easily accepted there as he was here?

Melissa and Victor breezed into the mess hall, where the rest of their Hive already congregated. The Commander waved them over and put her hand on Melissa's lower right arm as soon as they were in touching distance. The touch registered on all his sensors, external heat and humidity flowing down through the metal skin-shell to warm the cables beneath. He found himself pressed into the space at her side, cleared of a chair since Melissa came equipped with his own.

She didn't spare him further direct attention. Too involved in an ongoing conversation. "I've signed Alan up to give a talk at a space-time physics conference in Mandarin space."

Maybe this camaraderie was what he'd been missing all along. *If I'd gone to drinks or dinner with the Rangers, the Marshals, the local Sheriffs, and they'd treated me like this. If I'd automatically been one of their own, my non-eating no different than a peanut allergy. If they had, could I have remained a Ranger?*

Victor jumped right in. "Can we make it out there in time?"

Luciano, desultory: "Do they speak English?"

Gavin and Alan began discussing the Alcubierre drive and how soon it could get them to their destination, punctuated by Alan's explosive worries about preparing a technical presentation so quickly.

The Commander's hand found Melissa's arm again, a quick contact to get his attention. "You settling in all right?" Her gold-dipped circlet reflected the overhead lights, lending a warm wash to the air around her. To Melissa's silvery skin where it came close.

I'm fine. Rangers adapt to any situation.

His identity. His surroundings. They were all changing so quickly.

"I don't know my name anymore," Melissa said. He'd gone by *Melissa* so long. It was his name, his model number. But also a symbol of whom he had been. A woman, a robot.

The Commander didn't reply immediately. She tilted her head as if weighing options inside of it, thoughts so heavy they pulled her head to one side. "I have multiple names," she offered. "In private, my friends and Hive call me *Rhiannon*."

Melissa had never called her such, but he would. He could.

"In public, they opt for *my lady*. On Dyfed, they care that I am Queen. Once, a man called me Ceri." She speared her newest Devoted with a glare. "Don't do that."

Melissa's visor turned a dark blue in response. "I suppose I could go by Mel for now." The beginning of his model number. *M3L*. Shorter, somewhat masculine, still synthetic.

Rhiannon raised her eyebrows. "Pick whatever you want."

"Mel," he said. Decisive. Even as his fingers all curled and uncurled. Curled and uncurled. "For now." Curled and uncurled.

Rhiannon gave him another measuring look, but left it at that, returning to discussing whether the Hive should attempt to learn basic Mandarin before arriving in that society's space. Mel spoke Mandarin, of course. He'd learned many languages in his time, vocabulary and syntax coming easily to his perfect memory. He'd have to find texts on Cymraeg next, the better to keep up with his Welsh Hive mates.

Mel turned to Gavin at her other side. "Don't suppose you have any spare memory chips?"

Gavin waved expansive arms, diaphanous sleeves dripping in the John Wayne fashion. "My dear sir," he proclaimed. "Ve haff all ze cheeps in all ze styles!"

Mel had no trouble cutting through the overblown accent. No trouble asking to requisition one of those many *cheeps* for personal use. What was the Hive's was his own, after all. And he needed to make a memory of this moment.

Of feeling like a part of a whole, without needing to be in authority to do it.

He needed a memory chip of this event, this day when everything changed. When he switched life tracks of his own accord.

It was time to make new memories.

Chapter Thirty-Two

Tomorrow and Tomorrow

The *Cauldron*'s dining room was thick with must from weeks of airless disuse. The stale particles coated Rhiannon's tongue. It was too unpleasant to breathe through the nose before the recirculators kicked on.

But Rhiannon felt more at peace than she had in weeks. She had her Devoted—and *only* Devoted, now that Gwyn had moved on—and had them all in one place. She'd missed this, these bonding moments.

On John Wayne, each of them had their own desires, their own priorities, their own schedules. They'd expended their energy and blood on projects that took them farther and farther apart from each other. So far apart that one had broken off entirely.

Gwyn had been right. When was the last time they'd talked?

Goddess Ceridwen, is this how you felt when your assistant stole your greatest potion? As though if only you'd paid more attention...?

When was the last time Rhiannon had talked with any of her Hive? Truly made a connection? There'd been a moment when Victor and Alan had teamed up to present her with the crown, but she couldn't recall any others. She'd stayed away from them, spent more time with the courtesans.

She hadn't even noticed.

Rhiannon tilted her head forward, planning to hide behind hair. Hair held out of her face by the golden circlet. An enforcer. A reminder. In letting Gwyn go, she had to admit that her best friend would be better off in her chosen situation and maybe that the Hive would be better off without her divisive, disinterested, presence.

Her newest Devoted's smooth, metal skin warmed underneath Rhiannon's touch.

I hope all changes are so easy as this. Mel needed to feel at home, to make a connection with the Hive. He was already close with Victor, so where should she start him making that next bond, that next connection that would stitch him in tighter?

At her side, Mel asked Gavin about memory chips.

For all Gavin's posturing, Rhiannon saw the deference, the willingness to *provide all to a superior* in his demeanor.

Her eyes flicked between the two. Yes! This was the place to start. Starting now, here, she'd make this Hive into the closest, most seamless Hive the universe had ever seen. They'd stitch themselves so tightly together, it would be like they'd come from a single bolt of multi-patterned cloth. Now was the perfect time to start.

We've successfully worked together to get our tensor jet back. We control our own destinies. No more waiting.

This pair's destiny was to live as equals in her eyes. They needed to get a feel for each other in a situation where

Gavin was the one in charge, but that was safe and fun. Where Gavin had no responsibilities other than to spend time with a new Hive mate.

"I have a game," she said.

Gratifyingly, all eyes turned to her. The focus. The Queen.

Victor leaned in, all interest. Gavin cocked his head. Alan rolled his eyes, but stopped the ever-constant bored tapping. Luciano tensed. *What is Luciano afraid of?* Mel, well, she wasn't sure about Mel, other than that his head swiveled towards her. She'd need to learn more about him now that he was more than just an acquaintance. Now that he was *hers*.

"It's just for Gavin and Mel first," she explained.

Luciano relaxed onto his bench and looked down at his hands. Away from her. Away from them all. Oh, she needed to bring him back into the fold. *Hard*.

But first, Gavin and Mel.

"All right, you two. I want you to sit back to back."

Of course, they did as she told them. No questions. Her own ribs and shoulders loosened at the immediate obedience, at how well this was already going. *Gavin's been so touch-y lately. This set-up with the enforced contact is even better than I realized!*

"Now, Gavin will describe an object only he can see, and Mel is going to draw it."

Mel laughed like a tossed pebble rippling a lake, all smooth sound and motion. Natural. Nothing out of place.

"With what?" he asked, four arms spreading wide to show his lack of materials. His arms were bare, purely metal and welding, silvery-grey in the ship's light. He made a Spartan contrast to the sway of Gavin's many sleeves. Reddish blond hair brushed against Mel's sidelamps, making them look like bizarre ponytails.

Victor passed Mel his pad to draw on without hesitation.

That relationship is strong. Good. Strange that Victor's leadership no longer seems like a threat to my own.

"What about me?" Victor's giant, too wide smile was slightly disturbing. "I want a game too!" He no doubt saw this for the team building exercise that it was. Victor had been trying to draw them all into bonding activities on John Wayne.

He'd been right.

She nibbled on her lower lip. Who was least close to Victor?

Luciano. Not to mention, they needed to bridge some cultural gaps.

"If you want a game, Vic, you'll get a game." She pointed at her two chosen targets. "You and Luciano are on dinner-making duty. Together. For the week."

Until that moment, cooking had been a solitary activity, but not anymore. Together, they'd have to decide what to make and how to make it. "Good luck figuring out what to do with the standard American foodstuffs the docking authorities gave us." Maybe they'd teach each other and become friends.

Luciano's dark eyes flattened like they'd been weighted with excess gravity, but he went where he was directed.

Victor followed with a stream of questions. "Can you show me how to chop herbs like you did with whatever that green stuff was that one time? Did you cook with your mom back home? My mom always tossed me out of the kitchen! But my younger brother—do you have any siblings?—he was always..."

The patter continued. Rhiannon tuned it out. She still had three other Hive members to look after. The kitchen-bound pair was safe enough for now.

Rhiannon stood to see how Mel's drawing was getting on. It looked like a pigeon.

There were no pigeons on the *Ceridwen's Cauldron*.

She'd have to break in on this and see how it was going. *Not that there's a lot to break into. Neither of them are talking.*

She refrained from shaking her head. They'd take it as disappointment. And the only way they could disappoint her was if they didn't learn from this exercise. "So, how's it going?" There. That was a safe, non-judgmental opener.

Gavin shot to his feet and swept her an ostentatious bow. "My lady. Our newest artist's hand is passing fair, but it fairly passes that—"

He'd continue in this vein forever if she didn't stop him. "Tell me about the pigeon," she said.

"My lady?"

Mel snorted. *Which of these parts is technically his nose?* He changed his leg posture so that he was standing. Or, at least, no longer at seating-height. "I think she means our drawing." He turned the pad so that Gavin could see the bird on it.

Gavin's smattering of freckles turned a darker shade and his shoulders shook. "That's what you got from *feathery edges* and *kind of claw-like?*" His large, blue eyes scrunched.

Keeping them on track, Rhiannon prodded, "This isn't what you meant?" Already knowing it wasn't, she didn't wait for an answer, but asked Mel, "Did you try to clarify with him?"

Mel's eye visor flashed white before calming back to blue. *What does that mean?*

"He agreed with me." Rhiannon's newest Devoted sounded aggrieved.

Gavin rounded on Mel, defending his honor. "Would you rather the drum and the fife than the tabor and the pipe, Claudio?"

Rhiannon was pretty sure that was an insult. Something about war, if the drum was any indication. She opened her mouth to ask for a translation from theatrical context to shipboard context, but Mel beat her to it.

"Am I truly the Claudio in this scenario? Or am I Benedick, wishing for a man who is once wont to speak plain and to the purpose?" All four of his shoulder sockets rolled.

Even in the face of such tension, Rhiannon's limbs loosened. She wanted to crow, *"At last! Someone who understands Gavin's allusions."* But she bit back the sound of happy victory. Time to use their newfound common ground. Besides, she'd got the gist from the context.

"I want you to try this again," she told them, prodding them back towards their seats. "The same object. But this time, Gavin, I want you to give what you think is too much detail. When Mel asks a question, assume he knows absolutely nothing about anything and school him like the smallest child."

They assumed their position, solidly back to back.

"Yes, my lady."

They spoke in unison. Her plan was coming together already. They'd learn to communicate, to let Gavin be the expert, in no time. They already used the same language.

Luciano and Victor clattered about in the kitchen, murmurs reaching Rhiannon's ears. Mel and Gavin sat close together, learning to work with one another. This left Alan, Alan who had near *begged* for her attention and consideration and direction back on John Wayne. She beckoned him to her side.

"Walk with me," she said.

They emerged together into the *Cauldron*'s halls, echoingly empty with stale-tasting air. Whether the staleness came from the weeks she'd spent pent up or from the quality of the American air, she couldn't say. Now that the ship belonged to their Hive again, they'd get green back into the atmosphere soon enough.

She said, "I did the right thing, signing you up to talk about your drive to the Mandarins." It was almost a question, but she knew he needed this. Needed her to look out for his career and his mind. Needed her to be in control. Needed her to read his mind. "You'll have the chance for fame. Plus, you can learn things."

"Will they know us there?" he asked, proving her right about his need for *fame*. They passed an intersection. Alan echoed her earlier thought about green and living air: "Don't you want to check on the plants?"

But she drew him past the turn for the garden on legs fast and free in in the *Cauldron*'s lighter gravity. "Later," she said. "This talk is for you, so we're going to your space." The warm blue halls cradled them. "And, no. We have to stay away from home. You know that. But going to a new place only means you'll have the chance to see truly divergent physics in action."

He grabbed her hand in his large, screwdriver-scarred one, and tucked it in the crook of his elbow. *Fostering closeness.* "Speaking of divergent engineering..." He trailed off, plump lips quirking up on the left in merriment.

Hugging his arm close to her side, she played along. "No, Alan. You can't upgrade your new Hive member while he's asleep."

She dropped him in the engine room with a kiss on the cheek and orders to draw up an invoice for John Wayne Station. The Americans ought to pay Alan a rental fee for the time they'd used his Alcubierre drive. She'd find out from Mel what counted as simply an obscene amount of money and what was truly unsupportable.

Returning to the dining hall, she found the four Devoted working together to make tessellations out of vegetables. As soon as they noticed her, each one wanted her attention.

Luciano: "Maybe we can start a trivia night?"

Victor: "To help Mel settle in."

Mel: "He wanted me to draw a pastry cone. How did that start life as a pigeon?"

Gavin: "Do you want some more costumes a la Cleopatra's Palace? I could make some."

She perched on the table beside their vegetables, wanting to be closer. "Good idea. Glad it worked out. No thanks," she answered in turn.

It was good to see her boys all cozy and happy. Hive bonding already improving their relationships. To each other and possibly to her.

She watched them before grabbing a carrot out of the pattern. In retaliation, Victor threw a celery stick at her. But this only led to Luciano pouncing on her attacker and knocking him to the ground in a mock-fight. *How dare you touch my Queen!* escaped between giggles. Gavin pulled her off the table and onto his lap, burying his laughter in her hair, while Mel stretched out his top two arms, lacing them behind his head and opening up his chest completely, vulnerably.

It only took a minute to slip from her flamboyant prison and dance to the door, leaving warmth and happiness in her wake.

She was halfway to the garden—she really did need to check on their plant supplies—when Luciano caught up. He had a furrow between his risen brows and a corner of his mouth pulled down, but she didn't press. Just waited for him to speak.

He pulled himself together with a flat smile that meant nothing.

"I need to tell you something," he said. "I need you to know about the druid and how I came to be with him. I should have never—"

His eyebrows crumpled further together, and he looked ready to cry.

Not today. Today is for celebration.

"You know I love you," she soothed, "and that I will do anything you—or my other Devoted—ever need. So take your time." She tapped her crown as a reminder of all the time they had. "Get your thoughts together, and we'll talk after dinner. You have kitchen duty, remember?"

"We'll definitely talk, though?" he pressed.

"I promise," she said. "I'm here for you."

Tomorrow and tomorrow and tomorrow. There would be time for Luciano's news and Mel's integration. Time to mourn Gwyn's loss and celebrate Alan's achievements. Time for Gavin's plays and Rhiannon's Queen-study. The path behind them closed up tight, but the stars opened ahead for *Ceridwen's* metaphorical sails.

And someday Victor and Luciano will actually cook something instead of playing with the food!

END BOOK TWO
TO BE CONTINUED IN BOOK THREE

Other Works

The Hive Queen Saga
Queen & Commander – IPPY award silver medal winner
for Best Science Fiction, Fantasy, or Horror eBook (2013)
Hive & Heist (2014)

Novellas
These Convergent Stars (2013)

Short Story
"The Robot Who Stole Herself" (2014)

About the Author

Photo by Jeremy Barton

Janine A. Southard writes speculative fiction and video-game dialogue from her home in Seattle, WA. She sings with a Celtic band and is working on the next book in her award-winning Hive Queen series. She's also been known to read aloud to her cat.

The cat appreciates all of these things. Maybe.

Visit her on the Web: *http://www.janinesouthard.com*
Interact on Twitter: *http://www.twitter.com/jani_s*
Join the conversation on Goodreads:
  https://www.goodreads.com/jani_s

You can stay up to date with Janine A. Southard's latest publications and events by signing up for her newsletter (on the website).